Before I Find You

Also by Ali Knight

Wink Murder
The First Cut
Until Death
The Silent Ones

About the author

Before Ali began writing she did many jobs, including waitressing, teaching English to foreign students, working in a knicker factory and answering phones at Wembley Stadium. She spent a decade as a journalist and sub-editor before she wrote her debut thriller, *Wink Murder*, which was chosen as one of the *Independent's* Books of the Year in 2011. She lives with her family in London.

Find out more about Ali and her psychological thrillers on Twitter @aliknightauthor, Facebook @aliknightauthor or Instagram @potteralison

ALI KNIGHT

Before I Find You

HODDER &
STOUGHTON

First published in Great Britain in 2018 by Hodder & Stoughton
An Hachette UK company

I

Copyright © Ali Knight 2018

The right of Ali Knight to be identified as the Author of the Work has been asserted by her in accordance with the Copyright, Designs and Patents Act 1988.

A CIP catalogue record for this title is available from the British Library

Hardback ISBN 9781473684768
eBook ISBN 9781473684782

Typeset in Plantin Light by Palimpsest Book Production Limited,
Falkirk, Stirlingshire

Printed and bound by CPI Group (UK) Ltd, Croydon, CR0 4YY

Hodder & Stoughton policy is to use papers that are natural, renewable and recyclable products and made from wood grown in sustainable forests. The logging and manufacturing processes are expected to conform to the environmental regulations of the country of origin.

Hodder & Stoughton Ltd
Carmelite House
50 Victoria Embankment
London EC4Y 0DZ

www.hodder.co.uk

To my family, with all my love

PROLOGUE

Maggie

The night of

I don't know what's happened but I know it's bad. It always is, when you wake up on the floor, a bad taste in the mouth and blood in your eyes. It feels like youth and I've been running from that for as long as I can remember. The summer heat has cooked the paving slabs so they smell of tar and oil and something nastier – I can't breathe.

I hear squealing brakes as I try and suck something into my shocked and emptied lungs, images are scrambling in my brain and I'm trying to put them in order. A new, sickening sensation overwhelms me – the dark shape next to me on the ground isn't moving. Panic forms a cloud.

A tear rolls away across my face. The last few moments are coming back to me in violent flashes. The figure next to me is never going to move again. I heard the pop, as clear as a boot stamping on a Styrofoam cup in a gutter, of spine snapping as we landed – as clear a death sentence as any. Someone screams. Dread fills me and I arch my back, desperate to know if I will ever get off this floor, out of this God-awful mess and even if I do, how much of this will have been my fault?

The yellow rectangle of light from the window above me shimmers through my tears. She's standing there so calm and still, looking down, and my panic is snuffed out by fear.

CHAPTER I

Maggie

Eight weeks before

I was always intrigued when a real bobby-dazzler walked into my office and asked for my help. It proved yet again that no one is immune from betrayal – no matter how rich, famous or physically blessed, every walk of life needed my services: a husband watcher. I was a snooper, a sex detective, a marriage doctor, a destroyer of dreams, a killer of happy-ever-afters. I had spent my career down amongst the grubby pain of love betrayed, of lies exposed. Beauty wouldn't save you, money couldn't insulate you from it. The woman in the doorway proved just that. She smelled rich and she was a babe.

'Don't be shy, come on in,' I said. I was in a good mood, joshing and joking with Simona, the studious young Italian who worked for me.

The woman in the doorway was blonde, casually dressed, hard to put an age to but somewhere just north of forty, and scared as hell.

She stepped uncertainly into the room and Simona jumped up and closed the door behind her. 'Please, take a seat,' she said, holding out her hand towards the sofa.

The woman declined our offer of coffee or tea so Simona gave her a glass of water.

The woman perched on the edge of a small sofa near the window, her ankles and knees clamped together in a pose that the royals used to guarantee no knicker shots. Her blue eyes roamed over the three desks in the room, mine, Simona's and Rory's, over my retro filing cabinet and the pot plants and the black fan that only gets used on the three hottest days of the year. I couldn't tell if she was impressed by my stripped wood floors or my linen blinds, but I was. I loved my office and I loved my job. 'How can I help you?' I asked.

There was silence for a moment. The woman looked at her hands helplessly, twiddled with her wedding ring and gripped her bag. 'God, this is so embarrassing.' She tailed off, her voice was quiet. She conjured up English country gardens and mellow stone walls, scones and cricket matches and all that Olde English stuff.

Simona gave me a conspiratorial look and made herself scarce by heading into the small kitchen off the main room to make fresh coffee and pull out some little Italian cakes that always oiled the wheels when a client came in. 'OK, let's start at the beginning,' I said. 'I'm Maggie Malone, I run the Blue and White agency, and I'm going to find out if he's cheating on you. I'll tell you who he's cheating with, where and how, I'll show you the video, pictures or audio evidence if you want to see or hear it. And you'll pay me.' I smiled. Her mouth fell open, but only for a moment. 'And then you get to skip all the bits where he claims it was a misunderstanding and he's innocent and all that. It saves you a lot of time.'

I usually got one of three reactions at this point: tears, anger, or an empty seat and a banging door. Very rarely I got a fourth: she sat bolt still for about three seconds and then she burst out laughing. It was the first cocktail of the evening, that smile. She put her bag on the floor and sat back, twirling a shapely ankle that poked beneath her trousers.

She ran her hands down her shiny hair, clasped them in front of her over her knees. Her beauty came out when she relaxed. 'I think you and I are going to get on very well.'

I'd always been Marmite, people either loved me or hated me. This lady was a snob and I was a yob, and often opposites attract. Some people disliked what I do, they found it grubby and underhand, but I say, wouldn't you want to know if he was cheating? Wouldn't you open that envelope, click on that video file? Of course you would and anyone who says otherwise is a hypocrite.

I stood up and came over and we shook hands.

'I'm Helene Moreau,' she said.

Of course she had a name like that. Exotic, classy, I guessed the husband was French. There was no 'which Helene?' for her. She was one of a kind.

'And how can I help you, Helene?'

Simona arrived back in the room with fresh coffee in a cup and a cake plate decorated with flowers, on which sat the Italian biscuits. This time she took both without hesitation. She sighed. 'I want you to tell me if I'm married to a cheating bastard.'

CHAPTER 2

Helene

Eight weeks before

There are just a few moments that remain seared into my memory for years – seconds that have changed my life. One of those was the revelation that my knight in shining armour had another life.

We were at the Café Royal on a Tuesday evening; a thousand of us were raising money for wells in sub-Saharan Africa. It was chandeliers and evening dress, black-tie waiters and curving staircases, and a temporary cloakroom on the first floor, in which I caught a glimpse of my husband skulking, slapping away the hand of a woman in a green dress. I saw the hard, tanned planes of his face turn with a flash of anxiety towards the far door, checking to make sure no one was watching. Her slim bare arm came up over his shoulder and brushed slowly down his dark hair as he pushed her away. A moment later he left through the far door and she followed. I watched her shoulder muscles moving in her backless dress as she followed him out, I saw the ripple of her blonde hair.

What I saw made me feel as old as the hills, which are such immoveable, solid things, but it made my marriage as insubstantial as sand in an hourglass, draining through till not a grain of it remained.

I hurried through the cloakroom, round a maze of coat rails and out the other side, tracking her green dress but I couldn't find her, my mind already doubting whether what I had seen was real or not.

'Helene, come and boogie!' A friend caught my arm and spun me towards a dance floor. I pulled away, trying to see the woman through the crush. Gabe danced towards us – well, my husband doesn't dance, he sort of sways his shoulders to any music that's playing, be it disco, reggae or rap, on the balls of his feet, this way and that, forward and back, his slim legs bending at the knees. He has a raffish charm from a former age, a hint of colonial hotels or boat docks on hot Mediterranean nights, the dirty, dirty old goat.

He was humming, his composure returned, handing me a drink. Gabe always wanted others to enjoy life as much as he did, even if they didn't have a heart big enough. He raised his drink to save it from the dance floor crush – I saw the liquid slosh over the sides, as if his cup literally runneth over. As I stood there marooned amongst the swaying throng I wondered if this was how it had always really been and I had just been too stupid to understand: him having a high old time, gin and vermouth and olives, women and infidelity, secret trysts and traumas and me in evening dress and a smile, standing by his side. A Russian phrase I was once told came to me – only an idiot smiles all the time. Well, I might smile on the outside, but it would be a grave mistake to think I was an idiot.

I hunted all night for the woman in the green dress, but I never saw her again.

That was three days ago. I told no one what I saw and I did nothing – I'm not a dinner service thrower, a cut-up-his-suits-and-hurl-them-out-of-the-window type of woman – why give the neighbours the satisfaction? I'm calculated, a watcher, I have my eyes on the long-term prize. I had never had reason to think he had done this before, he had been a perfect husband. Which made what I saw all the more devastating. And I couldn't confront him, because I couldn't bear him lying to me. I knew all about liars. When it comes to sex I was one myself, and a good one, so I can spot it easily. I didn't want to have to watch him flailing in his deceptions. I was done with that.

But I hadn't slept for three nights as I pored over Gabe's every look and gesture, his behaviour and habits – his increased drinking, his blank looks, his open eyes in the darkest part of the night.

And then at three a.m. this morning I cracked. I Googled private investigators, and up popped the Blue and White, run by a woman named Maggie Malone. I liked the name and I wanted a woman. I had a wishful idea that she would under-stand me, that there would be some homeopathic trace of sisterhood, women together, united against the cheats.

That was how I ended up on Praed Street, Paddington, walking up a set of poky stairs past a lot of foreign-looking men loitering outside a lawyer's office. I could hear a woman laughing like a sea otter. I turned on the landing and saw the Blue and White sign on the open door. A big woman with dark hair caught sight of me and swallowed her laugh double-quick. She probably felt enjoying oneself didn't fit well with the business she was running – like giggles in a funeral parlour.

'Don't be shy, come on in,' she said. A petite younger woman with long dark hair got up and closed the door behind me.

I ended up on a sofa, which meant I was staring at a box of tissues on the table more suited to the back shelf of a minicab. I felt ill. I had already done something I never thought I would, walked into this office. It was all wrong, what was I doing here? The bigger, older woman was saying something to me, but I didn't even hear it.

Then she got my attention by outlining what she could do for me. What she could discover. She was blunt – rude, in fact. I thought about actually sleeping through the night again. And I thought, yes, that was what I wanted. That was what was just. I saw the flash of the green dress, of strappy, gold, fuck-me shoes. I heard that woman's throaty laugh, the way that her hand on my husband's hair had implied an ownership she didn't have, and I thought, Gabe Moreau, you have caused me pain. Husband dearest, you have broken my world, and I'm going to find out the truth, and then we'll see. I think I was laughing. Nerves, that's what it must have been.

Maggie was smiling. 'How can the Blue and White be of service to you, Helene?'

And out it tumbled, the whole sorry saga. 'My husband's having an affair. Well, I think something's going on. I want you to find out the details. Who she is, where . . .'

'OK, Helene. We need to get some information—'

'I'd rather you didn't write anything down.'

Maggie nodded and put down the pen and paper and leaned back. 'Tell me about your husband.'

'He's thirty-seven, we've been married for six years.'

'Do you have children?'

'No. He has a daughter from his previous marriage. Alice is eighteen now, she's just left school and is about to start an internship at Gabe's company.'

'Why do you suspect your husband?' Simona asked.

'I saw something I didn't like at a charity function. He was in a cloakroom with a woman . . . There was a woman who . . . I couldn't see who it was. Just a flash, but . . . but . . .' I tailed off and started again. 'There was definitely something not right about it. Not at all.'

'That's OK,' Maggie said. 'Has there been any other behaviour that's changed lately? Coming back late or not at all, business trips he's going on?'

I shook my head and closed my eyes. I ran my hands up and down my arms as if I was ashamed. Like this, I was just another client to Maggie, just the humdrum day-to-day business involving liars and cheats.

'It can even be the opposite – is he being more attentive to you? Happier with you?' Simona added. 'That's standard behaviour too.'

'I would say he is stressed and drinking more. He's distracted, but that could be work.'

'What does your husband do?' Maggie asked.

'He owns a property company. We're doing a big redevelopment south of the river in Vauxhall.'

Maggie nodded. 'We? You sound quite involved.'

'I work at the company too. I make sure we're contributing the right proportion of profits to charity, that kind of thing.'

'So you're in the office with him?' Maggie asked.

'I do it mainly from home. I go in occasionally.'

'But you know the people in the office?'

'Yes. She's not one of them.'

'OK, that's good, and rules out a lot of people.'

'Have you looked at his mobile phone messages?' Maggie continued.

'Yes. I know his code to get into it, but there's nothing incriminating on his phone.'

'I'm afraid that means nothing. He'll have another one. Or another sim at least.'

I was shocked. Maggie was talking as if this was all normal behaviour.

'Have you ever had suspicions about infidelity before?' Simona asked.

'No, none at all.'

'So, until the cloakroom, everything seemed normal with your husband, your family?'

'Of course,' I lied. Maggie looked at me with those big

brown eyes. 'Alice and I love each other . . .' Despite trying to sound certain I tailed off; I was beginning to question everything about my home life. Did Alice and I get along? She was a moody teenager, the truth was she often drove me into a rage with her thoughtlessness and selfishness. But rage never looks good on anyone, so Maggie was not to know. I ploughed on, burnishing my lie. 'She's a wonderful step-daughter and she adores her father.'

'Why did his last marriage end?'

'His wife died. Sixteen years ago. The car he was driving skidded through a barrier and into a river. She drowned.'

I could feel the pause in the room as what I had said sat heavily.

'That's terrible,' Maggie said. 'Had he been drinking?'

'They had been at a party, but he was breathalysed and had drunk nothing.' To my horror tears welled up. It was the lack of sleep, the stress, it was thinking about Alice and what she had suffered through the loss of her mother, it was my marriage hanging like gossamer. I was so ashamed, I couldn't breathe. Large, bitter tears rolled down my cheeks. Maggie reached over for that box of tissues and pulled three out with a flourish and handed them to me. 'Do you want to know the truth, or don't you?' she asked quietly. 'That is the only question that you need to answer. You don't have to feel guilty about that.'

The silence was punctuated by the roar of buses on the street. Maggie was holding my hand now, patting the palm. It felt lovely. She could have been a therapist – no, that wasn't right, she was much better than a therapist perched on some distant chair. She was that touchy-feely, big-hearted woman who gathered you up in her breasts and pressed you there as you inhaled perfume, cigarettes and sweat and she flicked on a kettle switch or pulled out a bottle of gin. It was a memory of women I had known when I was young, in a different time and a different life.

'You're shaking,' Maggie said.

I looked up at Maggie and into her large brown eyes and sat back and blew my nose. Simona handed me another glass of water.

'Have you told anyone about what you saw?' Simona asked.

I shook my head. 'No. I don't really have the words. I'm going to pay you in cash, I want no trace of this coming back to the house.'

'Cash works for me,' Maggie said.

'Alice must never know, of course. Never.'

'This is between you, me and Gabe. There's no need to be scared,' Maggie said.

I dabbed at my eyes, pushed back my hair. Composed myself. 'Of course I'm scared. I'm worried that once you show me the truth, I'm going to kill him.'

CHAPTER 3

Maggie

Eight weeks before

Helene's threats to kill her husband were run-of-the-mill. Everyone said that, or a version of it. Everyone. Jealousy was a killer. I had a client once shout at me – after he threw his coffee, his briefcase and half the contents of my desk across this room – that he would have rather his wife had been raped than slept with her tennis coach. You see, anger to eat up the world.

Cheating is the great leveller. It brings all who suffer from it – rich or poor, the beautiful or the ugly – to the same place. It makes us small, bitter shadows of ourselves, of what we thought we could be. That's the problem with love, it raises you up, like a Mississippi preacher, and it casts you low, lower than you ever thought you could fall. And it leaves you with nothing to cling to when you've got there. I know, I've been there.

As I watched Helene dab at her eyes with my tissues I thought about my chance encounter with Danny and how he had set me on the path to hearing the most intimate secrets of rich, cuckolded wives.

Twenty years ago I bumped into Danny in a bar. He had elbowed in front of me to get a drink, so I stood on his toe.

I was wearing stilettos and that got his attention. 'Fuck, that hurt!' he shouted, wheeling round, searching for and ready to deck whoever had caused him pain.

'Bet your girlfriend doesn't scream that very often,' I retorted sourly. I had been waiting for far too long in a three-deep throng of punters, all of us waving tenners, desperate to get the attention of the two lazy sods behind the bar in a dive in Camden Town.

'What is your problem?' he shouted.

'It's simple. You're not getting a drink before me, because I might die of old age before this useless barman ever serves me.' I was hollering back at him, because the music was terrible and the acoustics bad. 'Try the blonde five down, she's bored enough with her date that she'll enjoy you swearing at her.'

Danny's eyes slid to the blonde as I finally caught the barman's sloth-slow attention. I ordered and was about to join my mate and begin the fight to get a seat but found Danny was still staring at me. 'See the bloke in the red shirt and the trilby?' he asked.

I looked along the bar. 'The peacock with a pint and a G and T and . . . is that an umbrella he's putting in that glass?'

Danny grinned, showing a gold tooth. 'That's the one. He's eyeing up a woman. Who is it?'

The peacock had weaved his way through the crowd and plonked his drinks down in front of an eager-looking woman and slid in next to her, his back to the wall so he could see the whole pub.

I watched the couple for a few moments. She was leaning forward and talking at him in an unbroken flow, twirling the little umbrella between her fingers and then stabbing the ice in her glass with its end. Every time she looked down, Peacock gave a smouldering look to a woman on another table. 'He's got his eye on the girl in the beret and braces.'

Danny rolled his eyes, disappointed. 'You're not telling me anything I don't already know.'

I frowned. I was competitive and I didn't like his brush-off. I scanned the bar again, checking out Peacock and his date, trying to interpret body language and mood. After a few minutes Peacock got tired of staring at the woman in the beret because she had turned her attention to a tall guy with a crew cut and bodybuilder biceps. Beret and braces turned full towards me and in the harsh light that passed across her face I saw she looked very young, probably too young to be in this bar legally.

I looked back at Danny, took in his dad-down-the-pub outfit, his bulky bag and that he seemed to be drinking alone. 'You're not in here by choice,' I said. 'You're working. I bet you a beer you're following Beret and braces cos her dad's worried and he's paying you to find her, or keep tabs on her.'

I saw Danny's big and generous smile for the first time. 'I don't know what you do and I don't really care, but you'd be a great private investigator.' He handed me his card. Despite trying to feign disinterest, I was intrigued. I had always wanted to join the police, but I was too impatient and cocky to want to waste my time marching up and down at the Hendon training ground.

'How much do you earn?' I asked.

It was his turn to sneer. 'Enough that I don't have to drink in here by choice. Give me a bell if you're brave enough. Now get the fuck out of my way so I can order a beer.'

I got bladdered that night and the rest of the weekend. But by Sunday night I was staring at his card, smelling a break. I was in a dead-end job going nowhere and I liked his upfront manner. I didn't phone Danny or send him a fax; low-key wasn't my style. I broke into his office on Monday morning – a supermarket loyalty card picked up from a pub floor and applied to the lock on his shabby Caledonian Road office door took twenty seconds – and waited for him to arrive.

He stopped in confusion when he saw me sitting there. 'You're hired,' he said. 'But this is important. Don't break the law. Ever. You're not doing this job correctly if you break the law.'

I've taken Danny at his word – more or less – ever since. Danny taught me everything about the business. He was passionate and cynical. 'Everybody cheats,' was his motto. 'And everybody lies about it. I get paid to show them that they cheated, and that they lied.'

Danny was bullying and volatile and erratic but he was loyal and funny and smart. I loved that job. I stayed for five years. We were the tabloid equivalent of the bedroom police, taking money from whoever wanted to know and was willing to pay. Insecure wives, jealous husbands, worried parents, even sometimes the benefits agency. There was a guy, an Irish bloke called Gerry O'Brady, he walked with a cane and the revenue protection boys at Westminster Council weren't entirely convinced about Gerry's permanent disability. They hired us to take a look. Poor old Gerry, it was his soft old heart that gave him away in the end: his daughter was getting married, and amid the many guests and the mountains of booze was me, and I caught him on video dancing with his beloved Nancy in her wedding finery. No cane, no bad back, just the love for his daughter and his pride on her special day, and Michael Jackson to seal the deal. Did I feel guilty that I got Gerry five months in jail? Not one little bit. Did I like exposing the truth? I had no doubt I was strong enough to take it. If I was ever stuck in the Matrix, I used to say, I'd be grabbing the red pill. Give it to me, show me everything, I could handle it.

When I gathered up the courage to tell Danny that I was leaving to set up my own operation, he swore at me, then he paused, his finger tracing along the top of a brown Leica that he was fond of using on his stakeouts. He understood why I was going. 'The business is changing, girl, new technology's going to make what we do a piece of piss. Work hard and you could do very well.' I wasn't beyond basking in the approval of others, particularly of my boss, and I was pleased. He pointed his tobacco-stained forefinger at me. 'The reason you could be the best of the best? You don't have any second thoughts about who you're going to fuck over.' It was a requirement of the business, I knew, but I had wondered then, as I wondered later, whether he had meant it as a compliment.

'Give your agency a feminine name. Something women can relate to. Make them think the business isn't grubby.'

I thought for a second. 'What about Before I Find You?'

He frowned as he began pacing the office. 'Before I find you I get paid the big bucks?' He shook his head. 'No, use the name of a flower or a pet or a Farrow and Ball paint colour. Women love that Farrow and Ball shit.'

I laughed. 'What's your favourite colour, Danny?'

'Blue and white. Like Tottenham football club.'

That's how the Blue and White agency came into existence. Football colours.

I'd like to be able to catch up with Danny, in the wake of how everything turned out, but he died windsurfing in Greece two months after he retired. He got trapped under the board as he was pulled out to sea on winds that were too strong for him. He didn't have the strength to right himself and he drowned, in the bright blue Aegean. I still miss Danny.

Two weeks after I parted company with Danny I found a dingy first-floor office on Praed Street in Paddington that shared the corridor with a travel agent's. It was central and cheap and I've stayed ever since. The travel agent's is now an immigration lawyer's – people do the leaving themselves and need help with the arriving – but little else has changed over the years. I did a simple refit, ripped up the carpet to get rid of the smell of fags, brought in pot plants and pale linen blinds and bought retro filing cabinets and that large black fan. I got tasteful calling cards printed and handed them out liberally. My first three clients all came via word of mouth: and it was far from glamorous. I was staking out pub car parks, a massage parlour in King's Cross, the men's public toilets on Clapham Common. That first year was hard. I wasn't making money, or not enough. I had big ambitions and I couldn't realise them. I had to get noticed. My costs were high too: I had a group of freelancers I used on occasional jobs, and in the office I had my part-time secretary/ office manager/helper. I wanted to pull in richer clients and do more complex cases. Higher profile cheats had more to lose and would be harder to catch, I reasoned.

I probably would have stayed as a struggling one-and-a-half-woman band, if it hadn't been for Mrs Farmley. What happened to Mrs Farmley still haunts me to this day.

I tuned back in to Helene and Simona and their conversation. 'How did you hear about the Blue and White?' Simona asked.

'I found it on Google. I liked the name. The Blue and White sounds like an old colonial hotel in Rangoon,' Helene said.

I smiled. I didn't set Helene right.

CHAPTER 4

Maggie

Eight weeks before

The day Mrs Farmley came into the Blue and White it was raining. The rubbish was flowing down the gutters of Praed Street and the odour of someone's omelette bap was trapped in the enclosed stairway.

Mrs Farmley had been married for nineteen years and had three beautiful children. She had shown me photographs of a happy family; they lived in a spacious detached house in a Hertfordshire village. Husband Hal worked at a large insurance firm in the City. He worked long hours and often came back late. Two nights a week he was at a branch office in Hampshire and he played golf on Saturday mornings. In the end, it's the smallest fissures that break a marriage. People talk about doubt as a seed. But that's wrong, seeds grow slowly and steadily. Doubt is a disease and once it's taken hold in your tissues, in your heart, nothing can stop it mutating and expanding until it destroys everything you know and love. Everything.

People think they're stronger than that, that they are immune, that vows and social pressure and routine and children – always the bairns! – can protect them from doubt's effects. They are wrong. And so was Mrs Farmley. Hal made a careless mistake, he left his mobile phone – he was new to that new technology and he left it on a shelf where his seven-year-old could reach it. The natural curiosity of his beloved seven-year-old son destroyed his life. His son opened a message.

While Hal was in the shower Mrs Farmley, knowing the mobile was valuable and worrying about it breaking, took it from the son's grasp and saw the message '24th no good x'.

The number was another mobile. That x at the end. X marks the spot. The 24th of October was the following Saturday and she was taking the kids to her parents'. He was travelling back from a conference out of town.

Mrs Farmley made her first mistake. She didn't ask him about it. She let the doubt swamp her like a tidal wave. She didn't confront Hal, she didn't give him the opportunity to lie and convince her of a false truth. She came to me.

I eventually found out Hal's secret with the help of a grey wig. I have a bag of tricks that help me do my job. A hi-vis jacket and hard hat – the public and the target obey without thinking when someone is wearing that kit – an ID badge pinned to a chest, a variety of hats, sunglasses and a short grey wig. A woman, if she's older than twenty-five and wants to become invisible and forgettable, puts on a short, grey wig.

Hal was used to parking his car in a hotel car park and doing a quick switch in the back corridor and driving away in another vehicle. The grey wig allowed me to follow him closely enough to see it. Three weeks later we found out that Hal wasn't having an affair with his secretary or a woman he met at conferences. He was married. Hal had a whole other family, two daughters aged fourteen and twelve. He wasn't at the other company branch, he was leading another life as a man called John Andrews. He was a front-page-of-the-paper bigamist.

I told Mrs Farmley that what I had found was serious, that this was not something to deal with on her own. I asked her to come to the office with a friend. She didn't do it. The reaction of clients to the material I presented to them was unpredictable. I assumed women were safer, they tended to cry out their shock and betrayal; their fists didn't tend to fly, but I'd dodged more than one tipping bookcase and phones shoved off desks to clatter at my feet. And what I'd found was as bad as it got.

Mrs Farmley stood by my desk when her world fell apart, nodded, tucked her handbag into her armpit and walked calmly out of our door. I followed her, pleading with her to call someone, have a friend pick her up. She insisted she was fine, really, as she stepped into a taxi.

I called her several more times that evening, and when she didn't answer, my misgivings increased. Eventually, against all my normal operating procedure, I went to her house. I was too late – I couldn't get past the police cordon.

The police told me later that Hal had come home from the office at seven thirty. Mrs Farmley had watched Hal kiss their younger daughter goodnight at eight. As he was running a bath, Mrs Farmley had rooted around in the cupboard under the stairs and found an electric bar heater and an extension cable. While Hal/John was relaxing in the tub, she had plugged in the heater and opened the bathroom door. The house had plunged into darkness as the lights shorted.

The lawyers argued for a long time about whether the smell of burnt flesh was admissible at Mrs Farmley's trial.

Never think that infidelity doesn't ruin lives, that our secret, domestic selves can't wreak the most vicious vengeance. Cheating ruined Mrs Farmley's life, the life of her children, those other children who knew Hal as John, but as a darling daddy just the same. And I had made it happen. Hal might have been the one who did the dirty, but I had been the one to pull back the stone and watch the raw pain of the secrets wriggling and scorching under the light.

Mrs Farmley got nine years for manslaughter. I had to testify at her trial. It wasn't the first time I'd been in court, but it brought back some bad memories. So, at thirty-five did I grow a conscience? Did I go and do good works in the community, did I go into battle for those less fortunate than myself?

No, is the long answer. I'm a striver – we have to be grubby on the way up before we can be magnanimous in our time and money; before we can become better people.

That spring the phone never stopped ringing. However sick I felt about Mrs Farmley, her children and Hal, I found out there's no such thing as bad publicity. Over the next five years the Blue and White became the go-to destination for anyone with a cheating spouse. I hired Rory, a lapsed young Catholic from rural Ireland who washed up in London, hoping he was far enough away from his parents and eight siblings that his sexuality could remain the only secret his family ever had. The agency began to pull in the dough. I hired Simona, a very well-educated Italian who spoke four languages who couldn't even get a bar job in Naples, a few years later. Danny had been right, women were in the driving seat now, they were earning their own money, running their own lives, they weren't standing by or shutting up and putting up with what those they loved did to them. I was rising up on the backs of other people's broken romantic dreams. Three months after the trial, I hired four more part-time staff.

I was the cocky, mouthy, hard-drinking, cheater-hunting weapon of relationship destruction. Before I find you, I get paid the big bucks, I sometimes hummed to myself.

I had a checklist of success that I measured myself against. I got a result on every case I took on. I was going to expand into other cities. I was looking into partnering with a spy camera store, maybe running a franchise. I'd got a hundred different ideas of how love gone wrong was going to make me rich and happy.

I was healthy, only forty-two, what could go wrong for a sex detective like me?

CHAPTER 5

Alice

Seven weeks and four days before

What a summer I had before me! I was so excited that I sometimes had to squeeze my eyes shut and open them and give a little laugh, because it felt as if a barista was going to overpour the froth on a cappo, or champagne was going to rise up and burst over the rim of its glass. School was over, Trinity term was finally done. The world beckoned and I was ready.

I assessed myself in the mirror in my room, dithering about whether to have my long red hair up or down. I'd put it up, otherwise I looked like a Pre-Raphaelite nutter about to drown herself in a river. Those women were weak. Not a good look for a first day at work. I'd got on the dark skirt and a white shirt with the buttons done up, and pearl earrings that Poppa bought me. When I told the assistant in the shop that I was buying the skirt for my first job she was keen for me to get the red and make an impact, so I bought the black one. You have to know your own mind. I didn't think it was smart to take career advice from a woman in her thirties who worked a shop floor. I was starting as an intern at Poppa's company – my eventual company – that day.

I came down into the kitchen; Poppa and Helene were

already up. Helene handed me a cup of coffee from the percolator. 'You ready?' She smiled and it accentuated the tiredness of her eyes. She hadn't been sleeping, I could hear her slippers with the bunny ears that she insists on wearing scraping on the hall carpet late at night outside my room and creaking in the office across the corridor from my bedroom.

She didn't hand Poppa a coffee and I noticed that after a short hesitation he went to get his own. Helene was being petty, but then most adults I meet seem to act like children, including my stepmother. Helene is being . . . I don't know how to say it . . . Helenesh. Like a verb! To Helene, I Helene, she Helenes. Definition: a state of suspended, continual agitation. She was uptight, like *really* uptight. I respected that. Helene likes things just so, and I think there's nothing wrong with that. Poppa taught me not to accept second best, and Poppa is a good judge of what is right.

'We're quite the family business today!' Helene said.

Helene went into the office two days a week; she directed some of the profits to charity, which helped reduced the tax bill, or something. It sounded small-scale. I thought Helene should be more ambitious. She certainly had lots of talents and what's the point in getting out of bed if you weren't going to try!

Yesterday we all went out for breakfast at a local café and sat at one of the outside tables, watching the crowds walk by. Poppa leaned across and tried to kiss Helene but she pushed him away, snapping 'don't'. It was as if she couldn't bear to have him touch her. They have been married for only six years. I don't understand marriage. I can look at Poppa's and I think – is that it? Really? Their relationship was like a balloon that was slowly deflating in a garden the morning after a party.

It made me wonder what Momma and Poppa's relationship

had been like. She died when I was two. I never knew her. I liked to think sometimes that I could remember her laugh, a particular high, short sound, but I know I've made it up. I dream about her, and in my fantasies she becomes whoever or whatever I want her to be – astronaut, model, fortune-teller, masseuse. Sometimes friends' mothers hug me and I think, did my momma smell like that? Did my momma fiddle with her hair like that?

I try so hard, but thinking about Momma made me sad, and I didn't want to be sad! April 19th. That was the date she died. A late frost made Poppa come off the road on a bridge and into a river in flood. It was an accident, but there have been nasty people who have tried to make trouble with it, some girls who should have known better.

Liana Boothroyd was one. She sat behind me in Latin and didn't like me getting all the teachers' attention. I was called Hitler at school, most likely because I always had my hand up to answer the questions. I heard her whispering to Georgia, 'Her dad killed her mum. How much do you have to hate someone to do that?' I said nothing. I had heard that kind of thing before from sad little people who were unkind. But she had laughed. I heard her giggling. 'She must have been a nagging bitch.'

I saw crimson red, and I stood up and turned round and let my fists fly. I wasn't proud of what I did, and after we had both been hauled in front of Mr Dewhurst, who was the head of year, and Liana had been given an ice pack for her bleeding nose, I apologised to Liana. They were only silly words she had used and they couldn't hurt me. I know the truth. My poppa loved my momma. He always said he did.

I was really scared about being expelled though, and once Liana had been excused I sat down with Mr Dewhurst and tried my best to convince him that I was truly sorry.

If you really want something you have to work hard at it.

That was the first time I got to know Mr Dewhurst better.

Poppa was still talking in the kitchen, brushing toast crumbs off his shirtfront. 'You're going to be taking a look at all departments – sales, finance, the architects' office – then we'll go and see some sites across London. You'll get the full picture of how this industry works – the good guys and the bad guys, the highs and the lows.'

'Bad guys?' I asked.

'You're making it sound like the Wild West,' Helene said. 'Your dad's hardly the gunslinger swaggering into town. You're a special, nice, wonderful girl, Alice, I'm sure you'll smash it.'

I smiled, because I am a forgiving person, but this was so typically Helene! It was a dig, a jabbing reminder of my privilege, of our money, of my elite education and my instant internship because Poppa was the boss. Sometimes I thought Helene didn't appreciate that Momma died in fear and pain – what's privileged about that?

'Come on, Alice, we can't be late on our first day,' Poppa said.

'Break a leg,' Helene added as we left.

Poppa drove. I have no fear of cars, but I have a big fear of drowning. That would be like, unbearable, literally. It was no surprise, I suppose, considering what happened to Momma. Mr Dewhurst's fear was drowning too. We had so much in common!

Poppa once said to me when I was little that the worst thing that could happen had happened to me, and so I would never have to go through it again.

I have chosen to believe that. I have lived my life since Momma's death with that in mind – the worst is over. The best is yet to come.

CHAPTER 6

Helene

Seven weeks and three days before

I hadn't been sleeping well for days and I was making mistakes – changing into the kind of distracted person I used to have no time for. Yesterday I lost my keys. I met a friend in a local coffee shop to talk about a fundraising event she wanted help with. The place was too crowded, with pushchairs being shoved past stools, and our conversation was often interrupted by the squawks of babies until a headache was drilling through my skull. I was keen to get home, but once outside the house I couldn't find my keys. I had to get the neighbour to let me in using her spare set. Once inside I spent a long time staring at my handbag with its baggy opening, thinking about the ease with which someone could have taken them, the vague sense in the café of someone being behind me, of a sunhat scraping my shoulder . . .

Did I need to change the locks on the front door? As soon as I had the thought I dismissed it. Pull yourself together, I intoned, you're becoming a nervous wreck. Keys get lost, life goes on.

I splashed some water on my face, opened my laptop and went back to my emails. But the feeling of something being out of place remained. Knowing that Maggie and others I had paid were out there, somewhere, didn't help. It made me feel I was being watched. At work I couldn't settle. I wandered the office corridors, sensitised to the ping of texts and the tapping of computer keyboards. I dropped in on Gabe's secretary more than I needed to – Soraya was always polite but distant, as if I was an irritating junior employee out to trouble the chief. She promptly apologised when Gabe was on a site visit with Peter Fairweather, the smooth-chinned boss of Partridger, an American building company. If Gabe was in his office he looked up from his desk, the phone often clamped to his ear, leaving his head cocked at the side, and smiled at me, an eyebrow rising into a question mark. He was silently asking 'What can I do for you? How can I be of help?'

And I smiled and shook my head and shrugged my shoulders and retreated.

I didn't know what I was looking for, I was terrified of what I might find. I was a coward, hiring Maggie Malone to do my dirty work for me. I thought I was a woman who acted, who stood up for herself, who trod her own path, however you want to express it, but that was before I fell in love. Love changed everything. I was very scared about whether I could live without him.

I glimpsed Alice, so formal in her dark skirt and buttoned-up blouse, hunched in the corner of the meeting room scribbling notes, a collection of much older men gathered round a table getting animated. Gabe was head of the table, the finance meeting was running over. He looked tired and drawn from this angle. Work was certainly stressful at the moment, but was it also something else?

I was scared because of Alice. I loved Alice. She was not my biological child, I couldn't have children, and I hadn't known her as a young child, but it mattered not at all. She was my life, my sun and my future. Sweet, damaged Alice.

What I saw in that cloakroom at the Café Royal upended my world, but Alice had her world destroyed in that car crash, and it had been long in the making to fix it again.

Alice adored her dad. With one parent gone, she had attached herself completely to the other. That was hardly unusual or surprising and it was not for me to damage that union, but I used to have principles: be truthful, be proud, be strong. Love unconditionally, love whoever you want. I was aware that I had become a middle-aged woman mired in compromise.

Alice's internship with the company was one such compromise – she'd walked right in to the job because Gabe could not refuse anything she asked for. They didn't see the thousands of letters and emails I got from less fortunate young kids, desperate for a leg up, a break. Alice was cosseted in privilege and connections, with a grade-A education – she was fearsomely bright – and natural drive, and I couldn't say no. I saw her little pout that starts when she is disappointed or annoyed, and Gabe gave in as quickly as I did. She had experienced so much upheaval for one so young, and my inner tigress roared – make an exception for her! Break yourself on the wheel for her!

She cast a spell over her dad, a spell over me too, I suppose. He had fought so hard to give his daughter solid foundations beneath her feet and in two hours – at lunchtime – I was heading back to the Blue and White, back to the snoopers who had the power to take it all away. That woman in the Café Royal was a threat to my family, to what I have tried so hard to create. Only by knowing more can I understand how to protect what I love the most. And I would do anything, absolutely anything, to protect what I love.

CHAPTER 7

Alice

Seven weeks and three days before

I'd been at GWM – that's short for Gabe Walter Moreau – for two days, and I'd tried really hard to remember the names of a ton of people. I shook hands wherever I went, introduced myself and smiled at everyone. I surreptitiously snapped photos of people on my phone and added names later, so that I didn't make any mistakes. I hated making mistakes.

On my first day Poppa handed me over to a man named James and he showed me all aspects of the business. A lot of the office is open plan and I eavesdropped like a pro! Of course a lot of my time was spent filing, but I expected that. Some people might think that was boring but I got to skim read a lot of stuff – I was a fast reader and a quick learner and I didn't mind at all.

Sometimes I saw a huddle of people laughing by the water cooler outside Poppa's office. One time I came out under the pretence of getting a drink of water, but really I had wanted to join in, but they smiled politely when I arrived and moved away. The same thing happened today. They knew I was the boss's daughter, so of course I understood. I just needed to work harder to win them over.

A little later that day James showed me the design studio where they mocked up beautiful images of finished property projects – line-drawn people standing by small-scale shrubbery in front of plate glass – when he got excited and picked up a magazine from a table. 'Look, it's Oblomov and his wife.' A cluster of people nearby began commenting on the Russian property tycoon and his wife. 'Hot doesn't begin to cover it', 'film star looks', 'silver fox', 'the wife's a bit plain' and 'mumsy' were bandied about.

I smiled. Best not to mention that Arkady Oblomov and Irina were coming to Helene's charity fundraiser in a few weeks. I'd never met them, but he was a competitor of Poppa's for the Vauxhall development site and had lost out because he had bid too low. Poppa had celebrated winning, but he hadn't crowed, he's not mean-spirited or cruel like these gossips here, he has always been respectful of Arkady and kept his doors always open to friends and business colleagues alike. I looked at the series of gaudy colour photos of the two of them in a large room with aggressively polished furniture.

All I could think was that Arkady was very handsome and his wife was well, less so, but I was at work and I wanted to be positive! 'He's amazing looking,' I said.

'Yeah, so how did that Soviet carthorse snag him?' someone scoffed.

'Maybe he actually loves her,' I said defiantly. I looked up from the magazine and saw that everyone was staring at me and no one agreed. When does cynicism take hold in a heart? How old do you have to be to think love is a lie and marriage a transaction?

I argued with my friend Lily about it too. I told Lily when we were lying around on my bed one afternoon that I was saving myself for the perfect man. She doubled over with amusement, her long dark hair sweeping along the carpet. I didn't see what was so funny. It wasn't something to be given away cheaply, I told Lily. When I found him our love would be magnificent. It would be perfect. I didn't like things that weren't perfect. For a while I had thought Mr Dewhurst was such a man.

Lily snorted. 'You'll be waiting a lifetime and then some,' she said.

Lily's parents were divorced. I was sure that's why she had such a jaundiced view of something so pure and important.

'And anyway,' Lily said, her face crumpled into a mischievous grin, 'for all you know maybe you'll fall in love with a woman.'

We squealed as if scandalised and rolled around on the bed.

Lily said she heard her mum having sex with her new boyfriend and asked whether I heard Poppa and Helene doing it.

'Never!' I lied. Truth was, I had heard them having sex. The violent, animal tone of it chilled me to the bone. I saw myself in a dark, meat-filled room, bloody carcasses touching my bare skin and making me recoil. It sounded like pain, it was a ritual I didn't understand, something denied me that made me angry. I would cover my head tightly with a pillow, hearing the roar of noise of my own thoughts inside my head. When I dared take the pillow away, the air cooled the tears on my cheeks.

Funny. I hadn't heard them having sex lately.

I was brought back to the design studio by James taking me to do more filing in the accounts department.

CHAPTER 8

Alice

Seven weeks and three days before

I was in Poppa's office sitting on a little fabric-covered chair in the corner, listening and learning. I was taking lots of notes, it was important to be able to keep a record.

There were three men in there with Poppa, the finance director and two lawyers. They were arguing about liabilities going forward and loan payments and due dates on the Connaught Tower development.

Poppa kept scraping his hand backwards through his hair and looked stressed. I really wanted to contribute and it was a real effort to keep quiet and just take notes. I felt Poppa should have been stronger with these other men, he should have stood his ground more.

The lawyer kept looking at me. I think he was wondering why I was in the room. I've more right to be in here than you! I thought. The lawyer asked for more coffee.

Poppa looked up from where he was flipping impatiently through a pile of papers on his incredibly messy desk. 'Alice, can you bring in a fresh pot?'

I stood reluctantly. I didn't want to be told to go and make coffee, though that was mainly what I had been doing for the past couple of days.

While I was in the kitchen, I convinced myself that making coffee was providing a useful service to the important people who ran GWM. But by the time I got back with the warmed pot and the clean cups and the hot milk, the office was empty, and I was frustrated about being cut out.

I poured a cup for Poppa, making it just as he liked it, hoping he would be back soon. I moved some papers to make sure I could set it down and it wouldn't spill.

I paused. From Poppa's office the hallway is partly visible through the sandblasted glass of the wall and from this angle I could see if anyone was approaching from the rest of the company. I began to casually lift the edges of paper, move sheets around, organise and tidy. I was a fast reader and could scan super fast. I had got to the bottom of the pile and had started on the next when I stopped. Buried under a stapled receipt for red wine was a handwritten note. The words made me take a sharp breath: 'You owe me. I'm not going away.'

The writing was scratchy and hard, each letter carved into the paper with such force it would have indented any paper below it. I instinctively looked up and around Poppa's office, but only bland walls and pale light reflected back at me. I took a photo of the message with my phone, put the pile of papers back as I found them and took the coffee cups to the kitchen. I was holding the handles so hard my knuckles were white.

CHAPTER 9

Helene

Seven weeks and two days before

I had to come back to the Blue and White because I had forgotten to bring a photo of Gabe with me the first time I came. I could have sent Maggie a photo from my phone, but there was an image of Gabe and me that Alice took a few years ago that I really liked, which sat on a shelf at home. I'm not vain, but it mattered to me that I showed our best side to Maggie. I liked the image of the perfect family, I liked people thinking I lived the dream.

Maggie took a long look at the picture, turned it over and flipped it out from behind the glass and Rory took it over to the photocopier and made a colour copy. 'We don't want to end up following the wrong guy now, do we?' Maggie had said as we waited for Rory to finish.

A disconcerting thought bubbled up then and must have been strong enough to show on my face because Maggie raised an eyebrow and asked if everything was OK.

'You follow the men, I get that. But how often do the mistresses pay attention to the family?'

'Pay attention?' Maggie asked.

'Oh you know, contact the family, follow the wives, perhaps.'

'Do you think this has happened to you?' she asked.

'No, I don't think so.'

'*Think* so?'

Maggie was the kind of woman who dealt in specifics, and I couldn't give her those. Now I had said it aloud, it sounded ridiculous. I was troubled by losing my keys but didn't want to tell her that. I was catastrophising. 'I'm being paranoid,' I said. 'It's a lack of sleep.'

'I'll be the judge of that,' she said. 'Has anything happened?'

'No, not to me. But have you ever experienced it?'

A strange look came over Maggie's face, and she looked away. 'Not in my years on the job.' She looked up at me. 'Were you married before Gabe?' she asked.

I shook my head, wondering at her abrupt change of subject. 'What about you – are you hitched?'

'No,' she said firmly.

I guessed trust was difficult when you did her job. I could see her on the hard end of infidelity and I imagined she wouldn't take it sitting down.

'My problem is,' Maggie added, 'I could never stay faithful.'

She didn't look embarrassed at all, and I thought, we are so much more alike than you realise.

CHAPTER 10

Alice

Seven weeks and two days before

I lay awake thinking about that note I found on Poppa's desk. Who could have sent it and why? What did it mean?

I knew about notes – it was how Mr Dewhurst and I communicated. Notes had a power that stays with them; I lingered over them too long.

When Poppa and Helene went out to dinner I decided to have a look around their bedroom to see if I could find anything else that might have been sent to Poppa. Some people might have seen this as snooping, but it was all for a good purpose. I respected people's privacy. After opening all the drawers and looking under the bed I found nothing, so I did the same in the home office; I checked under and above things. Then I rummaged through the wastepaper basket. At the bottom I found a collection of bits of ripped paper. I began to set them back together again on the desk. Slowly the picture became clearer as with each piece of paper more letters and words appeared, eventually spelling out 'You owe me. I deserve better.' I also managed to construct an envelope from the remaining paper shreds. Poppa's Bosnian surname, Gabe Buric, was written on the front. It was a name and a past he escaped a generation ago. There was no stamp, the message had been hand-delivered. I opened my phone and looked at the photo of the note I had found in the office. The writing was a match and the dark pen and thin white paper was the same. I took a photo of the note.

The doorbell rang and I jumped so high that the pieces of paper scattered across the floor. I threw them all in a hurry back into the wastepaper basket and opened the front door. It was an Amazon delivery for Helene. I stared at the box, suspicious. Even though I knew I shouldn't, I opened it. It was six wine glasses. I carefully taped the box together again and left it by the front door.

What was it that Poppa owed? Was somebody trying to hurt him? Did Helene know about it?

I balled my hands into tight little fists. No one was going to hurt my beloved daddy, I thought.

CHAPTER 11

Maggie

Seven weeks before

Helene wasn't surprised that I had never married. I could see her calculating the impossible odds of falling in love when I spent my days unmasking love gone sour. I was glad she thought my single life was down to what I spent my waking hours doing. There was no way she would ever need to hear the name Colin Torday. I certainly wasn't going to tell her the truth.

There's a reason why I was good at my job. I've done what those I tailed did. I knew that for some people, it was impossible to stay on the right side of their marriage vows. They are condemned for that, exposed and divorced for that, but it doesn't mean they aren't sometimes victims too.

But it's hard to feel sorry for a victim like that, and I didn't see Gabe Moreau as a victim. I saw him as money to be made and a reputation to cement.

We had started Operation Gabe Moreau on Monday morning and went at it for five days straight. With the basic details that his wife provided we had the means to completely open up Gabe Moreau, to strip him of his privacy and scrutinise his every move. And it was all legal. There's no privacy in the Internet age. If you care about that kind of thing, invent a time machine and go back to yesteryear.

To watch someone, really watch even the devious and careful ones, required two people working the day shift and often someone at night as well. We did a lot of our tailing work in a London taxi; no one gave a second glance if they saw it hanging around in a street. It also doubled as a convenient space to change outfits. I took the day shift with Simona, Rory always preferred to work nights. When he wasn't tailing our clients' spouses he was falling into or out of an all-night bar or club.

It rarely took more than ten days to get irrefutable evidence of an affair. It was like playing hide and seek with a small child; they stand in the middle of the room and put their hands over their eyes. They think, if I can't see you, you can't see me. Cheaters are like toddlers, running full pelt towards their sex sessions with no regard for who is standing by, recording their every move. And for the record, most cheaters like to visit their lovers every five days. Human beings are funny creatures – full of enough vanity to fancy they are original when really, we're all the same.

When we first saw Gabe and Helene's home, Simona and I knew we'd got lucky. It was three floors of Georgian property porn designed to turn on those of us who squeeze into poky spaces or wake to the roar of trucks on the A40. The house was part of an elegant, curving terrace and sat three in from a quiet corner in Islington, north London. A small alley ran from the corner down the back of the houses and gave access to the gardens and we had several parking options that enabled us to watch the front door and alley simultaneously. Large London plane trees were accommodating enough to throw a pleasant shade over the taxi. I thought this job might even be enjoyable – staking people out at home is often a challenge of double yellow lines and nosy neighbours.

Gabe came out the front door at five to seven with a young woman with red hair. Helene had told us this was his daughter Alice. They drove away in his car.

Gabe Moreau looked better than his photo. He was taller, with a little less hair and a little more attitude. He wore a suit but carried the jacket over his arm. He opened the passenger door for his daughter and smiled as she got in. He cast a look around the street before he folded himself into the car, but his gaze never rested on us.

It never did. I prided myself that Gabe would never know I was there. I was bloody good at my job.

The next few days were routine – we waited for long periods outside his office in a large building on Upper Regent Street, north of Oxford Circus, followed him into coffee shops, sat at the bar at busy restaurants and endured the crush of after-dinner pubs and bars.

We took photos of the people Gabe met.

One evening after work he walked to a private members' club in Soho. For all the places you cannot follow someone or the private rooms you cannot enter, there is always a bribe you can pay. Always. For doormen, bouncers, fixers, cabbies and drug dealers, the cash-in-hand enticements work wonders.

Moments after Gabe had gone inside the members-only club Rory and I approached the door. While he acted silly, distracting the girl on the desk, I went over to the doorman and shook his hand, making out I knew him. I palmed a fifty into the breast pocket of his jacket while asking who the man who had just arrived was drinking with.

The doorman did a quick calculated glance left and right, smiled and walked away. A few moments later he stepped outside to tell me that he was drinking with a middle-aged man. It was the easiest fifty quid he had ever earned.

I thought about the people I tailed all the time. I spent time anticipating what they were going to do, how they would act. It was a power trip. Certain things immediately stood out about Gabe Moreau. He was effortlessly popular. Riotous laughter would often erupt from his restaurant table, making other diners look over in envy at the good time a group that didn't include them were having. It was often his arm up calling the waiter for more wine, more desserts. He was an exhibitionist, a showman, the centre of attention. He was a big tipper.

On the Friday I wanted to check the inside of his office building and followed him. GWM Holdings was on the fourth floor. I went up to five and walked down the fire escape. I glanced through the doors of GWM and saw a normal-looking office. I walked to the top floor of the building and called the lift. Several people got in with me and I rode down and stopped on four. The doors opened and Gabe got in.

Not good. There's one rule about tailing a target – don't ever let them see you. Ever. A private investigator should be as invisible as air, as quiet as smoke. And less than a week after I'd started the job, he was staring right at me.

And then he wasn't. His gaze didn't linger, his eyes swept across my face with as little interest as if I were an office chair or a cup of coffee in a bin.

He turned round to face the doors and I knew then that he wouldn't remember me. My face was one of thousands he saw every day as he forged through life. It was crowded in the small lift, and Gabe's neck was inches from my face. I studied the shape of his head, the fall of his hair, the shadow of his shaving line, the knife crease down the back of his blue Oxford shirt.

I smelled him; a faint whiff of aftershave, something expensive. He spoke to the woman next to him but kept looking straight ahead. She was eager to please, smiling and answering his questions. They shared a comfort that comes with many hours spent working with someone. I made her as his secretary.

The woman turned and looked round at me. Was that some

animal instinct of self-preservation? An atavistic reaction to scrutiny – like being hunted?

Cheats are opportunists, because they are human. They end up close to home. They cheat with their colleagues or family friends, or with people they pay. And the first suspect on the list is always the secretary.

Helene had seen him with one woman, but that didn't mean there weren't others. I once tailed a grandfather who was seeing five women.

This lady was middle-aged, wore a wedding ring, high heels that looked like they would be giving her grief by the evening. She wore a peach blouse in a drapey fabric and her hair done up in a tight bun.

I knew it wasn't her. Gabe had a pack of papers in his hand and the lift was crowded. He adjusted his hand and brushed against her arm. She instinctively reeled back, a small, delicate movement that preserved her private space. Everything a person I was tailing did could be read by me.

They were professionals. His hands hadn't slid over the most intimate parts of her body; she was a foreign country to him.

By the end of that first week, we had nothing. I wasn't worried. What Helene didn't understand was that Gabe Moreau was a slam-dunk cheater. In my business the client was usually right, because ninety per cent of the time, if someone came through the door wanting my services, it was because there was something to find. There was no smoke without fire with infidelity.

CHAPTER 12

Helene

Six weeks and three days before

I knew the Blue and White had been following Gabe for a few days. Maggie, Rory and Simona were watching his every move. It was a strange sensation. When darkness fell last night I imagined they crept up the alley at the back of the house and watched us in the kitchen from over the back fence. I had no idea what they witnessed, how many secrets or embarrassments they were privy to. It made me try and behave better. It made me wish Gabe would.

What would someone think, looking in on our evening together? I had thought we enjoyed a happy family, a good relationship, but is that how Maggie would see us? How big is the gap between appearance and reality? When Gabe and Alice got back from work he was called next door by our neighbour who was in a jam trying to erect a trampoline for her grandchildren. I started listening over the garden wall as she tried to help him with steel supports and badly translated Chinese instructions. In the end she good-naturedly gave up and went to make tea to help him along.

There would be balloons, she said, and Gabe had described how he would like to play balloon tennis with the kids across the garden wall. I wouldn't normally have eavesdropped on their conversation, but I see Gabe in the cloakroom with that woman and every scenario takes a new and dangerous form. Even when he was giving our elderly neighbour a helping hand. Every failure of mine is accentuated including my inability to have children. Gabe would have loved nothing more than to play with our own children. His innocent neighbourly chat is like a screwdriver being pushed into my heart and twisted.

Hurry up, Maggie, I thought, hurry up and find me some answers.

There was clattering by the door and Alice let her friend Lily in.

It was a hot evening and while Alice was still dressed in her work clothes, Lily had spent the day outside somewhere. She was wearing hotpants and a crop top and her hair was tied high on her head. She was a show pony, large doe eyes staring up under a thick mane of dark hair. Alice is a serious girl and I was intrigued she was hanging around with someone so flighty. It was faintly comical to see Alice in her dark and sombre office clothes and Lily in little more than a bikini. But they seemed happy enough, nattering away about something I didn't understand and throwing fruit in a blender.

I was trying to get Gabe to pay attention to the charity auction we were planning in a couple of weeks. He came in from next door's garden and washed his hands.

'Shall we do wagu beef or the chicken satay at the auction?' I asked him.

'Is that how you pronounce it? I thought it was wayju.' He tried a Japanese accent on for size.

'It's wagu,' Lily said confidently as she threw chia seeds into the blender.

'Sorry,' Gabe confessed. 'It's not my first language after all.' He opened a kitchen drawer and pulled out a spatula. 'Can't we just have beef burgers?' He mimed flipping one and then tried to poke me in the ribs to get my attention.

'Put it away,' I said, irritated, 'it's not like you can cook with it.'

He was not taking this seriously. We were doing this party to try to oil wheels with our financial supporters so that they will lend us the money to finish not just Connaught Tower but Connaught Two. We paid above the odds for the site, and we beat a lot of competitors. We were stretched, with high debts and onerous repayments. And I understood what made businessmen – make that most men – tick. They didn't like to lose. Partridger, the American conglomerate, lost and Peter Fairweather, the east coast CEO of the company, would be angry. He'd have dented pride, shareholders and even more senior managers in New York to placate. Partridger wanted the Vauxhall site as the first wave of its expansion into London. Questions would be asked, doubts would be sown, his place in the Partridger hierarchy would be less secure. He would feel more paranoid; every morning he walked in the office he would secretly wonder if it would be his last. I knew how he would be feeling because I once had the ear of other men like Peter Fairweather.

For the Russian, Oblomov, the loss was more personal. Because he owned his entire company, he was the father of every success but also every failure. How Qatari Futures, the third losing bidder on the Vauxhall site, were reacting, I didn't know.

Gabe was not paying attention to my arrangements for the party, he was asking Lily about her plans for the summer. Her mane of hair swung from side to side, her naval ring glinted, her luscious flesh, ripe as fruit, hung heavy, ready to pluck. Gabe was a flirt; Lily was young and beautiful. It was a story as old as time. I didn't bear Lily any ill will. She would grow to learn which attentions to ignore and which to encourage. If she knew what was good for her she'd avoid married men. But the glimpse I got of the woman in green showed me she wasn't young, she was around my age – old enough to know better, mature enough not to care. This scared me more than Lily explaining to Gabe about spiralising and clean eating and him pretending to be interested.

'Has everything been going OK at work?' Alice asked Gabe. 'I'll always have your back, you know.' It was a strange question coming from Alice, she couldn't usually see her Poppa as anything other than heroic and irreproachable. 'If it's to do with work you know you can talk to me, I really want to understand how it all works.'

There was something ghastly about his face, a look I'd never seen before. Who are you? I thought. Who is this man I sleep next to every night? We all have secrets, but what are yours?

'This house is just so mega, Mr Moreau.' Lily was spinning round in her socks on the slippery kitchen tiles.

The conversation was killed by Lily turning on the blender and a deafening noise reverberating off every hard surface in the kitchen. I slammed my hands over my ears, tension jumping up my spine. Gabe and I were left staring at each other, my suspicions swirling as if the noise was our marriage crumbling to rubble.

I turned and closed the curtains so Maggie couldn't look in. Some things had to remain private. She didn't get to know about Alice's life. Alice had nothing to do with my disintegrating marriage.

CHAPTER 13

Alice

Six weeks and three days before

When I got back from work Lily came round, hunting for ways to relieve her pressing boredom. I suggested a job. She flopped back on the bed as if exhausted and then began to try on lots of my clothes, then left them lying round my bedroom like litter at a festival. Her boredom left her roaming from subject to subject, until she landed on Momma's death. Most people didn't ask, or didn't dare, but Lily was either more curious or didn't care about offending me. I gave her the benefit of the doubt. I said it was difficult.

'Do you ever cry about it?'

I hesitated. 'Yes,' I lied. I often lied about Momma. I gave them a version I thought they wanted to hear. The truth was, I didn't shed tears over her; I had been too young and I had never known her.

She asked how I got on with Helene. She was watching me, waiting for me to join her in a bitchfest about my step-mother. But just because she wanted to do that didn't mean I was going to comply. I was better than that, I reassured myself. I felt loyal to Helene. 'She's great,' I said. I sensed a moment of disappointment from Lily, who threw her phone in disgust down on the bed and turned to stare at the ceiling.

'I'm so bored,' she sighed. She pulled herself on to her elbows as a new thought struck her. 'Your dad is really hot, who would have thought it?' I felt weird when she said that. I hated her for a moment, really hated her. 'What?' she said defensively. 'Sometimes when you look at me like that it's kinda creepy.'

'He's just a wrinkly old bag of bones.'

Lily screamed in scandalised delight. 'Alice! Yeah, he's kinda old, but he's got charisma. It's like he *notices* you when he looks at you.'

I felt the old pull of protection. I needed to change the subject. 'We could go for a walk.'

She looked blank. 'A what?'

'Never mind.' I said there were lollies in the freezer and she asked if they were Innocent ones and I said I think so and then she was kinda interested and we ambled downstairs to loll about on different designer furniture.

Helene was fussing around with a checklist for a fundraiser she was holding and so we decided to make smoothies. Poppa came in and mixed himself a stiff one. I could see the gin glugging from the bottle. 'Has everything been going OK at work?' I asked Poppa. 'You seem a bit distracted.' I was thinking about the notes I had found.

Poppa escaped having to answer as Lily started the blender and the crunching ice cubes roared in the machine. It was too loud for anyone to speak.

I saw Helene putting her hands over her ears. That wasn't necessary, Helene! You were Heleneing! My stepmother thought this kitchen was acoustically challenged but she was wrong. It was modern, it was now, it was *right*.

I was the driver behind the makeover of this house from a warren of damp rooms and skittering spiders into the sleek, Cubist flow we enjoyed now. Lily loved the white tiles so much she did the splits on them in her socks. When Poppa or Helene expressed reservations about the cost or the upheaval (it took six months living in a rented flat while they took the back wall away) I had to put them right. No half measures, no compromises. A property developer had to practise what he preached. His house needed to exemplify the happy domestic fantasy; he needed to be living *in* the dream. And he was.

The house was unrecognisable when we'd finished. I even had to show Helene how to use the remote-controlled fire in the living room; she kept saying it was too modern and complicated, but she was only a few years older than Poppa and he didn't have a problem with it. Honestly, she seemed to create problems where none existed. I've always suspected that Helene is a closet fantasist. It goes hand in hand with egotism. She thinks it's all about her, but that's a view held by only one person.

CHAPTER 14

Alice

Six weeks and two days before

Today Poppa drove us to a site visit in Vauxhall. We got to see how Connaught Tower was progressing, how it was leading the regeneration of a forgotten and run-down part of inner London. Lily was here too as Poppa invited her last night.

From the car I could see the skyscraper soaring skywards. 'Wow, it's amazing, Poppa.'

'It's important to remember, Alice, that what you're looking at are homes, not just steel and glass. This is where a new community will put down roots. This is the future – mixed developments like these make the new London, and I'm so lucky to be part of it, in shaping a world city.'

He's like that, my poppa – when he turns his attention on you, it's as if you're basking in the glow of a thousand suns.

I could understand how Helene fell for him, how he fell for her. When he dropped the fateful line, 'There's someone I want you to meet,' my world screeched to a violent, shuddering halt. I hated him then, so much, and oh how I wanted to loathe the very guts of this Helene! But I didn't. I couldn't. You couldn't hate someone who tried. She was nice. More than one person said I was very mature for handling it so well.

Soon after I met her, Helene became my stepmother. It was a small wedding. There were Poppa's friends from work and a scattering of Helene's friends from here, there and everywhere – but no one from when she was young and no family. Poppa and Helene are quite alike in that respect; it was one of the things that brought them together, I imagined. They don't cling to the past. But it was important to note that I don't hold a life of many different incarnations against anyone. Reinvention was no bad thing, I believed. If you want to leave a place and people behind, why not? Why do we assume loyalty to those who happen to come from the same place is important or a sign of a good character?

Helene and Poppa have never had children. She couldn't. She would have been a good mother, I think. But if I was being selfish, I guess I was glad. It meant there was only me to dote over!

Poppa parked and we got out and that was when I noticed the protestors, about thirty of them, waving placards and shouting.

'Who are they?' Lily asked.

'Luddites,' I spat.

'Now, now, Alice,' Poppa said. 'People always protest when change happens. It goes with the territory, but we're trying to get a deal that suits everyone. They want homes, we want to build them—'

'But homes can't get built unless we can make a profit!'

'Yes, but it's a question of degree. How much profit is enough? We have to strike a balance that suits everybody. They say we make too much, the company directors say we make too little.'

Lily was listening with her head cocked to one side, her curtain of dark hair flowing over her shoulder, but I was annoyed, I thought Poppa was too nuanced. He needed to see things in black and white if he was to continue being successful. He needed to get with the binary idea of good versus bad. I was standing on the side of good. I had never had any problem with that.

The straggly crowd, comprised of shapeless men in track-suits and women pushing buggies, was chanting 'hands off our estate'.

I turned my back on the protestors and walked into the marketing suite set up in the unfinished building. Men in suits and women in high heels milled around. Lily and I looked at computer-generated images of what the building and the larger area would look like when completed. It was pleasingly ordered and regulated, clean and tidy.

Poppa came back from shaking a series of hands and led us through into the foyer of Connaught Tower. It was lit with arc lights as the plate glass was still on order and the windows were covered with board, but we could see a soaring ceiling and a wide, shallow hole in the ground where a fountain would one day burble and flow. 'It's been designed by an artist in Shadwell,' Poppa said. 'It's going to be the biggest indoor fountain in London, and the wall over there,' he waved his hand across the hole, 'is going to be clad in limestone, quarried in Wales. This building is a celebration of British craftsmanship.'

I was saying how amazing it all looked when Poppa caught the arm of a man passing by and introduced us. 'Girls, this is Milo Bandacharian.' A guy in his twenties with olive skin and very dark green eyes held out his hand. God, he was so hot he made my stomach flip! I mumbled my name and stood there awkwardly, but Poppa came to the rescue. 'Milo is a local resident. He helps keep communication open between us and the people who live nearby.' Poppa's attention was taken by a woman with a clipboard and he left us to talk to a group of men.

Lily began to talk to Milo. 'Aren't you hated by the buggy brigade out there and ignored by the suits in here?'

Milo shrugged. 'The way I see it, you have to try and negotiate the best deal with developers, make sure the community's voice is heard, otherwise you can end up with nothing,' Milo said. 'When this area where we're standing was going to be redeveloped, there were originally going to be twenty-three social homes out of seventy, now because we helped GWM win the bid, it's up to sixty-three. Every council home saved is a new start for an ordinary family.' He paused. 'It's nice to see that Gabe's daughter is taking an interest in the family business.'

'I'm not his daughter,' Lily said, 'she is,' and pointed at me.

Milo looked round and I felt uncomfortable, but not in the way I had with Mr Dewhurst. There were a thousand things I wanted to say, and no hope of saying any of them.

'Where are you from anyway? What kind of name is that?' Lily asked.

I wasn't sure that was a particularly polite question, but I really wanted to hear the answer.

'One of my grandmothers was French Polynesian by way of New Zealand, my dad was Irish, my mother's half Pakistani and I grew up here in Vauxhall.'

'Wow,' grinned Lily. 'Sounds like there's been shagging on nearly every continent.'

I was shocked but Milo laughed. 'Let's hope they had a lot of fun.' He turned to me. 'I like your dad. He listens and he lets me keep him in line.'

'Everyone likes him. There's nothing original in that,' I snapped.

He grinned and didn't seem to be put off by my barb and suggested we all went outside. I thought we were going to stand in the sunshine but he invited us to go and meet the protesters. 'Oh no,' I began, but Lily seemed keen and followed Milo over. Lily is the kind of girl who would poke an ant's nest, just to see what happens. I was forced to follow.

The protesters were less intimidating up close. Everyone smiled and said hello and mingled. I drank in every movement of Milo's, from the way he shoved a hand into his jeans pocket to the shrug of his left shoulder, but the sun tracked round the edge of a building and shone directly at me and I had to shield my eyes with my hand.

'That's amazing,' I heard Milo say. 'The sun has made a halo of your hair.' The look of rapture on his face made me put my hand on my head as if I was so stupid I had to check that my hair was still there, when really I should have been putting it on my heart, to stop it jumping into my throat. Milo was distracted by a guy stretching an arm over his shoulder and he turned reluctantly away.

A few moments later he came towards Lily and me and handed me a flyer. It listed bands and artists I'd never heard of against a swirling blue background. 'You two should come to this. There are so many vacant buildings round here waiting to be demolished, they're the best places for parties at the moment.' He pointed behind him at a crumbling Victorian-style building with a large weed growing from the side of its roof. 'The demolition order on that has been approved. We're having an event in there on Friday night.'

'This is so cool,' Lily said, staring at the flyer. I could see the gleam in her eye, her voracious need to experience life, as Poppa walked towards us. 'We are *so* going to this,' Lily whispered as we retreated back to the car.

Milo would be there. Nothing was going to keep me away. Nothing.

CHAPTER 15

Maggie

Six weeks and two days before

On Wednesday Gabe drove Alice and her friend who we'd seen throwing some indecent gymnastics moves in the kitchen of Moreau's house to his construction project in Vauxhall. We passed the usual hoardings advertising luxury flats to the tax dodgers of the world who laundered their money through London bricks and mortar. We drove into a schizophrenic neighbourhood, one of the many in the capital that were in the process of being cleansed of everything that had been before. A scrappy city farm giving off the stench of manure cuddled up to a collection of low-rise, rain-stained council blocks with faded signs telling kids not to play ball games on an inviting patch of grass. Beyond sat a half-completed tower of glass and steel where Gabe parked and got out and disappeared behind high wooden hoardings. Many of the doors and windows on the estate were boarded with steel screens, the council's anti-squatting paraphernalia nailed in place. The former inhabitants were being moved out and away to cheaper locations.

There were a collection of official-looking cars parked outside the tower and knots of well-dressed people entering it. A short distance away a group of protestors with home-made banners were shouting 'Hands off our estate'. A little later Alice and her friend came back out with a young guy in jeans and began to talk to some of the protestors and then Gabe arrived, and shortly afterwards the protesters began to disperse. Less than forty-five minutes after he arrived, Gabe was driving back to the office.

That evening Gabe drove back to Vauxhall alone. The sun was a low ball of fire on the Thames as we crossed over to the south side of the river.

Gabe parked in a different place this time, tight to a white van and out of sight of the road. I watched in my rear-view mirror as he cut across the scrubby grass surrounding Connaught Tower and let himself in. He seemed a different man now, furtive and watchful; he looked behind him several times as he fiddled with the padlock key on the door in the wooden protection wall.

I debated following him in and leaving Simona to watch the outside, but then we didn't need to. A short while later Gabe appeared on the fifth floor, a solitary figure standing amongst exposed steel girders and scaffolding and full in the wind; the windows were not in place yet. He stood there for nearly ten minutes, staring out across London at the setting sun.

'What's he doing?' Simona asked.

'Hell if I know.'

He stopped staring out at the city and fumbled in his jacket pocket for his phone and began to text. A few moments later he was distracted by something in his trouser pocket and he pulled out another phone and answered it. At that moment I knew I had won. Helene had never mentioned two phones – I was sure that one of them she didn't know about. I knew I had rumbled Gabe Moreau. I had the feeling I would need just a couple more days to wrap it up, if that.

The conversation was short, less than a minute, and Gabe

remained unsmiling throughout, before he hung up and moved out of sight. A couple of minutes later he was getting back into his car. A short call normally means a meeting is being arranged. And we would be ready and waiting to get the damning evidence we needed for his wife.

That's all it takes to deliver the fatal blow to a marriage.

CHAPTER 16

Helene

Six weeks before

Earlier this morning I went back to Praed Street for a follow-up meeting. Maggie was in a look-at-me-and-fight-me-for-it outfit: tight-fitting red skirt, a silver blouse and black stilettos, and radiating a good mood. We were alone, Simona and Rory presumably out tailing my husband.

'Tea, coffee, me?' Maggie said suggestively, but her attempt at a joke fell flat. I sensed she was attempting to forge a friendship of sorts, but I wasn't in the mood. She retreated to her office chair. I thought she might put her feet on her desk, but she leaned forward, elbows on the desk, and got serious. 'First, we need to go through some photos to clarify who people are.' I nodded and she handed me an iPad and I swiped through a series of photos. I swiped past Soraya, Gabe's secretary; Lily; a couple of colleagues from work and two women I didn't recognise at all. The photos ended. 'She's not here,' I said, frustrated.

'Not yet.' Maggie paused. 'He's pretty popular, isn't he?'

'Everybody loves Gabe.' I couldn't keep the sarcasm out of my voice, and tried hard to tamp it down.

Maggie stayed silent, watching me with her large, dark eyes. She didn't miss anything. Maggie would be arrogant enough to believe she could winkle secrets out of people before they'd realised they'd given them up. 'How did you meet Gabe?' she asked.

'At a charity event. We were raising money for women's education in the Horn of Africa. He was on my table. There was a man sat between us and we just joked and talked right over him all night. I got home and realised I hadn't laughed like that in longer than I could remember. And that was it, we were off to the races. I was thirty-five, never married. Friends said I was lucky, after so many years, to find a man like Gabe. "He's a keeper," they said. Gabe was rich by then, powerful I suppose. But I fell in love with him because he was kind.'

How embellished are the stories we tell after the event to make sense of our lives? Much is omitted, and other bits exaggerated. Gabe had in fact swapped places with the boring man in between us. It was if a colourful butterfly had unexpectedly landed on my wrist and at any moment I expected it to fly away. It was intoxicating, laughing with Gabe that night. Our dinner guests were ignored, we only had space for each other.

I stared straight back at Maggie, but I blushed, and she saw it. I was remembering what had happened after the dessert; the unaccountable intensity of it. Gabe and I had stood together, napkins thrown aside, and he had taken my hand, and pulled me down a flight of back stairs. His hand was so warm, a physical comfort for someone like me who is known for cold hands and feet. And we had kissed out on an empty balcony, his eyes glittering sparks of possibility. And I had pushed him away, suddenly fearful, because I could feel my self-control falling away, like a silk dressing gown off a naked shoulder.

He had paused, smiled his lopsided smile and whispered in my ear, 'What are we going to do now?'

I knew how to play the seduction game better than anyone. My self-control was something I'd cultivated meticulously over the years, and it had not been easily won. I had worked, and worked hard, to get to that charity auction, to being courted by Gabe on that balcony with him that night. I knew exactly how to play him to get him wanting more, to send him wild with frustrated desire. But with his breath in my ear and his hands on my waist I simply gave in. I threw away the rulebook. I haven't felt like this in years, I thought. We had sex up against the wall of the stairwell, like a couple of teenagers in the pub car park at closing time. I cried. It came out of nowhere, as if that emotion had been hovering, just beneath the surface, for years. My legs were shaking, and I felt sick in my stomach. He didn't recoil in horror, he wiped my tears away, as if he was used to women reacting that way. I have always wondered, when I think back now, whether I should have paid more attention to his response at that moment. But I was already lost; love, when it hits, grinds every precaution to dust. I realised that with him, the usual conventions didn't and wouldn't apply; giving myself to him was just something I had to do.

Outside the back door of the venue he hugged me. And let me go. He walked away a few steps and seemed to change his mind and came back and put his hands behind my head and kissed me again.

And that night had promised all the good bits that had come after. He phoned the next day, and we married six months later.

But I can't forget, sat here in Maggie's office not seven years later, that Gabe had taken me somewhere that night where I had never been. If he could do that to me, a woman who had made it her life to never give something for nothing, what could he do to other women? To that woman in the green dress?

Maggie was still staring at me, waiting. I needed to fill in the silence. 'Gabe is the kind of man who when he wants something, he goes all out to get it. And I guess that included me.'

'So, as romances go, it was straightforward,' Maggie said.

'Yes,' I lied. I chose not to tell her the downsides, the sceptical faces when people heard I was a woman with nothing who married a younger, rich widower, six months after meeting him. 'Gosh, you make it sound so easy,' a woman casually let slip to me at a party. It's not easy. Lying next to the man you love as he cries himself to sleep over his dead wife, as he murmurs Clara's name in his sleep.

Try that for easy.

We tailed off into silence. Maggie watched me for a few moments, then shifted in her seat and began again. 'Gabe went to Connaught Tower yesterday and stood around on a high floor for a while, looking out. I was unsure what he was doing, do you have any idea?'

I was back on safer ground and felt more confident again. 'That's a ritual of his. Gabe is Bosnian but he grew up in Vukovar, in Croatia. The town was completely destroyed in the Balkan war of the 1990s. The population was decimated, his parents were killed in a mortar attack on their house. He fled to London. The night before he and his wife Clara left, they climbed the water tower, the highest point in Vukovar, and looked out through the mortar-shell holes at their destroyed world. The sun was setting. And I think at that moment he swore that he would never stand to see destruction like that again. Clara and he came to London as refugees, like so many before and after them.'

'I thought Moreau was a French name.'

'He changed his name and Clara's. He wanted to obliterate his painful past. He was called Buric. He picked Moreau simply because he liked the sound of it.'

'It's some story,' Maggie said. 'He's done very well for himself.'

'He worked very hard, worked three jobs, took risks and got lucky. He went into property right when prices started rising and it has paid off. But only in the last few years has he really made his money. We've built thousands of council homes, good quality homes, all over this city over the years. His life now is very different from where he started when he first arrived here. After Clara died, he took to going to stand at the high places, always looking west, to take a moment, I suppose, to think about his dead wife, his old life.' I tried very hard to keep the bitterness from my voice. 'Did you notice how he holds his right arm?'

'I was going to ask you about that,' Maggie said.

'He injured it when the car went off the bridge and into the river and it's never been right since. He has restricted movement in the lower arm and constant pain.' There was a pause, Maggie was content for me to keep talking. 'I was lucky to meet Gabe. He allowed – well, his money allowed me to really expand the charity work. I've always wanted to give kids in this country – this city – the opportunity to make their lives better, to overcome their disadvantaged back-grounds. He and I saw eye to eye on that. We have achieved great things. We're very passionate about that.'

I didn't tell Maggie that I couldn't have kids. That Gabe and I tried, over and over again for years when we were first together, but it never happened. We tried one round of IVF, and that failed too. And then we accepted our defeat, and we smiled bravely for Alice, and I forced myself to believe that she was enough. When I saw couples with toddlers, and the jealousy threatened to overwhelm me, I scolded myself that I was lucky to have such a beautiful daughter. That she was the child I would never have. And I pretend now that our failure doesn't matter; that he and I had moved on. But the fact remains Gabe had a baby, and I never did.

'Why did you never have children?' Maggie asked.

I swallowed and shrugged. 'It just never happened that way.' I gave Maggie a pathetic smile that stank of an apology when none needed to be given.

She moved on, like it was too small a detail to dwell on. 'He made a call from Connaught Tower on what I think is another phone. If I'm correct, the next few days should give us something.'

'I've searched every inch of the house, I haven't found an extra phone, or even an extra contract.'

'They are easy things to hide.'

I didn't like hearing that. 'With your cases, how often have you found something by the end of the first week?' I asked.

'With the majority we have some kind of lead to go on. A flat they entered that we then check out, a hotel room that needs further investigation.'

'You could take it as a compliment,' Maggie said. 'If he is having an affair, he's keeping it very, very quiet. His behaviour so far is all within the range of normal,' she added.

I felt a flash of anger. I opened my handbag and pulled out the envelope with the cash in it. I handed it over and Maggie pulled out the notes, licked her finger and began to count, the bills feeding through her adept fingers.

'Don't ever underestimate him, that would be a mistake,' I said.

She didn't pause until she got to a nice round number. 'Why do you say that?' She turned the money sideways and knocked the notes together on the desk and placed them in the drawer.

'He killed the woman he loved when his car veered off the bridge and went into the water. He suffered life-changing injuries. Anyone who can live, survive and thrive, after that, is easily a match for you.'

CHAPTER 17

Alice

Five weeks and six days before

It was late afternoon when I woke up with what can only be described as the back of my head shot away.

Oh my God, what a night out in Vauxhall.

It had been coming back to me in vibrant staccato images that weren't linear. There was a dwarf on stage! And a bar that was set up inside an old camper van – it was so amazing! And jugglers. Were they throwing fire? There was fire somewhere. Lily kept dragging me away from the wall into the middle of the dance floor where two women in silver catsuits were dancing.

Lily was shouting in my ear and giggling; she made me down a red drink in a plastic beaker. We danced a lot, I think, but I couldn't really remember. I felt scared and then I didn't want to let go of her hand.

Lily dragged us over to talk to Milo. I felt so good, being there with him. I couldn't remember what he was saying. He had lots of friends, everyone was so nice to me. He was fist-bumping this guy and that, his voice sonic-booming, his hand on my arm warm and cold at the same time.

I had been so happy then!

Somewhere in that endless night of noise and lights, Lily

and I left with Milo and other people and went back to his flat. As the party ebbed and flowed around us we gravitated towards each other, ending up squashed on a sofa together.

We started talking about our mums, for he had lost his at a young age, just like me. And I had started jabbering at him about Momma and how no one understood what it was to lose her so young. And Milo had listened, he hadn't pretended, he had really understood. We had talked for so long! I had found a kindred soul, someone who understood my pain.

When his hand touched my forearm the hairs on my arms stood up like sunflowers on a cloudless day.

I couldn't remember exactly what I had said to him after that. From Momma I must have moved on to talk to him about school, about Lily, about all my life goals that I wanted to achieve and at what age I wanted to complete them. I remember him smiling, I remember a sensation overload, my lolling head, the warm sticky leather of Milo's battered sofa, the room turning, slow and stately as a Ferris wheel.

Then later, or maybe it was before, Lily's face was looming over me, she was laughing hysterically, high pink spots on her cheeks. 'You're tripping off your nuts, Alice! Dance, come on!' Her face split with a smile and she twisted away, her long slender fingers moving in a wave.

Later, back on the sofa again, Milo picked up a lock of my hair and ran his fingers down the squeaky strands. He bent over and kissed my neck, the ridge of my collarbone. His lips were so soft and warm and I felt the strongest pull of desire in the pit of my stomach. I feasted on the mesmerising curve of his eyebrow, the white tips of his teeth as he spoke. And then the room was spinning fast, the Ferris wheel had become a rollercoaster and I didn't like it and I couldn't get off and he was asking me questions, more and more questions, I couldn't remember what about, and then my hands were freezing cold and I was shaking and engulfed by hot, shameful tears. I was so scared, more scared than I had ever been, because emotions I couldn't control were tumbling over themselves inside my head and heart.

I saw a look on Milo's face I didn't like and suddenly he was dragging me to the window and trying to get it open and I vomited repeatedly out of the window as people pushed and fought to get away from me.

I woke up in just a pair of knickers in Milo's bed, my head in his armpit, our bodies sticky with sweat and tangled in a sheet. I needed the loo and slipped away from him, plucking one of his T-shirts off the floor and holding it to me as I went. I stepped across the narrow corridor into the toilet. He was still asleep, his arms thrown trusting and wide, when I came back into the room. I needed to find Lily and bent down to pick up my bra off the floor. When I stood up, his eyes were open and he was staring at me from the bed.

'You're holding that bra like it's a weapon,' he said.

I grinned, held my arm up high and twisted my bra round and round like a rodeo rider at a Texas fair. I saw his eyes widen in appreciative surprise. Some women would have been embarrassed at how we had awoken, wondering at the cross-currents after a night together, but I refused to be one of those girls. I loved Milo, and he loved me. He grinned back and sat up in bed, the muscles in his back and arms catching the sunlight. He gave his hair a good scratch with both hands and threw the sheet off and stood up. He was puppy-dog bouncy.

'Well, good morning,' he said, coming towards me with his erection pushing at his Y-fronts. We played an amusing game of him trying to kiss me as I struggled into my clothes. Eventually he sighed in defeat then hurried into his jeans and threw on a T-shirt that had been balled up on the floor.

'I guess you're feeling better now?' he asked. 'You were pretty ill last night at one point, ranting and raving all over the place.'

'Better out than in, I suppose,' and we both laughed.

I moved down the stairs and Milo followed, holding my hand. A huge black man in a scuffed leather jacket came out of the kitchen holding a can of Red Bull. 'Boo!' he said loudly, and I jumped back against the wall. 'I'm only kidding,' the man said, 'girl looks petrified, Milo!'

'Leave her alone,' Milo said good-naturedly. 'This is Larry, by the way.'

Larry held his hand up in a flat-palmed American Indian salute.

I slid along the wall past Larry and into the kitchen; I rinsed the dregs from a plastic cup and drank some water. Milo put his hand on my back and I turned round. He wasn't like any guy I had met before. He didn't talk earnestly about university options or brag about how well he skied. He was older and rougher. There was a raw energy to him that suggested dangerous possibilities.

He didn't take his eyes off me, his earlier jokes abandoned. I looked at him and I couldn't look away. 'There's just something about you,' he mumbled. He pulled me slowly to his chest and held me against his T-shirt, which smelled of smoke and late nights and promise. 'I feel like I already know you,' he said. And the Ferris wheel journey of last night began again and I softened against him. He leaned down and kissed me.

I felt myself falling, plunging through delicious barriers until I stumbled backwards, my eyes wide open with the shocking possibility of it. 'You're so gorgeous,' the words were out of my mouth before I could even think what I was saying, what the effect of them might be. He grinned and put his hand on the wall, his jokey demeanour signalling his victory.

I blushed to the roots of my hair, which made his grin wider. 'You're laughing at me!'

He began to protest and put his hands on my hips, drawing

me closer to him. He kissed my ear, but I twisted away, a flare of anger igniting in me. I headed for the front door, the heat of the day hit me as I opened it. I heard Milo behind me.

'Don't go,' he said, burying his face in my hair, but I was keen to be gone now, to preserve what little dignity I felt I had left. He kissed me as I pulled away.

I was nearly at Connaught Tower when I heard Lily's voice.

'Slow down, Alice!' I waited for her to catch up. She grabbed me and linked arms and we stumbled in a slow meander across a patch of scrubby grass. Her face had ballooned on chemicals and not enough sleep, her glossy mane was a lank tangle round her shoulders. 'Oh God, I'm desperate for a wee,' she said. She pulled her pants down and squatted on the grass.

'Lily, someone might see!' I glanced nervously around, astonished at Lily's lack of decorum, her lack of control. The headmistress at school flashed before me, all that money that had been spent and here was one of her pupils, fanny being tickled by the grass.

'Who gives a shit. Just be thankful I'm not in a playsuit.'

And suddenly we were laughing uncontrollably, rolling around on the floor flapping our arms.

'What a night!' Lily said, half lying on the ground. 'That'll go down in the book.'

'What book?'

Lily slowly got to her feet, testing to see how steady she was. 'The book of living, Alice. You're finally beginning to read it. Losing control, Alice, it's fun. You need to have more *fun*.' She leaned into me, hoping maybe I could steer her upright. I felt the warmth of her arm through my skin. It felt so good. 'Milo likes you,' she said, digging her elbow into my ribs and giving me a conspiratorial look.

I felt a surge of triumph. Lily was right, Milo *did* prefer me to Lily, and it felt like victory. We staggered across soft grass in the wan London sunshine, kicking litter and dirt from our sandals, and it was exquisite.

CHAPTER 18

Alice

Five weeks and six days before

By the evening I felt I had been so fucking stupid I was lost for words. When I thought about last night in Vauxhall – and I had been thinking about literally nothing else – I had to put my hands over my face, I was so ashamed. I had fallen at the first grown-up hurdle I had tried to jump. I paced around my room in an agony of remorse and rejection. I burst into tears. I had been weak, I had been gauche. I had shown Milo I was just a stupid little kid, a dull child who couldn't take her drink or her drugs. I had stood there roaring like an idiot, topless in his bedroom! Milo didn't like me, he couldn't like me after that, he didn't care about *me*, he was probably making a YouTube short about me right now. And underneath it all I was thinking about what ammunition I had given him that he could use against GWM, that he could use against Poppa. I would be the intern who brought bad publicity on the company. I would become the girl who had made her family lose millions.

FFS, you are just a dumb bitch, Alice! I was so unhappy I wanted to die.

Milo didn't text, he phoned. He actually phoned me! That was so retro! I didn't remember giving him my number, maybe he got it off Lily. Yeah, maybe she gave it to him, or maybe he was hunting me down all over town! I had forgotten how good his voice was, he had got that kinda flat, rough London thing going on.

'How are you feeling?' he asked.

'Fine. Fine.' I was trying to not give anything away, to make up for earlier.

'It was a shame you ran off this morning, I could at least have made you a cup of tea.' I could listen to his most banal sentences over and over.

'Anyway, there was something I was going to mention to you but you had split before I remembered. There's a protest meeting on Tuesday in the community centre here, I'm speaking and so is Gabe. Why don't you come along? I'd really like to see you again.' I felt such a surge of pleasure that it sucked the breath from me and I couldn't answer. 'You'll see all sides of the arguments about development that are going on down here. It'd be great for your work experience. You'll realise that we're in a fight for the soul of the city.'

I sensed danger – the liberation he was proposing was novel.

I forced myself to tell Milo that I'd think about it. He didn't pressure me and that was something that also surprised me.

'Well, give me a call when you decide. Catch you later, Alice.'

And he was gone. After half an hour of feverish Internet typing, I had watched two YouTube videos of Milo delivering speeches at council meetings, viewed fifteen hundred times each, found his Insta and Facebook pages and read everything on his blog, Homes are for Living In. I was not naïve; if he could get close to me, perhaps recruit me, the developer's daughter, to stand on protest lines, it was a coup. Was that why he was interested in me? Or was it something else? It had felt so right being with him it couldn't possibly be a lie, could it?

And suddenly Tuesday seemed a lifetime away and I couldn't possibly wait that long to see him again. But first I had to get through the charity fun run that Helene had organised. I felt on such a high I felt I could fly it without my feet even touching the ground.

CHAPTER 19

Helene

Five weeks and five days before

There were ten thousand of us amassed in central London on a Sunday morning in a road that was closed off to traffic. There was an air of excitement and fidgety preparation as runners warmed up, adjusted ear buds and tied shoelaces tighter. Alice, Lily and I were stood in a loose circle. I took it as a point of pride that I could recruit both of them to get out of bed early and get involved – I can be manipulative when I need to be. The glow of raising money for a good cause was the headline argument, but thinner thighs and tighter butts ran a close second.

I was dutifully doing stretches while Alice was fussing about fixing her race number straight with four little safety pins. Lily was finishing off a last cigarette, causing mutters from competitors surrounding us as her smoke drifted over their faces. Sunglasses obscured her eyes. The girls radiated low energy, catching frightening loud yawns off each other and using each other's shoulders as props to stay upright. They had been out a lot and I had hardly seen Alice all weekend.

A man with a loudhailer began issuing instructions that were so distorted by feedback no one could hear what he said, but we all knew it meant we would imminently be

underway. We were boxed in among a large crowd of competitors far back from the starting line, but even so I felt the
familiar pulse of adrenaline at the start of a race. 'You'll smash
it, Alice,' I said. 'You'll be so much faster than me.'

'Yeah, like, *of course!*' she answered, rolling her eyes, as if
the result was a foregone conclusion. I felt a flare of competitiveness. Just you wait, I thought, I might surprise you, I
want to win.

The runners in front began to move forward like a wave,
and everyone around us cheered and took off at a tremendous
pace, far too fast to be maintained. I kept Alice in sight in
front of me, her perky ponytail bouncing to my rhythm. I
kept pace with her until I saw the four kilometres sign, then
felt thirsty. I grabbed a bottle of water from the race helpers
that lined the route as the crowd behind the street barriers
roared us on.

Somewhere in that crowd was Gabe, offering his support.
I began to feel lethargic and heavy. Running, which had
always come so effortlessly to me, became more difficult. I
saw Lily on my right catch up with Alice and she beckoned
her with her hand, and the two of them suddenly took off,
their long legs carrying them away. They were swallowed up
in a moment in an undulating sea of runners.

I tried to stay positive – there was still a long way to go –
but I felt so tired, my lack of sleep catching up with me, the
stress of my problems with Gabe robbing my body of vitamins
and energy. I felt very alone.

I tried to push myself forward through sheer force of will,
but my body refused to cooperate. The markers for eight
kilometres appeared and went. The crowd of runners
surrounding me began to age, the young were nowhere to
be seen. A giant Teletubby waving at the spectators and
enjoying their cheers nearly tripped me up; a speed-walking
woman in her seventies overtook me.

The gap between how I saw myself and the reality was growing bigger all the time. I became prone to unsettling thoughts as the tarmac jarred below my feet. I was middle-aged. I was barren. I was done. No wonder my husband was having an affair.

The nine kilometres sign appeared. I felt so drained I wasn't sure I could run the last thousand metres. Finally the finish line took shape up ahead, and I gamely tried to speed up to cross it in style, but there were so many people ahead of me I had to queue to get into the enclosure.

I stood alone, a pain in my chest, my legs wobbling, surrounded by runners being embraced and congratulated by friends and family. I saw Lily with her arms around a reality TV star, his hand on her taut thigh as someone took a photo. I searched in vain for Gabe, but didn't see him.

I caught a glimpse of Alice's red ponytail, got a partial view of someone she was talking to. The crowd parted and I could see it was a woman in high heels. Her face was turned away. The crowd thickened again and my view was obscured.

I was sure it was the woman from the Café Royal. A wave of panic swamped me and I pushed against the crowd, desperate to get to Alice. She moved in and out of view as the crowd surged like water. My leaden legs wouldn't carry me to her, as I saw the woman put her hand on Alice's shoulder. A tall man blocked my view and I shoved him aside, his shout of protest echoing in my ear.

I was roughly shouldered from the side and nearly fell over.

'Fantastic job, you're a star!' Gabe had his arms around me as I tried to push him away, desperate to get to Alice, but now I couldn't see her at all.

'Where's Alice?'

'Oh, over there, I think, did you see Lily with that guy, honestly—'

I started forward to get to Alice when she came up along-side me, her face split with a smile and her eyes bright. 'That was great, wasn't it? I roasted you!'

'Alice, thank God,' I breathed, putting my hand on her arm. 'Are you OK? Who was that woman?' I was hunting for her in the crowd, but could no longer see her.

'What woman?' Alice asked.

'The one who was just with you, what did she say, are you OK?'

Alice gave a shrug of irritation. 'I don't know what you're talking about.' She drew back and pouted. 'Jesus, Helene, it's not all about you, you know. I ran in a personal best time, you should be happy for me.'

She put a heavy emphasis on happy as Gabe enveloped his daughter in a hug. I desperately searched the hundreds of faces surrounding us, but couldn't see the woman anywhere. I momentarily wondered if I was losing my mind. The crowd began to swim in and out of focus and I had to put my hands on my knees.

I felt Gabe's palm on my back.

'Helene, are you OK?' Alice asked. 'Oh dear, maybe it was all a bit too much for her,' she said to Gabe, 'it's quite a long way to run at her age, isn't it?'

CHAPTER 20

Maggie

Five weeks and three days before

After watching Gabe in Connaught Tower and finding the second phone, I had thought we'd get a breakthrough imminently and see his lover, but it didn't happen. We got through the weekend and the family's fundraising at a 10K run and then in the early evening on Tuesday, Simona and I followed Gabe from the office back to Vauxhall. The day was muggy, the evening light beginning to fade. His car pulled up outside a three-storey building with bars across the ground-floor windows and a rail line level with the second-floor windows. The Vauxhall Gardens community centre was pulling all comers in through its open doors – mothers with double buggies, students and shuffling old men, people of every race and creed. Outside, kids on bikes, teenagers on mopeds and youths with pitbulls competed for space.

Simona nudged me to point out a new black Mercedes with blacked-out windows that pulled up under the railway bridge. The driver's door opened and a heavy-set man in a dark suit got out and opened the rear door. A tall man got out and stood taking in the scene. He turned and I saw his face – he was middle-aged, but looked good on it.

'He's a cross between Colin Firth and George Clooney,' Simona breathed.

My reply was more to the point: 'God, he's fucking hot!' I shot back.

The wealthy passenger from the back seat wore a thousand-pound suit and had a sheen of wealth and importance. I thought he looked Russian.

'The City that takes all comers,' Simona added in appreciation as we followed him into the centre.

There were a lot of angry people sat in rows of chairs and a lot more angry people crowded into the spaces at the sides. The room was stifling and the ceiling low. A Lambeth councillor took to a small stage that had been set up at the far end of the room but he took too long to open the meeting and try and establish an agenda – he was drowned out by boos and catcalls from the audience.

The Russian stood near me at the back of the room, his face impassive. Gabe got up to speak. The atmosphere was poisonous and felt on the brink of getting out of hand.

'Leave our estate alone!' someone shouted.

Emboldened, a heavy-set woman stood up. 'My kids haven't had an afternoon kip for three years because of the drilling! It's driving me round the bend!' she began but Gabe interrupted her and forced her into silence.

'I'm Gabe Moreau. I own GWM Holdings and we are redeveloping Reg Jones House. Many of you know me as I've spent a lot of time here with you over the years.' I noticed several nodding heads in the audience. 'Reg Jones House is going to be knocked down and a tower built in its place. The plans are freely available for you to have a look at. But plans do change, because the cost of materials and the cost of demolition vary. As you are well aware, we are the company that accept the lowest profit margins and have promised to deliver more social homes than any other. But there are going to be changes to the original scheme.' There was a ripple of discontent through the room.

Gabe began to walk around the stage, his voice becoming slower and more intimate. 'I want to take a moment to tell you a story. I come from a town in a small country far away that was completely destroyed by war, where my family was killed and my house was bombed to rubble. My dad asked me once, when I was young, "What is a home made of?" I thought for a moment and I answered. "Bricks." "What else?" he asked. "A chimney and glass for the windows?" And my dad shook his head and he said to me, "A home is made of none of those things. It is made of love and hope and dreams." I don't build tall towers because I like steel or glass or square footage or aspect. I build homes because I believe in hope and family and renewal.' The room was quiet, he had their attention.

Simona leaned in and whispered, 'I'd make love to him.'

'I'd certainly fuck him,' I whispered back. It was impossible not to be impressed by Gabe Moreau that evening. It was the first time I'd heard him speak and his charisma stood out like salt on the rim of a margarita. When Helene and Gabe fell in love it would have seemed a relationship in balance – she provided the class and he provided the money. He had been a grieving widower being offered a new start and a new beginning. And I was being paid to pull it all apart.

'But there is a problem. The new costs mean that the number of new homes for council tenants has to be reduced—'

There was uproar. 'But we need more low cost homes, not fewer!' a young woman near the front said. It was a mournful plea that had people nodding heads.

'You have a choice, but it's not a nice one,' Gabe continued. 'The way I see it, we can spend the next ten years letting the lawyers argue about who is responsible for the changes, while your homes don't get built and the lawyers are the only people who get paid, or we can agree to the amendments.'

'You're stealing our homes from right under our noses!' a man shouted.

'Milo Bandacharian leads the tenants' rights group,' Gabe continued. 'I came from across the world to this city, Milo grew up right here. Let's hear from him.'

The man I had seen talking to Alice and Gabe the week before stood up. He wore a loose-fitting white T-shirt, battered Nikes and faded jeans and had a light London summer tan. 'I was born here in Vauxhall. I live in Reg Jones House. I have known many of you for years.' He looked tired, and was probably fighting off a hangover and too many late nights. 'I more than anyone want more homes, but I don't think there is any other way. We will have more homes under this developer than any other.'

It was all too much for a guy at the front who'd had too much to drink. He stood up chanting 'homes not profit' and the meeting began to crumble as others joined in. A councillor pleaded for calm. The Russian left.

Simona and I headed out the door. The mood was ugly and on the brink of getting out of hand. A hot summer night in the city, a brooding sense of injustice and grievance, this was how riots started.

'You follow Gabe, Simona. I'm going to walk a bit.'

'Here? I'd watch out, it's not somewhere to hang around.' She looked nervously at the long dark underpass by the community centre where suburban rail lines roared above.

'I can take care of myself.'

She shrugged, knowing better than to persuade me once my mind was made up. Why did I walk around the estate that night? Because it reminded me of where I grew up, the past reaching out to drag at my heels. And yet my estate was not like this. Whatever my problems – and there was a list as long as a toilet roll – I had security. Our scruffy patch of south-east London wasn't slathered over by developers like Gabe and that Russian, it wasn't seen as a patch of ground where millions could be made if you just knocked down the old and built the new. I crossed a playground, where the urban foxes were dining on the rubber of the swing seats, to an abandoned row of shops plastered with graffiti and wreathed in metal shutters. I vaguely followed the curve of the river east, the sound of passing trains from the nearby tracks competing with the cries of children and the barking of dogs.

I was in central London, the richest, most vibrant city on the planet – the flats towering in the distance were worth millions – but that wealth had never trickled down to here. To governments, to developers, here was human detritus to shove aside by the machine of progress. Gabe Moreau was expounding a different vision, but how different was he really? How different could he hope to be? Helene had told me to be careful about her husband, to not underestimate him. He had suffered the emotional explosion of his wife's death, but was she warning me about something else? You didn't become successful and get rich that young in the London property game if you weren't ruthless, smart and maybe more besides.

I was always careful on my jobs; love and exposure created a perfect storm that gave people licence to act badly, to be violent, to show the worst sides of themselves.

I walked east, bound up in my thoughts, until I got to St Thomas' Hospital, the Palace of Westminster and Big Ben lit up like a fairy-tale castle across the river. By one of the service doors of the hospital were a huddle of cleaners on a fag break, others streaming out at the end of their shifts. I saw the workers of the world in the 21st-century city, and they were limitless in number.

It wasn't until I got into work the next morning that I heard about the murder.

CHAPTER 21

Alice

Five weeks and three days before

It was awful hearing a crowd call Poppa a liar and a thief, and watching them stand to cheer. I wanted to jump up and down and fight back, grab little fingers and bend them backwards, grab a clump of hair just behind an ear and yank, hard.

But I did nothing. These people were intimidating and angry. I had crossed into a new world of difficult business decisions that changed lives, not always for the better.

Poppa was a fighter, he had come from little and made a lot. This central thing about him was something that had dawned on me slowly as I had grown older. I saw the other girls' dads pick them up from school, and Poppa wasn't like them. They were old and muted, with low voices and plain faces, sombre clothes and greyer hair. The teachers fawned over Poppa, turned and smiled at me as if thinking, Wow, who would have thought that the little mouse had this hidden away!

And I would put my arms around his waist and think, little mice can roar. His charisma and charm have been passed down to me, they're in my DNA too!

Sometimes I loved Poppa so hard it hurt. Seeing him here, trying to win over the crowd and show reason, I had a glimpse into what his job entailed and why he did it. He enjoyed the cut and thrust, because he had been battling all his life.

Poppa was one thing, but Milo was another. He was the reason I was here in this angry place but while I was desperate for Milo to see me – to think I was brave for coming! – I didn't want Poppa to and I was terrified he might spot me. The meeting had not gone well and he would see it as a failure. He would never want me to witness that failure. I shrank back behind the entrance doors until I saw Poppa hurry away into a waiting car with some other men.

Milo had clambered on to the stage to shout at people to stay, but no one was listening. I hung around outside the centre and Milo caught sight of me. He came over and kissed me hard on the cheek, but he looked worried, with tired lines around his eyes. He grabbed my elbow and pulled me away from the chanting crowd. 'It's going to get ugly, stupid idiots.' The night was hot and breathless and sour. Mopeds revved aggressively and teenagers hung around in huddles. 'We need to get out of here.'

He put his arm protectively round my shoulders and I felt the delicious sensation of being pulled into a protective circle by him. We hurried back to his flat with several others, including Larry. Huddles of people arrived and left in a constant stream. I heard the short burst of a siren somewhere nearby. I wanted it to be just Milo and me but he became distracted, texting and phoning a ton of people.

The living room was crowded, the kitchen empty. I tailed him into the kitchen. A chorus of shouts drifted from the living room. He lived life in a constant party, in a maelstrom of causes and strategies and front-line activism.

'Alice, how much do you know about your dad's business?'

He had opened the fridge and pulled out a beer, popped the top and stood leaning back against the wall.

I shrugged, because I had nothing to say. Should I have been embarrassed that I knew nothing?

He looked away and I felt with a stab of recognition that he was impatient for me to be gone. 'How many people do you know who work at GWM?'

'I don't understand.'

'I mean, there's your dad obviously, but do you know the others?'

'Yes, I know them. Well, I don't really know them. Why?'

Milo gave me a funny look. 'I thought you were working there.'

'I am! But I haven't been there for very long.' Larry shouldered his way into the kitchen, reaching round Milo to open the fridge.

'Give us a minute, Larry, will you?'

Larry glanced at me in surprise, took a four-pack and left. Milo stared at me. His eyes were dark and dangerous and I was torn between wanting to jump into his arms and run away. 'So, do you know all the departments? How they work, that type of thing?'

'Yes, I do.'

'It's just that far more people are robbed at the point of a pen than the point of a gun,' Milo added. He shook his head, as if to dispel something unpleasant. I reached out and touched his T-shirt, felt his warm skin beneath. He said something under his breath that I didn't catch. He looked at me with those startling green eyes. 'Do you have a boyfriend?' he asked quietly.

'Me? Of course not!' I said. I want you to be my boyfriend, I was thinking.

He said nothing and a dark little thought came to me. 'Why? Do you have a girlfriend?'

He turned and opened the fridge door and shrugged sadly. 'I don't even know,' he said quietly.

I took a step backwards. I was astonished. He had misled me! I felt shame crawl across my skin at how I had let my feelings run away with me.

He looked at me, offering me a beer from the fridge. He saw my face and became defensive. 'Look around you, Alice, look outside this door! Someone's making a ton of money, and it isn't anyone in this room.'

I took the beer even though I didn't want it. I had been dreaming of this moment with him for so many hours, for days, but it wasn't turning out how I hoped. He was ruining it by insinuating things I didn't understand about GWM. The problems of the world, and the problems here in Vauxhall, were not my fault. But then he reached a hand out and touched my cheek, his features conflicted. 'Oh but God, you're lovely,' he said softly.

This was how it was meant to be, his soft hand on my cheek, his adoring eyes on mine. He was the handsomest man I'd ever seen, and he would be mine. I deserved it, so it would be so.

As I tried to catch hold of him the sound of smashing glass from the other room brought Larry through to get stuff to clear up.

Milo got distracted and pulled away from me. He bent down under the sink to pull out a dustpan and brush and began asking Larry about someone I'd never met. It was as if the moment shattered. I saw him in his tiny, crowded flat, full of hangers-on, trying to use me. For every kiss another piece of information, for every embrace, a name and number, for every smile and compliment, a video taken or photo shot.

I walked backwards out of the kitchen, waiting for Milo

to plead with me to come back, but he was talking with Larry and he didn't even see me go. I was out of the flat before I heard him call my name, but he didn't appear. I tested him, waiting in the dark outside, but he never emerged. Sour and painful thoughts roiled around inside my head and I had to run the gauntlet of menacing groups of young hooded guys lingering by walls and gathered in clumps beside benches and on the greens. The smell of skunk hung heavy in the air. With every step I got angrier that something so glorious and intense had been snatched away. I hurled the beer bottle at a wall, watched in satisfaction as it smashed into pieces, foam spraying up the brickwork like sea spray.

CHAPTER 22

Maggie

Five weeks and two days before

It was Helene who told me Milo was dead. She phoned, her voice high and fluttering; she was floating on a wave of disbelief and what sounded like panic. She couldn't get her story out, but I realised that was because she had no story to tell, she had what most people did at a moment of bad news – a desire to know more, to know less, and to repeat over and over. Gabe had phoned to tell her, police in white paper suits were at Milo's flat, there was uproar on the estate and shock at GWM.

'This is bad, Maggie, this is very, very bad,' she said.

'I'm sorry, this is terrible news,' I said. 'Did you know him well?'

There was a long shuddering sigh. 'He was a wonderful man, a passionate, unique individual,' she said. I could hear her voice catch in her throat.

'Are you OK?'

'No, of course not . . . Yes, I don't know,' she said. 'I feel this is an attack on Gabe, on all of us. It's like we are all one step from disaster.'

'I'm not sure I know what you mean,' I began, but she interrupted me and said she had to go. The line went dead.

I put my mobile on the desk and turned to Rory. Before I could even ask him a question, he gave me a full rundown of what he knew of the night before. Simona had followed Gabe home after the meeting in Vauxhall and he had stayed there all night. Rory had taken over her shift at two a.m. after he tipped himself out of a nightclub, but he hadn't left until he came into work this morning.

The three of us speculated a bit on the news, but we got more information a couple of hours later when two detectives came to the Blue and White. Detective Inspector Dwight Reed was large, black and bald and his colleague, Gary Burton, was small, white and hairy. I knew they were approaching because I heard a flurry of clanging feet as frightened illegals visiting the immigration lawyer's next door clattered down the fire escape at the back of the building. You can smell a policeman, even one in plainclothes, from fifty feet.

It was nice of the police to come to the office, they could just as easily have made me wait hours at the station among the drunks and the drug addicts to take my statement. As a private investigator it's important to keep on the good side of any police inquiry, and I wanted to give them a statement that I had been on the estate that night as I didn't want them wasting hours tracking down a taxi someone remembered seeing there. It was also a way for me to find out more information about the case and they knew that.

The coppers I've dealt with over the years have been distant and disinterested. They think PIs are failed police officers, people who couldn't make the grade. When they find out that I specialise in infidelity they become sullen and suspicious. Too many of their friends are the people I investigate. There's a high incidence of domestic violence amongst policemen and high divorce rates too. They're swimming and drowning in the stress and emotional pain of their jobs.

Dwight had been one of those statistics – a man whose marriage had failed when his wife left him for another man. I knew that because five years ago he and I had had a thing. Strange word that, as if what goes on between consenting adults is impossible to describe. We had a great time, he wanted more, I couldn't give it to him. I played out the usual 'It's not you, it's me' excuses. Ours was a story as old as the beds we did it in.

If he was embarrassed at seeing me again he didn't show it. But then he didn't seem that pleased either. He looked good, his divorce long behind him now. In my office he threw me some tidbits of information. Preliminary reports estimated that Milo had been killed between two and three a.m. He had been found the following morning by a mate who had keys and often dropped in as they shared the costs of a printer. There was no sign of a break-in or of a struggle. The crime scene was still being examined, but he had let the killer into his home. It was someone he knew.

'But then,' as Dwight explained, 'that doesn't narrow it down, as Milo was a party animal, had people back in a constant stream to that flat, had friends and acquaintances from a hundred different protests and causes and was very active online.'

'Did he work?' I asked.

Dwight smiled ruefully. 'He was a part-time social worker. There are lots of angles to pursue.'

'Did you find the murder weapon?' I asked.

Dwight shook his head. 'He was hit with a heavy object. He would have been killed instantly.'

There was silence for a moment as Dwight and I sized each other up.

'Did you see anything worth reporting last night?' Dwight asked.

I told him about my walk as closely as I could remember,

relating who I saw and where. Dwight seemed impressed at my detailed descriptions. I have a good memory for faces, places and times. 'Is Moreau a suspect?' I asked.

Dwight ran his hand across his bald head, feeling the contours while he considered the question. 'Everyone's a suspect until things become clearer.'

Something struck me. 'Does Gabe have any previous convictions?'

'I'm not here to make your job easier, Ms Malone,' Dwight began, but he was being playful now. He was the kind of man who stayed late at a party, hogged a dance floor, showed a woman life was worth living. His partner Gary looked like he'd already booked and paid for his bed at Dignitas.

'Come on, Dwight. Let's help each other. Spread a little love.'

He knew that was underhand, but he kept his control. He had been keen for us to carry on, get more serious, but back then I sensed a wellspring of anger about his ex-wife that meant he wasn't ready. Which was convenient for me, I guess, since I've never been ready. Not since Colin. But I kept that fact to myself.

'He's got no convictions, he's whiter than white.'

This news didn't help the feeling I had that there was something I should be seeing that was obscured. I kept thinking about Mrs Farmley, still in jail for throwing the heater into her husband's bath. She would have bet her life that Hal wasn't married to someone else. Finding out he was upended her world and made her do something unspeakable. We think we know the people we live with, and we know them not at all. Most of the time we don't even know ourselves. We certainly don't know the people who hire us or who we follow.

'I've got something to show you,' I said. 'A man turned up at the meeting in this Merc.' I showed Dwight a mobile phone photo of the Russian's licence plate.

Dwight was less than impressed. 'We've had ten calls to the incident line about that car already this morning. No one drives around in that if they don't want to be remembered.'

'So who is he?'

Dwight exhaled loudly. 'That's Arkady Oblomov's car. He's a Russian billionaire who develops riverfront property, it's how he made his fortune.'

'So what's he doing turning up at a community meeting in Vauxhall?'

Dwight shrugged. 'Unclear. Him and his wife are in the copy of *Hello* that's by the coffee machine at the station. There's never been any chatter about him being dodgy, and I imagine Milo's community protests are too small-scale for him, but we're looking into it.' He gave me a level look. 'So what's your connection to Mr Moreau? My guess is you're doing surveillance on him.' My silence was his confirmation. 'The wife's hired you, hasn't she? She's suspicious of her handsome property millionaire husband. Let me think, she can't wait for you to catch him red-handed so she can take him to the cleaners in the divorce.'

I don't mind that Dwight is bitter. He's had experience of a bad divorce. My days are filled with bitter men and women. It shows they can feel. It shows they can love. 'I spend a lot of time with cheats and liars, that's true.'

'Being unfaithful isn't against the law.'

'But it's against the rules,' I snapped back.

Dwight gave me a look I quite liked. 'It can feel good to break the rules,' he quipped. The stir of transgression I felt deep inside was broken by Dwight's partner Gary muttering, 'What the hell is this?'

Dwight felt he needed to explain. 'Ms Malone and I already know each other.'

I could have added 'in the Biblical sense', but I held back. 'She's one of the best private detectives in London.'

That was sweet of Dwight, no contest. I was reminded of one of the reasons we had got on so well.

'So where did Moreau go after the meeting that night?'

Simona spoke now. 'I tailed him home and Rory took over at two a.m.'

'He was there all night,' Rory said. 'So were his wife and his daughter,' he added.

'So the Blue and White agency has given Gabe Moreau an alibi for murder.' Gary Burton said it as if we'd done something wrong.

We had reached the end and Dwight and Gary got up to go. 'A friendly piece of advice, Ms Malone, don't overstep your remit,' Dwight added. 'I will be very unhappy indeed if something you do jeopardises any future case we have. I mean it.'

Rory and Simona said their goodbyes and I opened the office door and Dwight and Gary and I stepped out into the corridor. The policemen began to descend the stairs. I saw a man's legs disappearing through the window of the corridor on to the fire escape.

'Please don't send the immigration boys round, you'll cause a breach of the peace,' I said.

Dwight turned back round and leaned his elbows on the banister. 'I bet you can deal well with chaos. You probably thrive on it.'

'I'd pull you out of a burning building.'

'I'd let you,' he parried back.

So I'm a flirt, deal with it. Gary threw his hands up and muttered something under his breath and walked downstairs. Dwight ignored him and stayed where he was, his smile on full wattage.

I didn't want him to go, I was having too much fun. 'There's something else,' I said. 'Gabe Moreau has got two phones. I'm trying to find out if one of them contains something interesting to me, and maybe to you.'

'Why, Ms Malone, you should have been a copper.'

'There's always time,' I said before walking back into the office and closing the door.

My smile faded pretty quickly when I saw Rory and Simona's faces.

'Ditch this case, right now. He's toxic. So is she,' Rory said.

I sat down, a bad mood beginning to wash over me. 'You're overreacting.'

'Rory's right. I think we should pull out,' Simona said.

They were both standing by my desk, like they were doing an intervention on me for alcohol or drug addiction. Rory handed me a sheaf of papers. 'Here is some of the stuff I've been working on. GWM is worth £150 million. It's majority owned by Gabe Moreau. He built the company from nothing. You don't make money in this kind of market with this kind of competition without being really ruthless. Now someone directly involved, standing in the way, no less, in one of his big deals has just been murdered. Whatever the real story is and whoever is responsible, I know for sure he's going to be paranoid, guilty, secretive and watchful. And we're going to be following him around 24/7 to find out if he's *shagging*. If he finds out about us—'

'I've never been rumbled before—'

'Let me finish, Maggie! He could easily discover us, and when he does he's not going to like it. That's bad for us, and probably very bad for his wife.'

I had to admit Rory had a point. No one liked being followed, not least by someone their spouse had hired. The consequences for their safety were important to think about.

Silence fell in the room. We were all thinking the same thing. If Gabe was involved, how much danger did that bring to the Blue and White?

'There's something else,' Simona added. 'Is Helene hiring

us just a lot too convenient? Has she set the whole thing up?'

'If there's one thing I hate, it's being used,' I muttered.

'You and me both,' Rory answered.

'Maybe we're reading this all wrong,' I added. 'Maybe Helene hired us to protect herself.'

Simona made a noise. 'She doesn't need protecting,' she added.

I made a decision there and then. 'Until she sacks us, we keep going. We've seen no evidence that he could turn violent, but we'll need our wits about us.'

Rory threw his hands in the air and slumped back down in his chair. 'You're a fucking fool,' he muttered.

Well said, Rory, but not well enough. My problem was, I was stubborn and contrary. I was getting paid good money, and I wanted a result. And I wanted this kind of result. Truth was, I liked hanging out in expensive bars in Mayfair and Marylebone where the drinks were doubles and the nuts and Japanese crackers complimentary, waiting on crowded West End streets being jostled by tourists from around the world who had paid a fortune just to come to see and experience London. It was what I worked for, and I didn't want it to end. And I wanted to discover the truth. My competitiveness and insecurity all played a part. But most of all it was professional pride. I found Gabe intriguing, attractive even. I didn't want him to beat me. I didn't want to be played. In the end it was as simple as that. I didn't want to be outsmarted. Not by a man; by a rich, powerful man, even less.

I've watched toddlers fight to get ownership of a swing, yank a toy from another's grasp. It doesn't matter at that age whether they're boys or girls. But by the time those children are teenagers, it's the boys who grab that seat, it's the men who get the toys, the reins, the controls. What I'd seen of life told me I couldn't win if I didn't fight.

CHAPTER 23

Helene

Five weeks and two days before

It takes twenty years to build a reputation and five minutes to lose it. And the bad publicity surrounding what happened to poor Milo could have pulled this company to the floor. And there Gabe was, a rabbit in the headlights, frozen into inaction. He needed to act swiftly, he needed to be resolute. But since we got the call that Milo's body had been discovered, Gabe had sat on a kitchen chair, staring blankly at the fridge, as if he might find a set of instructions as to what to do stuck there with a magnet. A man you worked with had been bludgeoned about the head! Move!

I was trying to formulate an appropriate response; there were so many moving parts that needed to be coordinated – the staff, the community groups not just in Vauxhall but all across the capital that we worked with – they all needed reassuring. Gabe should give an interview to the local news, I believed.

I understood that Gabe was shocked and upset by what had happened, but it was as if this news had completely knocked him over, it was as if a bomb had gone off behind his eyes and rendered him mute.

But all of this paled into insignificance once Alice got up

and asked us why Poppa looked so odd. I told her what had happened and she collapsed into hysterics.

And out tumbled a story that Gabe and I knew nothing about. That when we thought she was out with Lily on Friday night the two of them had spent the night at some kind of rave in Vauxhall with Milo himself, and Alice had gone to the protest meeting on the estate last night.

That finally got Gabe moving. He was furious, channelling his grief for Milo into anger at his daughter – telling her it was dangerous and she was being naïve. That she didn't understand drug dealers and muggers out for her phone. And I felt like retorting she's a woman – unlike you she knows everything about personal safety because she *feels* the danger. And an even darker thought bubbled up, like gas from a badly digested meal: unless your memory has failed you, Gabe, the greatest danger Alice experienced was where she was supposed to be safest – at school.

In reply to our barrage of questions, Alice had started shouting that Friday night had been the best night of her life and she had felt that for the first time she had really lived but it was all ruined forever. Then Alice did the thing I hate – the flopping on the sofa and the screaming - and I was made out to be the cold bitch by trying to get her to calm down while her dad ranted and raged just like a spoilt kid, just like her.

Her furious little face was scrunched up, as his was, and they looked so shockingly similar, mirror personalities. I was the interloper, forever the outsider in their intergenerational spat, as their helixes of DNA spun and twisted round each other. I appealed for calm as I tried to put my arms around Alice's shuddering shoulders. She pushed me violently away and I watched from the door as they gathered energy for round two.

I needed a bloody cigarette and wondered why I had

bothered to give up. If this didn't send him into the arms of that bitch from the Café Royal nothing would.

Maggie had saved me. She was the saviour of this whole family. The Blue and White had given us all an alibi for last night, which meant we would escape intrusive and hurtful investigation and my husband didn't even know it, could never know it. The feeling of a sense of threat tightened around me. It turned out we all knew Milo, some of us better than others. But he united us all, and now he was dead. Why was Milo killed? Was it a crime of passion? It seemed impossible, yet the alternatives were almost worse – was he not the man he seemed?

'If anyone calls at the house or on the phone, don't answer,' Gabe said.

Alice stopped her screaming and stared at him, still as a puppet in a shadow theatre. 'Why?'

'Because it might be the press.'

'The press?'

'Journalists who want—'

'I know what the press is—'

'Well then—'

'He's been killed and all you can think about is what they write about us? Poppa, you're a monster—'

'I don't mean it like that, as you well know—'

We were interrupted by the doorbell. There was a stunned silence then Alice was up and moving across the room, giving both of us a look of such withering hatred I was momentarily stunned. 'It's Lily, for fuck's sake.'

I opened my mouth to correct her appalling language, and stopped myself. Now is not the time, I counselled.

The wailing and exclaiming started anew in the corridor, long teenage hair flying in the wake of sobbing, Lily calling over and over, 'I can't believe it, I can't believe it', and I felt my old enmity for such emotional vomiting. I wanted to say, but you hardly knew him, you knew him less than I did, far less than Gabe. I felt contempt for their Twitter and Insta generation, the empty public competition to be more affected than each other. And then I was appalled at my cynicism and I wanted to cry with them. They were young and emotionally green, they were privileged enough to have the freedom to feel. The tragedy was living a life, as I used to, where it served you better to not feel anything at all.

I left them to it and headed out the back door into the summer morning. It was so blue and beautiful, but I saw none of it. I shed a tear for young Milo in silence and alone. By the time I came back inside, Lily had left and Alice was locked in the bathroom. A long while later she emerged, pink and lethargic, her phone dangling from puckered fingertips.

'You OK?' I asked. She stared at me, the steam and the fighting having robbed her of energy to speak. She blinked at me, her eyes expressionless discs. For a terrible moment I wondered if she had already forgotten who Milo was.

CHAPTER 24

Alice

Five weeks and a day before

The day I had to give a statement to the police I hadn't slept well and was nervous – I wanted to make sure I told them as much as possible and remembered everything that might help them catch Milo's evil killer.

In the end it was straightforward. Two policemen came round to the house and we sat in the study because it seemed the most sensible place. The first policeman, DI Reed, had huge muscled arms and was very big. He led the interview and the second, Burton I think his name was, was small and tired and never said anything much. He looked like he was half asleep to be honest, which I didn't think was very respectful to Milo. I felt they should have impressed upon me that they were working night and day to reach a conclusion and get someone behind bars.

Helene sat in on the interview with me. She suggested it and I was happy about that. I didn't want to feel intimidated. The way the police look at you it's as if you've done something evil or wrong even when you haven't.

DI Reed asked all the questions, so I stopped looking at the other man. He asked me how I knew Milo and for how long and where I'd been with him. I stumbled when I had to describe the party and tried to keep it vague – what if they asked about the drugs? Could they arrest me for what happened that night? For what I took? Was that against the law? I mentioned more than once that I was eighteen in case he thought I had been drinking.

But they didn't seem interested in me, only my relationship with Milo. I felt so sad, when I think about the potential that has been snatched away from me and him. I believed that I was in love with him. I don't care if that sounds presumptuous or naïve. I know how I felt. It was such a different feeling from Mr Dewhurst, Milo felt like an equal to me, he was closer to my age for one, and my poppa liked him. I bit back tears. What a tragic waste.

DI Reed asked about the last time I saw Milo, the night of the protest meeting.

'In his kitchen,' I said. 'There were lots of people there at his house, we were trying to have a conversation but kept getting interrupted.'

'What were you talking about?'

I swallowed. 'We were just talking about this and that, talking about the party. Remembering the funny things that happened.'

Out of the corner of my eye I saw Helene looking at me and then looking away. I wondered if she didn't approve.

'Did he sell you any drugs?'

I took a deep inhale but Helene interrupted me sharply. 'Don't answer that.'

'He didn't take drugs or sell me any,' I said firmly. 'Milo said to me quite clearly he was against hard drugs.'

Helene asked DI Reed in a tone of outrage, 'Are you telling us he was a dealer?'

'It's a line of inquiry we're—'

'Rubbish! He wasn't a dealer. Not in any meaningful sense. This is a distraction, or slander at worst,' Helene added.

'Please, Mrs Moreau, if we can continue. Did he say he was worried about anything, or anyone?'

I answered straight away. 'Not that I know of,' I said.

I had to name the people at his house, but apart from Larry and a couple of other familiar faces, I knew no one.

'What time did you leave?'

'I left about nine thirty and came home.'

'Did you go out again?'

I shook my head.

There was a pause and I thought that was the end of his questions. 'So you came home at nine thirty. That's an odd time to leave,' DI Reed continued.

'What do you mean?'

I sensed something wasn't right because Helene stiffened beside me. 'Well, it's neither here nor there, neither early nor late. Did you guys have an argument?'

I realised I was gripping the seat really hard. I tried to keep my voice level – how dare he insinuate! 'No. Nothing like that. I wanted to stay longer but there were so many people there I thought another time would be better to talk.' I caught a sob in my throat and had to put my hand over my mouth. 'But there never would be a next time!'

Helene put her hand on my back and murmured comforting words. A tissue was put in my hand and I balled it and shredded it and wiped my eyes.

Then before I knew it the chairs were being moved and legs were being stretched.

'Thank you for your time,' DI Reed said as he stood. 'Do you have anything else you want to say or add?'

I shook my head and we all began to move towards the door but DI Reed spoke again.

'One more thing. Did he ever talk about a woman he was seeing? A girlfriend?'

I shook my head and that would have been the end of it,

but at that moment I glanced at Helene and it was her face I remember – like her oldest friend had betrayed her over something hideous and she was trying to recover.

CHAPTER 25

Maggie

Five weeks and a day before

Dwight was the kind of blunt, plain-speaking man I've always respected. So when he phoned the next day he just got right down to it.

'Did you know the daughter, Alice Moreau, knew Milo?'

'Alice? I saw her with him briefly at some official function in Vauxhall.'

'Turns out they were more friendly than that. She went to a party with him, stayed the night at his flat, was at the public meeting and back at his flat again on the night of the murder. The way she talked, I think she'd got a crush on him.'

This sat awkwardly with me. No one liked being blindsided. It was as if Dwight was calling me out on not doing my job properly. I hadn't seen Alice at the meeting, but I hadn't been looking for her; I hadn't even considered that she might have been there. 'I didn't know that.'

'Fill me in, Maggie, what's she like?'

'She lives at home, insulated from the day-to-day problems any normal person has to face. She'll never have to worry about money for the gas meter, so to speak. She's interning at her dad's company. She's strait-laced, well-educated, I'm sure.' I tailed off, there was little more I could add.

'She says she came home at about ten. Does her story check out?'

'Hang on.' I asked Simona for the notes that she had jotted down while being outside the Moreau house the night of the murder. 'Yeah, that's what we've got, give or take fifteen minutes.'

Dwight didn't thank me for my help. 'The Moreaus are keeping secrets from you. Welcome to policing.'

I slammed down the phone, furious with Helene and pissed off at Dwight.

Five minutes later I phoned him back. 'I want to see Milo's flat.'

'Nothing doing at all, Maggie! Why are you so interested in the detail of Milo's death?'

'Come on, Dwight, he's connected to a case I'm doing, don't run down my job.' We argued back and forth for a while, with me trying to tell Dwight I might have something useful to add to the investigation, and him almost laughing at my ego-fuelled presumption. I like to think in the end I convinced him by being a professional and with my razor-sharp debating skills, but he only agreed once I said I owed him a ton of drinks and would buy them for him.

I got down to the station in double-quick time and as he drove us to Vauxhall we talked. 'What's the working theory? Was Milo's murder anything to do with the redevelopment of the estate?'

'Lots of residents think so. The bad feeling and paranoia around here is running high; my officers have heard every theory going about his death, from Polish builders desperate to keep their jobs to serial killers. One guy spent twenty minutes trying to convince an officer that it was an MI5 cover up, because their big building on the river there isn't real, it's here on this estate and Milo found out about it. Everyone living in Reg Jones House is a spook in disguise.'

I smiled as we walked up to Milo's door. 'Problem is,' Dwight continued, 'Milo was a controversial figure. He was born and lived all his life here, the council flat was his mum's before she died. Some of his neighbours hated him, said he was too noisy with his constant parties, others claimed that he was some kind of Ghandi for council house occupants – the little guy facing down the corporate raiders. There is talk that he was a dealer, but also records show that he had beef with the drug dealers on the estate. Called the local station many, many times to report dealing in the stairwells and in that playground that he looks out on; he used to get angry when they didn't respond immediately.'

'So would I,' I said in defence of Milo.

Dwight looked resigned. 'Everyone has sympathy with that, but drugs is just one of a myriad problems there – you should see the call sheets about antisocial behaviour, joyriding, noise issues, dangerous dogs. The drugs squad busted thirteen Vietnamese guys running a dope farm from a council flat. It goes on and on.'

'Careful,' I said, 'I grew up on an estate like this, so did you.'

'And what did we do?' Dwight parried. 'We left. Maybe that social dream has failed.'

I didn't agree. I watched a young guy in a grey hooded tracksuit a distance away with a small, muscled dog with a gold chain-link lead. The man was bending down with a little black poop-a-scoop bag to pick up his dog's mess. I would have argued the point with Dwight, but I was conscious of being short of time. 'Do you see this as a drug-related crime?' I asked.

We were at the door of Milo's flat now, ducking under the tape. Dwight was silent for a long moment, weighing up his answer. 'No, not really.'

'Someone murdered him. That's fact, not speculation.

What's the CCTV on the estate show for the night of the murder?'

'We've got the film from every camera that was working in a wide radius from Milo's flat. The estate's very well covered, the only problem is that some of the cameras are out of action because of the building work.'

'And?'

'So it's possible to leave Milo's flat and be away anywhere without ever coming into view of a camera, if you know what you're doing. According to some of Milo's friends, there was a woman he might have been seeing, but if he was, it was very hush hush, as no one can describe what she looked like. It's all a work in progress. But at this moment a drug dealer nicknamed Bee-Sea, short for Battersea, is in custody. Some low rent grassed him up. He's done time for GBH, ABH, pimping, etc. I could go on. Believe me, he's quite capable of murder. It would be our pleasure to put him away. So you get ten minutes in here.'

I nodded and we entered.

Milo's flat in Reg Jones House conformed to a standard layout I'd seen a hundred times: a small entrance hall with stairs up to the top floor that would contain two bedrooms and a small bathroom, a small kitchen off to the left and past the stairs a lounge with a picture window.

Dwight followed me into the lounge. The room faced west and the place was cooking in the heat. The room was large, with a gas fire set in the wall with a thick-framed mirror above it, and square plastic tiles on the floor that Milo had painted bright blue and covered with a rug.

There was a tatty leather sofa and an armchair, a coffee table and a desk in front of floor-to-ceiling shelves made of scavenged planks and stacks of bricks. The desk had space for a computer, I saw a printer and a shredder. I opened the shredder and found it empty. There was an overflowing wastepaper bin filled with old banana skins, beer bottles and fag butts.

The walls of the lounge and parts of the carpet were covered with Post-its and tape marks that pointed out blood spray patterns. Milo's body had fallen across the carpet and hit the coffee table and lain bleeding on the rug.

I looked at the items on Milo's shelves: photos of him as a boy with his parents, a smiling woman that was probably his mother; a mocked-up retro newspaper front page with the headline 'Agitator who must be stopped' and a photo of Milo holding a banner on a student loans march.

I felt the terrible loss of that young man's life, which had been ended so violently in the flat he had been born in and grew up in. The sun moved behind Connaught Tower and the light in the room shifted to darker hues.

'Did you find the shredder empty?' I said.

'Yes. And his computer's missing.'

'That's hardly a drug dealer profile, is it?'

'It is when he used to video the dealers who hung around by the playground you can see from the kitchen window.'

'Are you saying his mobile is gone too?'

'And all his cash, though according to his friends he never carried much around with him.'

'Why would a bloke like Milo bother to empty his shredder when he leaves his bin overflowing right next to it?'

Dwight sighed. 'Maybe he never did. Maybe he never used it, or maybe someone stole everything in it. We have to work through. Every bin within a large radius of this flat has been searched, for the murder weapon and any other items. We've found nothing of Milo's yet.'

'This whole thing makes me crazy,' I said, shaking my head.

Dwight came and put a consoling hand on my arm. 'It's how we do it,' he said quietly. 'We work methodically, we keep a cool head, we rule nothing out, but we don't indulge in fantastical theories either.'

I didn't have Dwight's self-restraint. I couldn't stay calm. 'How about this for a theory. I lie every day to get my job done, but there are bigger liars and bigger cheats competing for millions, even billions, and maybe Milo got in the way, maybe the people on this estate are being cheated of their homes by powerful groups—'

'I didn't have you down as a people's crusader, Maggie,' Dwight said.

I wiped my hand across my face, shaking with emotion. 'Me? Give me a fucking break. Like you said, I ran the first opportunity I got.' I looked back at the nasty stain on the carpet, the last struggles of a beautiful young man with everything to live for. What an utter, pointless waste. I felt small then, grubby and irrelevant. Truth was, I couldn't become a police officer, not because I found something better, but because it would push buttons in me that for the good of everyone around me should never be pushed. And then there was the small matter of my criminal record.

We walked into the kitchen and I looked across the children's playground at the block of flats opposite. 'How often did Moreau come here? What did the neighbours say?'

'They say they'd seen him sometimes, but not the night he died.'

I turned and opened the fridge, used my foot to pull the salad drawer and saw the usual bag of leaves disintegrating in its plastic coffin. I closed the drawer pretty fast. Dwight looked at me, non plussed. 'Force of habit,' I said by way of explanation. 'I once found a mobile phone used by a wife to cheat on her husband in the salad compartment. My client said afterwards that in all their years of marriage he had never once opened it, which was exactly the reason she chose to use it.'

Dwight looked at me with fresh appreciation. 'I don't think I've ever opened mine,' he said.

It was the only revelation in that sad and sorry visit.

CHAPTER 26

Maggie

Five weeks before

We tailed Gabe for another day and got nothing interesting, so I called Helene. 'This other phone that we saw Gabe using in Connaught Tower is troubling me,' I said. 'I don't think he has it with him every day, which means he's hiding it somewhere, most likely the office or your home. If we can find it, we'll basically find out everything.'

'Do you want to come here and look for it?' Helene asked.

I hadn't expected her to be so accommodating, but finding that phone was beginning to get me itchy and scratchy so I eventually agreed. And after hours of waiting outside the Moreau's house I was genuinely interested in seeing what lay inside it.

Helene opened the door in her 'at home' uniform of track pants in a colour probably called Dove and her hair up in a casual ponytail. She looked decades younger than she was. She led me into the kitchen and made me a coffee from a machine more suited to a NASA spaceship and poured it into a wobbly artisan cup in dullest pewter that probably cost the same as the GDP of a small African country. She couldn't find any sugar, which made it quite the worst and most expensive coffee I'd ever tasted.

As I pushed it aside politely she said, 'I don't want this tragedy with Milo to stop you doing the best job for me.'

'I'm a professional: you pay me, I work for you,' I said neutrally.

'Come off it,' she almost snapped. 'You must have been pissed off being kept in the dark about Alice knowing Milo, but it was as much a surprise to us as to you. Imagine, she was with him only hours before he was murdered, how much danger was she herself in?'

None, I wanted to say, but didn't. That was the thing about rich people, they thought the world revolved around them and for them. Maybe it did. 'I've got a question,' I began, 'do you think his murder has anything to do with the redevelopment going on—'

'Absolutely not.' Helene was adamant, interrupting me to claim it so.

'It'll be one of the theories that the police are working on.'

'I'm aware of that.' She shook her head, as if to dispel bad thoughts. 'I just refuse to believe it could be.' She put her empty cup down on the island. 'But then that leaves even more unpalatable options – that Milo was involved in some kind of illegal activity, drugs, or he was badly in debt or something.'

'Well, there's always a third option,' I said.

'Oh, what's that?'

'It could be a crime of passion. He rejected someone, and they didn't like it. Not one little bit.'

She almost snorted with derision. 'Don't be ridiculous.'

'It happens all the time,' I said.

She shook her head. 'Men aren't murdered over that, only women.' She sounded sure of herself, but she had turned away towards the corridor so I couldn't see her face. 'Why don't you come and see the house?'

It didn't disappoint. It gave, and then it just kept on giving.

It made the five-star hotel bars I'd followed Gabe into look shabby. As Helene showed me round it, despite knowing I needed to keep my distance from her and maintain my critical faculties about the motives of the Moreaus, I fell completely under the spell of that house and the family lucky enough to live there. I felt a hunger to feel the plumped sofa cushions, to stroke the nap on a velvet chair, to run my toes through spotless calfskin rugs, to be able to say something, anything, about the pictures – sorry, Art – on the walls. Up on the first floor I let a fantasy carry me along for a few more moments – of imagining I was slipping between those smooth bed sheets, pissing in that marbled bathroom, bathing in a sunlight glow from those tall windows, running my hand across the soft cashmere of a husband's sweater.

I knew Helene wasn't keeping this domestic show on the road herself, she was ordering staff about to achieve it for her, getting them to buy into her vision. There was effort required to keep it up. The high standard of presentation went deep – as she showed me the upper recesses of her vast domestic playground it made me appreciate what Gabe had chosen – he had married a woman who enjoyed order, who was ruthless about getting what she wanted. And who kept a fucking beautiful house.

That was until she opened the door to Alice's room. And I understood the messy compromises that families – even ones headed by Helene – were subjected to. Helene had told me that Alice had helped refurbish the house, but grand visions and day-to-day reality don't always marry. That room was like a festering spot on the back of a beautiful woman.

CHAPTER 27

Helene

Five weeks before

'We need to talk about Milo,' Maggie had said when she phoned. She was clipped and controlled, but I sensed a deeper level of suspicion than she had shown previously. She tried to hide it but failed. I was paying her, but she still had the right to be angry.

I told her to come round to the house. Gabe had taken Alice into the office about an hour earlier, to take her mind off Milo, and Alice had agreed.

Maggie didn't like the idea. 'I shouldn't be seen at your house,' she said.

'Oh come on, you think I can't lie convincingly in the unlikely event one of them comes home?'

Maggie to her credit hadn't pretended to protest. Half an hour later she was standing at the door. I brought her into the kitchen and as we drank coffee I found I couldn't stop running on about Alice and Milo. 'Alice met Milo for the first time when she went with Gabe to see Connaught Tower. Apparently Milo invited her and Lily to some party at the weekend and then she went to the public meeting. Lily didn't go to that. That's why she was back at his flat the night he was killed. There were lots of other people there too, they were never alone.

'Gabe's hit the roof. I told him she's eighteen, like it or not she's a grown-up, her head's going to be turned, she's going to fall in love with inappropriate people, do stupid things, but he doesn't like it.'

'You should have told me straight away.'

'You know what, Maggie? It wasn't a priority. Things have been hell here. There were policemen here all day, Gabe had to give a statement, they were probing Alice, there were reporters at the offices today.'

'How well did you know Milo?' she asked.

I could see her watching me carefully, sizing me up, trying to see what made me tick. She had been around enough liars to spot them easily. 'I've known him for about a year. Gabe and I got introduced to him shortly after we won the bid for the Vauxhall site. He was my type of guy, passionate, kind, funny. We had meals with him, we met him at his flat, I went with him when a petition was presented to Parliament about the housing crisis in London—'

'You went without Gabe?'

'Yes. It was just Milo and me.' I could see she was surprised. Well, she could shove her suspicions where the sun didn't shine. 'So I knew him quite well, and I am devastated that this has happened.'

She didn't answer that, but got off her stool and began wandering round the kitchen, her stilettos making hard clacking sounds on the tiles. 'Can I see the rest of the house?'

I showed Maggie the living room and the six bedrooms and the en-suite bathrooms and the study.

Maggie paused in the doorway of the study and looked around. 'Who works in here?'

'Me mostly.'

'What are these boxes for?'

I had piled them along the walls and tried to create more space. 'When we renovated, the cellar had to be cleared. A lot of it is Gabe and Clara's old stuff. Since Gabe had no desire to sort through any of it – it would have been too painful – it all got dumped in here. I've been trying to go through it but honestly, I'd rather not.'

'It's a good place to hide a phone.'

I shook my head. 'I already looked.'

Maggie stood on the landing of the house looking around, like an animal sniffing a predator on the wind. She looked back at me. 'I'd put it in the place you're least likely to go, the place you feel you shouldn't go.' I frowned, I wasn't getting it. 'If it's in the house, it'll be in Alice's bedroom,' she said.

A moment later I'd opened Alice's door.

Alice was as messy as her father. I took the decision for family harmony that I wouldn't get involved in either the nagging of her to clean her room or ever giving in and doing it myself. It was a cesspit. Alice's cloyingly sweet perfume mixed with a base note of sweat had nowhere to escape as the window was shut against the hot day. Her bed was a rumpled take on Tracy Emin's – minus the condoms. Her collection of soft toys and dolls sat in a straggly line on her headboard, their glass eyes shining dully. Her desk held a clutter of books and a photo of three teenage girls in school uniform; Alice was the figure leaning in from the left-hand edge. I watched as Maggie took a step forward and pulled open the desk drawer. I glanced at a chaos of pencils, childish rubbers, bits of paper, hair bands and a half-empty packet of Tampax – here was a room where a child had become a woman.

Maggie got down on her knees and looked under the bed. Her arm reached under the base and I heard the muffled sound of objects being moved. A moment later she stood up again and turned to open the large cupboard.

'Stop it,' I said sharply. She turned to look at me, her hand on the knob. 'I can't do this. It's not right. She has nothing to do with this. I can't invade my stepdaughter's privacy and root through all her things. We'll have to find another way.'

It took Maggie a few seconds to reply. 'Well, the tailing hasn't worked, so we can employ another tactic.'

'What's that?' I said.

'We can try a honeytrap.'

CHAPTER 28

Maggie

Five weeks before

'With a heterosexual man we put a woman in his way – say in a bar or restaurant, a private club, even on a train, and see whether he comes on to her. We record the conversation and sometimes have someone else in the room taking pictures. If he takes her number and then calls her later, it shows a pattern of behaviour, which is indicative of a cheating mindset. It colours in the picture, if you like. It's not proof of anything, and our honeytrap never meets the man again, she just waits to see if he calls or suggests another meeting.'

'How much success have you had with honeytraps?' Helene asked.

'A hundred per cent.' I could see that this shocked her, but it shouldn't have really. Once a client comes to us, the cheating has already started.

'So, who would do it?'

'Either Simona or I.'

There was a pause as Helene searched for an elegant way to say something she thought was rude. 'But neither of you are his type.'

'Experience has shown me that it doesn't really matter

what a honeytrap looks like. It's the availability that's
important.'

'That can't be true.'

'I'm afraid it is.'

'A hundred per cent success rate? Jesus Christ.' Helene
was pacing around in her shiny kitchen, absorbing what
I was saying. 'You know what's been bugging me about
that night at the Café Royal? It was how brazen it was. I
was so close by, so were our friends, and he does it right
there. That shows such arrogance, such confidence,
doesn't it?'

I didn't reply, because it was better that way, but she was
right. To be wanted sexually is the biggest ego booster I know.
For some people, to flirt with risk is to live. Gabe was playing
for high stakes. Everything was on the line: reputation, career,
family and fortune.

'So where do we do this honeytrap?' Helene asked.

'Sometimes Gabe drops into the bar beneath the office at
the end of the day. That would be a good place to make an
approach, if you want to pursue this tactic.'

It didn't take her long to agree.

So how did I get a man to notice me when he's met, wooed
and married someone very attractive? When his life is a
succession of beautiful, cultured women and endless choice?
It's so fucking easy, that's the shame of it. Plumbers, CEOs,
footballers, pensioners – in the end they all crave tits and
attention, even if they don't know it. If their predilections
veer towards Rory, it's cocks and attention.

Here's what we did.

A few days later Gabe went into the bar under the office
and Rory and I swung into action. I was the one who
honeytrapped him simply because he was in the bar when I
was outside on my shift instead of Simona or a freelancer. In
the back of the cab I changed into a tight, black worky-style

dress with high heels, nude tights, a plunging neckline and loose hair.

Luckily Gabe had placed himself at the bar on a stool rather than at a table where it would have been harder but not impossible. Rory went in first and took the stool two away from Gabe.

I came in a few moments later and approached the bar, looked hesitant, and began to sit down next to Rory and a seat away from Gabe.

'My mate's taking that,' Rory said to me rudely.

I paused, making it clear I thought he was an asshole. I turned to Gabe and pointedly said, 'Sorry, do you mind if I sit here?'

Gabe glanced at Rory who was slouched with his elbows wide, glanced in faint pity at me and said, 'Not at all.'

'Thank you so much.' I began to get on the stool, then dropped my bag and bent down, collecting the things that had spilled out, apologising. I flashed him my chest; it was all quite straightforward.

He got off his stool immediately to help. Rory ignored us both.

I finally got back on the stool and faced him full-on. I pretended a double take and smiled. 'Haven't I met you somewhere before? I'm sure I have, but I can't place you.' I gave him a long stare, which he couldn't ignore. I'd reeled him in.

I know a lot about pushing the right buttons. Is this manipulation? Entrapment? It's a human right to flirt with the opposite sex, to make a fleeting contact that makes our lives worth living. But taking a number and phoning up later is something else. That's cheating. That's what a wife pays me to find out.

'I'm not sure,' Gabe said diplomatically.

I ordered a whisky from the barman. I saw it was what

Gabe was drinking and mirroring behaviour is a successful tactic when flirting. I've learned over the years that men like you to drink whisky because most women don't. It sets you apart from the Chardonnay gluggers – and from their wives. I took a sip and stared at Gabe again. 'I've got it, I've seen you in the building. You work in Sentinel House, don't you?'

'Yes. I'm on the fourth floor.'

I faked a puzzled look. 'Let me see, is that Something Holdings?'

'GWM Holdings. We do property.'

I nodded. 'That's it. What's that like these days? Boom times I bet.' He nodded politely, his interest pitched at low. I held out my hand. 'Melissa Fulton. I'm on the sixth floor, with the PR lot. I do high-end electrical goods, if you're interested.'

He shook my hand. 'Gabe Moreau.' His hand was warm, his skin smooth.

'Pleased to meet you, and cheers.' He half raised his glass with mine. 'So, you having a stressful start to the week, to be in here at five forty-five, or are you a lush?' I asked.

That made him smile. Up close, it was a good smile. 'Well, my work has been unusual lately, to say the least.'

'Oh? How?' I asked.

He didn't bite. If I was hoping for something about Milo or Vauxhall I was set for disappointment. 'What are you doing in here?' he asked.

'I'm off to a launch of a new range of French-made blenders – you know, the type stocked only in Selfridges and Harrods and sold direct to high-end show flats, that type of thing.'

'Oh, that might be useful,' he said. 'Do you have a card?'

'Of course.' I pulled out my purse and got out a card that I'd had made in the Underground a few hours before. I could feel the thrum of excitement that he was walking into my trap. 'How many show flats does GWM have at any one time?'

'About twenty that are live now, more coming on-stream over the next six months.'

He picked up my card and began to tap it on the side of the bar.

'Well, you should give me a call, maybe there's something we can do for you.' I held up my whisky. 'Cheers again.' This time he chinked his glass against mine. 'Here's to four walls and a roof. There are worse ways to make a living.'

He didn't agree or disagree.

That whisky tasted good sliding down. 'So do you live in London? I can hear the trace of an accent.' He nodded. 'Do you like it?'

'That depends.' There was a pause and he put his drink back on the bar as he formed a thought. 'Listen, when you go somewhere high – I don't know, Primrose Hill, or Greenwich Park, and you look out, what do you see?'

'The skyline of London.'

'But what in particular?'

'I don't know, the Post Office Tower, the Shard . . .'

'Exactly,' Gabe said, becoming more animated. 'You see high things. But you know what I see? Cranes, the machines that build the future. The future of this city is up. I see the buildings that aren't even there yet. And I get excited about the worlds to be created in that air, the homes and jobs that will be seventeen storeys up. The love stories, the legacies that we can create.'

'Wow.' It wasn't difficult to look adoringly at a man high on his own theory and passionate about expounding it. 'You certainly like your business,' I breathed.

'To me it's not a business. It's a vocation.' There was a small pause. 'I come from somewhere where for a while it was all going backwards.'

'What do you mean?'

'Every day someone was killed, families were destroyed, history was obliterated. The world was unravelling. It's hard, being here, now, in such a safe place, to imagine such a thing.'

'It sounds terrible. Where is this place you're talking about?'

He ignored my question. 'Where do you live? I don't mean which part of town, I mean in a big place or a small flat?'

'Well, I live by myself.' I made sure to get that information out there. 'Hell, isn't everywhere always too small?'

Gabe shook his head. 'I don't think so. We need to transform how we live in spaces. If you took all the objects out of your house, how much bigger would it be?'

'Well, a lot.'

'That's the challenge. You see, I don't want to build houses, I want to build dreams. I want people to be able to fulfil their potential, be who they want to be in the greatest city on earth.'

'Just a small-scale ambition then.' I took a slug of whisky.

He looked at me penetratingly. 'I find English people funny and also quite charming. They always deflect. Just when it gets interesting they have to make a joke.'

'I've got one: an Englishman, an Irishman and a Scotsman go into a bar . . .'

He didn't laugh. 'See, sliding away from the stuff that matters.' I began to feel the tingle of success. He was flirting. I sensed Rory leaning forward to not miss anything. 'Anyway, I believe housing is a problem that just needs to be looked at in a different way. It's not about money or planning – although those things are important – a home is where people build on the past, renew their family histories. I want to build innovative, new homes that will last a thousand years.'

'Bad news for my blenders. I'm afraid we work on the assumption that consumers think it looks dated in three years.'

He laughed at that. 'I thought those beds that came out of

the wall were the naffest thing ever.' I was laying a trail, seeing if he would bite.

He nodded and drained his drink. 'But a bed that transforms into a sofa at the touch of a button? Now that could be great.'

A phone beeped and he pulled it out of his jacket pocket and read a text. I glanced down at his trouser pocket, but could see nothing that looked like the other phone.

'Let me get you another,' I said as I tried to catch the barman's eye.

'Make no mistake, there's a battle going on at the moment over the soul of this city and it's all to do with housing and where everyone is going to live. If housing is done wrong, you can't ever recover from it. It's there, looking at you, its ugliness staring down at you. It's a bit like families, I guess, the mistakes hurt for generations.'

He could hold a room, could Gabe Moreau. 'I guess so.' I tried a little giggle. I'm not the giggling type, but it's a winning flirting strategy. 'It must give you the biggest buzz when you work hard and compete and win?' Flattery see, it gets you everywhere. It gets a man caught by a sex detective.

He looked rueful. 'It's supposed to.'

'So it doesn't work with you?' His mouth pressed into a hard line. He gave me a sideways glance full of a meaning that I wasn't sure I was interpreting correctly. The last of my whisky flamed down my throat. 'So what does give you a buzz?' I asked.

He ran the tip of his finger around the rim of his empty glass. I held my breath.

'Making up for past mistakes.'

'Do you have past mistakes you regret?' I asked.

'Doesn't everyone?'

'I certainly do. But I thought it was as my mother always said, because I've always lacked self-control.'

He had leaned nearer to me, and I caught a faint trace of his aftershave. His forearm on the bar was inches from mine. He was flirting with me for sure. Rarely had it been so much fun. The barman headed towards me. 'This round is on me,' I said.

But he pulled his phone towards him and put it in his jacket pocket. 'I have to go. Enjoy your blender launch.'

It was so sudden, such a switch of mood that I felt the pang of disappointment. 'Do you have to go so soon? I was enjoying our conversation.'

He smiled. 'Bye.'

And he was heading for the door with not a lingering glance or moment of regret.

Rory waited a full three minutes to make sure he was really gone before he hopped over a seat and put a consoling hand on my shoulder.

'So, what did you think?' I asked Rory. 'He seemed bang up for it, didn't he?'

'Jesus, Maggie, could you make it any more obvious? You need to flirt with them, not jump in their lap!'

'What? He was coming on to me, I'm sure of it.'

Rory made a scoffing sound. 'It's debatable.' In an exaggerated American accent he said, 'Hot for you, honey? Not in a million.'

I said nothing, feeling strangely resentful about Rory's interpretation of what had just happened. Gabe had left my fake card on the bar. It sat there like a rebuke. And I couldn't hide the prick of disappointment in my stomach.

CHAPTER 29

Maggie

Four weeks and four days before

My failure spurred me on. I ditched my tailing of Gabe, leaving Rory to go back to the taxi and wait for him. Having a drink had loosened something in me, I had an itch that needed to be scratched. I phoned Dwight. I told myself that it was for professional reasons, that I wanted an update on the Milo murder, but anyone who knew me could have called me out for that. I just didn't like to be rebuffed.

He sounded pleased to hear from me. 'You got a recorded confession yet?' he asked.

'Ha ha. Wishful thinking never hurt.'

He suggested we meet for a drink later in the week and I pushed him to bring it forward to tonight, to right there and then. An hour later I walked into a pub on Palace Street in Victoria to find him sitting at the bar.

I got on a bar stool next to him and ordered a double gin and tonic. Dwight got in another beer.

'So let's talk about your case this time, not mine,' Dwight said. 'The suspicious wife still paying you?'

I nodded. 'But I've got no joy yet.'

'So is he or isn't he cheating?'

We were knees together on our stools. I thought about his

question. 'Oh, I'm sure he's cheating, but you know, I can't work him out. I tried a honeytrap and got nothing. I thought he was going to take my card, but he left it behind.' I took a drink. 'And then the wife, she's hired me, so she's hard as nails behind this English rose exterior. She's calculated, yet I think she's vulnerable too.'

'Relationships are messy. You win some, you lose some.'

'I hate losing.'

Dwight made a noise. 'So do I. Losing in my job means having to face a family that haven't got justice.'

'Gabe seemed a bit preoccupied when I had that drink with him, but then after what's happened recently that's not a surprise. Of course the other way to look at Milo's murder is it could be serving as a warning to Gabe and his company.'

'It's far-fetched . . .' Dwight tailed off. 'Unless he contacts us and says that, we've got zilch. I wonder how he'll feel if he discovers his privacy has completely disappeared.'

'Orwell would have been horrified.'

'Indeed. What's your Room 101 moment?'

I smiled and took a large gulp of alcohol. I could feel the evening sliding away into an alcoholic haze. 'That's easy. Not being believed. Seeing something, clear as day, and everyone else saying it never happened. Being fitted up by the CIA or MI5 of whatever, your prints somewhere you never were, your DNA on a murdered body. You know what's true, and no one else trusts you.'

'OK, you're paranoid, I get it. Mine's more straightforward: falling. Off a building, a cliff, out of a plane, I've got a terrible fear of heights. You ever seen Sylvester Stallone in *Cliffhanger*? *Vertical Limit*?' Dwight grinned and shuddered.

'You ever worked a jumping case?'

He shook his head. 'No. I think I'd find that difficult.'

Somewhere in the distance was the sound of large-scale drilling, the area round Victoria – once a grubby amalgamation of faded mansion flats and civil service buildings – being razed to the ground and big ugly buggers of buildings thrusting skywards, another part of the crazy paving of London's building boom.

'You hear that?' I said. Dwight looked confused. 'So much concrete being poured, foundations metres thick. How many bodies are under this new city, do you think?'

'Jesus, woman, I thought policemen had twisted outlooks. We're positively happy clappy compared to you.'

'Before I find you, I make the clients pay the big bucks,' I said under my breath.

'What's that?' Dwight asked, and I shook my head.

'Nothing, just a silly phrase. Come on, let's drown our sorrows with another drink,' I grinned.

Dwight was studying me over his beer glass. 'Tell me, how does it feel when a honeytrap fails?'

'You're asking me if I take it personally?'

'Do you?'

'Of course not, it's just work.'

He grinned. 'You're lying. But you know, Maggie, if you'd honeytrapped me, I'd have failed.'

I love that moment, when the cards are laid out, intentions made clear and a new road back to a warm bed is opened. 'You got a girlfriend?'

'Not at the moment.'

'Then you've failed nothing at all. You're simply being a man and thank heaven for that.' I reached forward and held his chunky knee.

He smiled. 'Let's have another drink.'

'Make mine a double,' I grinned.

Three hours later we were back at his flat and I got a closer look at those powerful thighs. They were every bit as good as I remembered. We upended a lamp by his bed and probably kept the neighbours awake. I peeled myself out from under sticky sheets as the morning light began to fill the room and headed home.

I have a man problem, I'm not gonna lie. I have a need problem, and I have a sex problem. I don't have to give my hard-earned cash to a shrink to be told it's a pathetic need to be wanted, to be loved. My family never wanted me. So, years later this is the result, I guess. Nothing or no one has ever been enough to stop me doing what I do. Maybe one day I'll meet someone who is enough, this mythical person who can tame me, who can make me stop looking, stop exploring. But I know he doesn't exist. The past has made me this way, and unless some seismic event can knock me off course, I'm sailing into a future of full-on promiscuity.

Dwight didn't wake as I closed his bedroom door. As I made my quiet and sated way towards the Tube my mind kept straying to a man's back clothed in a blue Oxford shirt. I'll catch you yet, I thought, I'll catch you yet.

CHAPTER 30

Maggie

Four weeks and one day before

Two days later we lost Gabe. Rory was in the taxi outside GWM's offices, Simona was in Praed Street, and I was in the toilet of the sandwich shop. According to Rory, Gabe came out of the building, spent a long time waiting in the sunshine on his side of the street, then weaved dangerously through moving traffic to the opposite pavement as the lights changed to red and walked away down a side street.

I got a panicked call from Rory on my mobile, telling me to leave it running down my leg. I hustled back out to the street to find Rory stuck at the lights. I knew from experience this light was long and we couldn't turn right because there was a line of traffic eager to catch the green. 'Go,' I commanded Rory, who got out and began to follow on foot.

I had to pull a U-turn, which would annoy the world and his wife. The lights changed, and I held up half of central London as I swerved into a new line of traffic. I eventually cut left a block north of Rory and stop-started down a slow-moving one-way street.

Five minutes later Rory rang, out of breath. 'I've lost him. He was ahead of me, he turned the corner, and he was gone!'

I drove around in an ever-increasing grid of streets,

searching left and right. Rory ducked into John Lewis, jogged through an underground car park in the nearby square, checked doors and windows, doubling back on himself.

We got nothing. Eventually I picked Rory up on the corner of Harley Street. I banged the wheel in frustration. We had a major fuck-up on our hands.

I left Rory on the street corner where he'd last spotted Gabe and drove the taxi back to wait outside his office. Two hours later I saw Gabe walking down the street from the direction of Oxford Circus Tube.

I couldn't be sure but I thought he might have been wearing a fresh shirt.

I felt a strange sensation then. Did he know about us? Was he yanking our chain? But the overriding sensation was that he had outsmarted me. My honeytrap had failed, and I'd lost him for a crucial two hours.

There was something about that man, but I couldn't put my finger on it. He was either the smartest cheat I'd ever tailed or the most innocent. And if he was innocent, what game was Helene playing?

I phoned Rory and five minutes later he was back in the cab, sweating and in a bad mood. 'I think he's changed his shirt,' I said.

'How can you be sure?'

'It looks fresher.'

'Where the fuck did he go?' wailed Rory. 'Does he know about us?'

'What do you think?'

'He can't! There's no way.'

We argued the issue for a while but I eventually sided with Rory. He didn't know about us.

We were still arguing the finer points of it when we saw Gabe come out of the office at five thirty and cross the road and go into the Langham Hotel.

I moved to get out of the taxi but Rory had his hand on the door. 'I'll go,' he said.

'No, I'm going.'

'But he knows you – it has to be me!'

I was out and crossing the street before Rory could react. I looked back and could see him throwing his hands up in frustration, banging on the window of the taxi and swearing inside the hot metal. I heard my phone beeping and turned it off.

As the door of the hotel swung shut behind me, all the noise and desperation of the city was sucked away. It was cool and quiet in the hotel. Gabe was not in the lobby. I glanced into the bar and saw him pulling out a stool.

I headed down the stairs to the toilets and fluffed my hair and sprayed some perfume over my sweat and drew on some lipstick.

I came back upstairs and threw open the door to the bar.

I love a hotel bar. It's the anonymity, the silence, the thick stylish menus brim full with enticing alcoholic combinations; it's not knowing where the evening will end.

I began to walk across the room and did an obvious double take and headed over to Gabe. 'Hello there.' He looked up, confused. 'Blenders, do you remember, for show flats?' I lamely explained. There was a beat of silence. 'I really do make a lasting impression! I sat next to you in the bar under the office a couple of days ago. I work in the same building as you.'

'Sorry, yes, of course!' He smiled and I tried not to look offended, though I was. I forced myself to relax. This was all good news for Helene, I reminded myself. I didn't sit, I hovered, as if I was leaving my options open. 'I'm waiting for a friend, but she's always late, and I always hope that she isn't going to be late.'

'Please, take a seat,' he said and grabbed a stool for me. 'How was your launch?' he asked politely.

'Really good.' Positivity worked best with men. No one liked a moaner. 'So, have you been sat at your desk all day in this heat?'

'No, I had to get on the Tube, worst luck.'

I grimaced. 'It's horrible in this heat. I hope you didn't have to go far.' He didn't answer. 'Arriving for a business meeting all hot and bothered just puts you on the back foot before you've started.'

The barman brought Gabe a drink, meaning he didn't have to answer. I had to let it slide. 'Are you waiting to meet someone, or are you having an affair with the barman?' It was a lame thing to say but I got a response.

He smiled. 'My daughter's on her way. She's just finishing up something.'

'So you and she are close.'

'I guess we are.'

'I love it in here,' I added, not having to lie at all.

'Yes, so do I. I used to work in a hotel. It brings back memories.'

'Oh? Which hotel?'

He looked at me with piercing brown eyes. 'Back in the former Yugoslavia. But there's not much call for a hotel in a war zone.'

'I see what you mean. Did you come here, during that war?'

He nodded and took a sip. 'It was more terrible than you can imagine.'

'I'm sorry, I didn't mean to remind you of bad times.'

He waved my comment aside. 'Life is full of good and bad things. They seem to go together.'

'Don't they just,' I added. 'I guess your daughter is one of the good things.'

He smiled into his drink, sad and fond at the same time. It was the smile a father gives his child, an expression of pure, intergenerational love. That kind of bond is uncomplicated, unlike romantic love, which is compromised, angry, deceitful and constantly negotiated.

He nodded. 'Yes.'

'Is she like your wife?'

'My wife?' He looked confused for a moment, as if I'd dragged him back from another mental place entirely. 'Oh no, she's not at all like my wife.' He saw my face. 'I mean, my first wife died.'

'Oh. I'm so sorry.'

'Don't be. It was a long time ago now.'

'How old was your daughter when your wife died?'

'Just two.'

'That's terrible,' I sighed. 'Was her death sudden, if you don't mind me asking?'

He nodded. 'Yes, it was.' He didn't look at me as he spoke.

'Was it difficult to rebuild your life after that?'

'It changed a lot of things.'

'Do you think your relationship with her is different from other fathers and daughters?' I probed.

'I think it's impossible to know. Other people say we have an intense relationship, I guess.' He shrugged. 'But I feel that I'm talking about myself. What about you? Do you have a family?'

I shook my head. 'No, that life isn't for me.'

'Well, that might change.'

'I like no ties. It's exciting.' I stared at him, but he didn't bite; he looked like he was thinking about something else.

He became animated. 'You know, I look at my daughter and I marvel, really. Her life is so safe, and that makes me so happy. That's what I work for every day, for that moment when I can lie down and go to sleep and know that I protected her, that the chaos I saw as a young man won't happen to her.'

I took a long gulp of my drink. 'I'm glad you feel that way, but chaos can exist anywhere, not just in a war zone. I mean, look at me, I never knew my dad, I never want to remember my mum and I don't have children. My relationships are all – in the moment, shall we say.'

'But are you happy?'

I made a snorting sound. 'Only the unhappy ask that.' I glanced up at him. He was staring at me over the rim of his drink, enjoying my discomfort. 'Jesus, I don't know. It's a work in progress.'

He smiled. 'Let's drink to a work in progress.'

'Too fucking right. Cheers.'

He took a long drink and took the cocktail stick out of his glass. He pulled the plump green olive off with his teeth, giving me a glimpse into his mouth.

There was silence as he chewed his olive. His eyes were roaming across my body, taking in my neck, boobs, hips and legs, but I sensed vague appreciation rather than hard, cold desire. I held my breath. I felt conflicted, which was unusual. If I did my job well I'd eventually catch Gabe out. Yet I didn't want to. He seemed like a nice guy. I wanted him to be the exception to my succession of cheats and liars. I wanted him to be good and I wanted Helene to be wrong. I looked away.

When I looked back up, his eye was on Alice standing in the doorway.

CHAPTER 31

Alice

Four weeks and one day before

I followed the old tart who was pushing her tits in Poppa's face to the toilets. The flush started and she opened the door and turned to the basin to wash her hands.

'I hear you work in Sentinel House?' I said.

She looked at me in the mirror as she flicked water off her hands. 'That's right.'

'I'll keep an eye out for you.' Her hands stopped moving. 'So I can make sure you stay well away from my poppa. Low-rent flirts aren't his style.'

She stared back at me and wiped her hands on a little square of towel. 'Does he have form?'

She stayed calm, she wasn't shocked or outraged, and I felt the anger building. I knew my instincts were correct, this woman had brawled in streets before, she had had too much to drink and swung at chins and cheekbones, she was dangerous to Poppa. 'Stay away from him or you'll be sorry.'

'With respect, I think that's for him to decide.' She threw the towel in the hamper and waited.

'Leave him alone!' I shouted.

I was sweating as I walked back into the bar. Men like Poppa are easy pickings for money-grabbing vultures like the slag in the toilets. They can smell his kindness and his money like rotting meat. They have no shame. Once again I see myself as Poppa's saviour.

Poppa was placing the drained martini glass down on the little circle of paper on the bar when I came back. 'Poppa, why do you end up talking to such random people when you're just trying to relax?'

'I was having fun.'

I made the barman get Poppa a fizzy water with a twist of lemon. 'Helene should thank me, is what she should do.'

'Why, darling?'

'Come on, Poppa, this family is like a seesaw. You and Helene sit at either end, and I'm the fulcrum in the middle. Don't look so confused. If I wasn't underpinning it all, you two would crash to earth pretty quickly.'

Poppa picked up the drink and took a sip but pushed it away when he realised it was water. 'I don't understand that analogy at all.'

'Poppa, you're so silly! Without me, there would be no balance at all. See?'

CHAPTER 32

Maggie

Four weeks and one day before

Rory had worked for the Blue and White for five years. Those years had by and large been a seamless meeting of minds, but he was a strong personality and sometimes Rory and I fought. And very rarely Rory and I almost came to blows over decisions taken or not.

I left Gabe and Alice to their family love-in in the hotel and headed back out to the street, seeing Rory parked on the far side of the road.

He did a U-ey in the street and swung round to get me. I grasped the handle of the taxi but he shunted the vehicle up the street and stopped, the engine running. I walked forwards, and he did it again, and again, and again, half the way up Regent Street.

I was simmering with rage by the time he finally let me get in the back of the taxi. He began pointing at me through the gap where the money passed, calling me every name under the sun and more besides. 'You fuckin' eejit' was just one he landed.

'I suppose you ran into the daughter too, just to blow your chances even more.'

'She called me a low-rent flirt.'

'Jesus H Christ! You'll have to hire some freelancers – you can't go anywhere near him now! What were you thinking? You've lost your head. You used to be so strict about following the rules – no contact more than once; what's so special about this guy?'

'Oh come on, Rory, it's not that serious.'

'I don't like it, not at all. And don't you ever run off and leave me to mind this metal prison any more – you hear me! I'm not your poodle that you get to kick every once in a while!' He turned away and slammed his foot on the accelerator, which threw me back against the seats in an untidy backwards roll, my legs and stilettos akimbo, my neck crunched.

I took my punishment like a man.

CHAPTER 33

Helene

Four weeks and one day before

'Has Gabe had an affair before?' Maggie asked.

It was the casual way the question was posed that gave me an atavistic sense of wariness. I was sitting by the window in Maggie's office on Praed Street, the rumble of buses outside making the windows shake, as if a faint earthquake was subtly reshaping the world under our feet.

Maggie was relating the details of her honeytrap on my husband and how she had failed. As she described their two after-work drinks she made it sound like she'd had a great time. She got out of her large leather chair and came round to the front of her desk and leaned her bum back on it and crossed her arms. I sensed disappointment and frustration that she hadn't been able to manipulate Gabe. What did you expect, I thought sourly, that I was married to an arsehole? Maggie was underestimating him, and me. I had already told her that that was a mistake.

'I mean it wasn't all a bust, I got somewhere – he talked a lot about his past before he came to the UK, so it was certainly fruitful,' Maggie said.

I was dumbfounded and covered my shock by hunting through my bag for a headache pill. Gabe never talked about his past with me. 'What did he mention specifically?' I managed to say.

'The hotel he used to work in, family, that type of thing.'

I drank some water and washed down the pill, watched Maggie through narrowed lids. These subjects were off limits to the man I married, areas where I had probed and prodded and always been rebuffed. I was vain enough to think that what he wouldn't reveal to me he wouldn't reveal to a passing stranger over a martini. I wondered if she was lying, or if Gabe was. But to what end? Maggie was smart enough and cynical enough to have wondered whether Gabe was tainted by Milo's death or if he was involved somehow. She would have talked through with Rory and Simona the likelihood of the Blue and White being used by me, but why would she need to lie to me here and now?

A darker thought came to me. Maybe Maggie's cynical heart was vulnerable after all. Maybe Gabe had simply turned her head.

'So has he ever had an affair?' she repeated.

I pulled out some chewing gum and put it in my mouth. It tasted like dust. I shook my head. 'Not that I know of.' I was being noncommittal, when I should have told her straight. Never. He would never do that to me. I had been that certain, would have staked my life on it, before I saw that woman in the cloakroom. But now? Now my chaos swirled around me. I had thought finding out this detail about Gabe would affect my marriage, but I hadn't realised that my life was a Jenga tower, where if one section is examined, other areas get pulled out of shape until the entire structure crashes to the floor.

I felt Gabe and now Maggie had stripped me of all my certainties, of my power. I was flailing, and I didn't like it at all.

Maggie walked back to her seat and sat down. 'I have to tell you something else that happened. We lost Gabe for two hours.'

I was stunned. 'Where do you think he went?'

'We don't know. It does sometimes happen that we lose someone we are watching, but it is unusual.'

She wasn't embarrassed or contrite that she had failed. What am I paying you for? I silently fumed. I shifted on my seat, looked out the window at the new high-rises looming behind Paddington Station. A thrum of anxiety began. 'Does he know you're following him?'

Maggie at least considered the question for a long time. 'Rory and I had a talk about it. I don't see how he can. I think it was coincidence. But we'll make sure it never happens again.'

'Have you seen him using this other phone again?'

Maggie shook her head.

There was a pause. She was waiting to see how I would react. It was time to put the heat back on to her. 'Tell me something, have you ever got involved with your clients before?'

'Involved?'

'Oh, I don't know, ended up liking them more than you should, that type of thing? I mean, it's risky to play-act, isn't it? You see movies about undercover cops who end up really becoming like the drug dealers they are trying to catch.'

'You're flattering me,' Maggie said. 'Undercover work for the police is different gravy. They are living twenty-four hours a day with constant threat for months on end. Catching a cheat usually only takes a few weeks, as I've said before.'

I gave Maggie a thin smile. The way she said it was dismissive, as if it was small-scale, humdrum. This was my life, my everything. Be very careful with the weight I am handing to you, I thought. 'Would you say that these meetings with Gabe are fruitful?' I pressed.

Maggie nodded. 'Yes, but there's just one problem. When I was having a drink with Gabe in the Langham, Alice arrived. She saw me.'

'Oh no.'

'She's very protective of her dad, isn't she?'

'Why do you say that?'

'I sensed she was suspicious of what I was doing with Gabe.'

Did she have a reason to be? I was thinking.

'But she needn't have been,' Maggie continued. 'He was literally telling me how much he loved his daughter.'

It was like she had punched me in my defective womb. I knew Maggie was blunt and could be rude, but she had no idea how much she had hurt me at that moment. I felt the absence at my centre, the children I never had, the love Gabe would have given them. Would the woman in the green dress have even existed if I had been able to have children? Would a child have kept him closer? I stood on shaking feet, keen to be gone.

'So we'll continue as we have been,' Maggie said and I nodded.

She crossed the room and opened the door for me. 'I'm not going to charge you for today. I'm sorry that I lost him. I know this is difficult for you, even if I don't show it.'

I was mute. It was too little too late. I wasn't big-hearted or generous enough to respond.

CHAPTER 34

Alice

Four weeks before

Success has many fathers and failure none. And I had to admit, Helene's charity event made me appreciate my stepmother anew. I thought she was prone to too much introspection and self-regard, but the way she separated the guests from their money that night was like watching a master at work.

As an intern for GWM, I helped set up the party. It was at the office because there was a function room with large windows with a view over the West End. The set designers arrived in the morning and were there all day creating a venue that shouted sophistication and fun. There was a small kitchen at the back through which a production line of workers unwrapped and prepared canapés, while crates of champagne were stacked in the corridor by the service lift.

There was a buzzy atmosphere at work all day, with people peering in and commenting on the transformation, though only a small number of employees would be staying for the evening.

Helene had exploited every connection she had in the TV and PR worlds and all week items that were to be auctioned off had been couriered in – autographed football shirts, never-used designer handbags, spa holidays in five-star resorts. Helene had curried favour with an auctioneer who worked at Sotheby's and he was overseeing the event. The target was to raise a hundred thousand pounds for a charity that gave educational opportunities to disadvantaged young people in the capital.

The lobby was filled with the most spectacular bouquet of flowers and someone had done something amazing with the lighting so that by the evening it looked more like a posh hotel than an office suite. The guests arrived in the lobby and walked through the office past the design studio and into the function room.

It was an amazing evening. I felt like such a grown-up! I drank champagne, gobbled the canapés and introduced myself to so many important clients and contacts of Poppa. They were all so friendly and pleased to meet me!

Oblomov and his wife Irina came, some members of the board of Qatar Futures were there, some well-known TV personalities came and I was told some premier league foot-ballers were there but I wouldn't have recognised them.

I drank a little too much champagne.

I felt sick and hot and left to get some air. I wandered around on my own in the empty offices, trying out different chairs in the design studio for size. One day I would be sitting in one of them for real, I knew. After a while I headed back to the party and as I came out of the design studio, I caught a low laugh from Poppa's office. I walked along the corridor and was a little shocked to see Peter Fairweather sitting in Poppa's chair. He was talking to someone who I couldn't see through the frosted glass, but after a moment the edge of Helene's floor-length purple dress appeared. Helene must have been sitting on the desk.

The wagu beef canapés didn't taste so good any more. I threw the little skewer with the frilled paper decoration that was still in my hand to the floor.

A couple of moments later the door opened and Peter appeared, with Helene following behind.

If Helene was surprised to see me there she hid it well. 'Alice! Have you met Peter Fairweather of Partridger?'

I shook his hand. 'I'm interning at GWM.'

Peter nodded. 'They keeping you busy?'

'Oh yes, I'm learning such a lot, all about the company. I know that Partridger's bid for the Vauxhall site wasn't high enough to win. But are you looking at other sites in London?'

Peter looked surprised.

'This is Alice Moreau, such a talented young individual,' Helene added, giving Peter a look I couldn't interpret. Sometimes Helene made me feel like a gauche little kid, and I didn't like it.

'Ah, now I see where she gets it from,' Peter said, smiling at Helene. Helene looked at me indulgently. I had a sensation they were sharing a private joke. I wondered if it was at my expense.

'But are you looking at other sites?' I asked Peter again.

'The feelers are always out,' he replied, looking at Helene again. I got frustrated; his answer was so vague and non-committal.

'Come, Alice, the auction is about to start,' Helene said. She began to walk down the corridor with Peter.

'Do you think Milo would be here tonight, if he hadn't been murdered?' I asked.

They both turned sharply, the bottom of Helene's gown swishing round to face me last. 'I sincerely hope so,' Helene said quickly. 'There are some members of his community rights group here if you would like to meet them,' she said in a tone I couldn't interpret.

Peter said nothing, and neither did I. We were spared the awkwardness that had begun to bloom between us as the door to the auction room opened and we were pulled into a sea of people and noise.

Despite the tension with Helene, the auction was great fun. There was a rousing cheer when Helene took to the stage to declare that we had surpassed our fundraising target by nearly double. Poppa looked at Helene with admiration and pride. Arkady Oblomov was the biggest spender of the night – he ended up in a bidding battle with Poppa for a signed photograph of Mick Jagger.

Soon we were left with one remaining auction item. It was so large that we were told we had to gather in the street below. There was a minimum bid of fifty thousand pounds. The room pulsed with exclamations and astonishment. It was genuinely exciting and completely above board – even I didn't know what the prize was.

The hundred guests filed downstairs to the pavement on Regent Street and Helene got up on a little makeshift stage and made a short and impassioned speech, full of heavy innuendo – that GWM was 'driven' to work with the local community and there were 'no brakes' on our ambition for the charity. The crowd roared their approval. The auctioneer took to the stage and two women in shimmering gold dresses held a silk covering over the car.

The auctioneer began the bidding and as the price rose the women began to slowly pull back the covering on the car. With a final flourish, the smiling ladies pulled back the covering to reveal an Audi convertible, its black paint gleaming under the street lights. Everyone roared their approval. The winning bid was eighty-five thousand pounds from an elderly Asian man with white hair who I didn't know. It was all so exciting, to raise so much money for such a worthwhile cause.

After everyone had clapped and cheered, Helene revealed that the car had been an extraordinarily kind gift from property development company Qatar Futures. There were shouts and demands that we get on the podium, so Poppa, Helene and I ended up in front of the attendees, our arms around each other, smiling back at a sea of iPhones and the official photographer.

I could feel Helene and Poppa's arms around my waist, and I realised that this was where I had always wanted to be, up high, surrounded by love, adoration and respect.

Poppa, Helene and I were of course the last to leave. We got an Uber home, flushed with success.

It ended abruptly when we drew up outside our house. 'For goodness' sake!' Helene exclaimed. 'Who has done that?'

On the garden wall of the house, 'You can't hide' was sprayed in capital letters. Even in the dark it was visible, and the spiky lettering felt threatening and menacing.

'I'll get someone to deal with that tomorrow,' Poppa was saying. I couldn't see his face as he was staring out the window at the wall.

'Is this connected to us?' I asked.

He took a long moment to turn round. 'No. It's just some vandal.' His face was hard, set in a way that I hadn't seen before. And with that he stepped out of the car. I didn't believe him. I began to follow him out and opened my door, but as I did so I caught a glimpse of Helene's face. She sat motionless, staring at the lettering. I knew I had had too much to drink, but I fancied at that moment that I saw fear in her eyes. And all the triumph of the night and the money raised for a good cause turned to ashes in a moment.

CHAPTER 35

Maggie

Four weeks before

The night of GWM's charity auction was something to see. Rory and I ate kebabs and drank beer in the taxi as we watched the line of long black cars spit out London's great and good: old rich men in penguin suits, women in glittering evening dress, some B-list celebrities, and an Arsenal defender and two Chelsea midfielders and their wives. And three hours later we watched them all file out again and cluster round that Audi.

We saw the little stage erected, and watched the bidding rise higher and higher as the covering was pulled off the bodywork by the models. We listened to the cheers and the laughter from the darkness of our cab. We saw the Moreaus on that stage, their arms around each other, the people clustered below them, the photos being taken, the huge amount they had raised for charity, the applause they received.

They had it all. Most people I knew had little more than nothing. I had never been so close to a family that could tick all the boxes, who could go to bed in financial security and still be smiling at each other when they woke. 'Is it so bad,' I said to Rory, 'to want a little bit of what they've got?'

Rory drained the last of his can of beer and rolled up the

remains of his cold kebab in its white paper covering. 'Everybody wants that,' Rory said, nodding towards the cameras and the crowd. 'And a lot of people will do anything to get it,' he added.

We tailed the Moreaus back to their house. We watched as they went inside and the door shut behind them.

'What do you make of that writing on their garden wall?' I asked Rory.

'His mistress is tired of being given the runaround and wants him to sort this shit out?'

'I swear, you are even more cynical than I am, Rory.'

'That's impossible,' he retorted.

The letters seemed to shimmer in the darkness of the street. 'Unlike you, I see two options,' I replied. 'It could be that jealousy has got the better of Gabe's mistress, or it could be something connected to his company, someone who thinks they're owed financially. If it's the first, he's running the risk of destroying his marriage, but if it's the second, he could be in personal danger.'

Rory scoffed. 'Don't you worry on Gabe Moreau's account. He can take care of himself. As long as Helene keeps paying us, I'm happy.'

CHAPTER 36

Maggie

Three weeks and four days before

At the start of the new week Simona and I were on the Monday afternoon shift and were soon following Gabe as he drove out of town, heading west. He pulled into Kensal Rise cemetery off the Harrow Road. I'd caught three cheats in cemeteries – the dead don't stop people being passionate, if anything they were an aphrodisiac.

Gabe drove towards a large building in the middle of the cemetery, got out and parked. Simona dropped me off and I moved closer, using trees as cover. I got my zoom ready and looked around, waiting to see if I could see an approaching woman.

He walked around the building to where a row of memorial stones were inset into a side wall and stood before one of the plaques and touched it with splayed fingers, head bowed. The grass made my approach soundless, so I pointed my audio microphone towards him, receiver in my ear.

His voice was a low incantation, which I took to be a prayer, but he was talking in a language I couldn't understand so his meaning was unclear. What came next shocked me. He was quiet for a moment, staring at the plaque, then he turned his fingers into a fist and ground it slowly into the metal square. A sob rang out in my ear before he walked away.

I was a snooper. A grubby, amoral pryer into people's darkest recesses and most passionate shames. Most of the time I felt nothing. Served them right, I thought, but sometimes, just occasionally what I did made me feel bad. Grief was not clean, or ordered, it didn't behave. Here was anguish and rage twisted into a tight helix. It wasn't my place to witness or intrude.

When he headed back to the cemetery gates I approached the plaque. 'In loving memory of Clara Belle Moreau. May you live forever in our hearts.'

He was mourning his former wife's untimely, violent death, but was he cheating? I wondered if he ever revealed to Helene how often he came here, or whether he told her at all.

The more I watched him, the more complicated and fascinating he was becoming.

CHAPTER 37

Maggie

Three weeks and three days before

It's ironic, I suppose, that the day we finally caught Gabe I wasn't even tailing him. I was in the office meeting Mrs Gupta, a new client. Her husband ran a chain of Indian restaurants and she was suspicious he was having an affair with her sister, who was part owner in the business. That was going to be a case that wouldn't end well for anybody, I knew.

I was glad when Rory phoned and distracted me from my dark thoughts. He had tailed Gabe from the office to Connaught Tower and then to Chelsea. Gabe was driving his own car, so he had been easy to follow.

'Look at this,' Rory had said, and pinged me a series of photos.

It was Gabe, standing by a door that had been opened by a blonde-haired woman. In the next photo the woman was smiling, her arm on the doorframe, and in the next photo she had her hand on his hair. The subsequent photos showed Gabe step inside the house and the door close behind them.

'Where are you?' I barked.

'It's in a cul-de-sac off the King's Road. I've checked the door: three bells, no names, can't work out which one is hers.

Blinds are drawn, I can't see in. I'm going back to the taxi to wait.'

I was out of the office and ordering an Uber to drive me to Chelsea as quick as I could. 'Finally, we've finally nailed him.' I could hear Rory's excitement at the realisation that our long operation was drawing to a close.

I arrived at the address Rory had given me in twenty minutes. Rory had moved the taxi out of sight and we took up positions crouched behind a wall about a hundred metres away.

'He hasn't come out since I called you,' Rory said.

'Any sign of which floor they're on?'

'Not yet.'

'Did you see him use the other phone?'

Rory shook his head. 'There's something else. He stopped at a cashpoint on the way over here. He took out a lot of money. A stack, maybe this thick.' Rory made a little space between his thumb and forefinger. 'You maybe want to get Helene to check whether he still has it on him this evening.'

'Fan-fucking-tastic.' I sat back behind the wall to wait for Gabe, the thrill of the chase pulsing through my veins.

Half an hour after Gabe Moreau had walked into the Chelsea flat, the door opened and he came back out. I photographed them with the long-range lens on my Canon.

The woman he was with was slim and blonde-haired, wearing a fashionable below-the-knee skirt and heels. She had the air of someone who was used to being looked at, who knew male appreciation was never far away. The sun was in her eyes and as she held her hand across her brow the gold bracelets on her wrist glinted. Gabe had his hands in his pockets and was looking at the floor. After a while she patted him fondly on the lapel of his jacket, ran a hand through his hair as a goodbye and turned and walked back into the house.

Gabe got into his car and drove away.

Rory stood up and began to walk back to the taxi. 'I'll stay on him,' he said.

'I'll go and ring that doorbell. Find out who we've got in there.'

Rory was smiling. 'I was beginning to think Helene had made it all up, but I guess she was telling the truth.'

I approached the door and spotted the intercom camera. I rang all three doorbells. There was no answer. I rang again and again but got no joy. I checked to see if there was another exit from the row of houses but there didn't seem to be one. What was it about me that she didn't like the look of? Why would she hide in there and not answer the door?

I walked away further into the new development, past rows of bland and uninhabited townhouses and large shop windows that were empty, and eventually found a marketing suite with more lifeless flags set up on poles on the pavement outside and went in.

A white man in a grey suit came round to the front of his white reception desk and shook my hand a lot too hard. His name tag said Jonty Belvedere. I told him some nonsense about being a kitchen designer looking to expand into a shop for clients. He showed me a lot of marketing brochures. Why was it so empty round here? I asked him.

I got the usual excuses about a big push coming in early autumn, and dubious numbers relating to occupancy rate. He knew it was bullshit and so did I, but he worked on commission and he would be keen to earn.

'This development is mixed-use residential and commercial?'

'Absolutely.'

'I saw a row of houses up round the corner over there. Are they occupied yet?'

'Oh yes, the first wave of tenants and owners have already moved in. I've got viewings every day, a lot of competition and interest.' He pulled yet another brochure out. I would get high on the print fumes before long. There was a Foxtons estate agent's logo in the bottom corner. I looked at desperate Jonty trying to sell property duds, and I could almost have felt sorry for him. As Jonty watched another potential sale slip through his grasp, it made me think that property development wasn't the quick route to mega riches that every normal person thought it to be. At Queen's Gate, as this area was called, someone was losing millions.

True to form, I didn't care, I was just glad it wasn't me.

CHAPTER 38

Helene

Three weeks and two days before

Maggie showed me a series of photos of the woman who was groping my husband in a Chelsea street. They were long range, slightly grainy, but the mood and intention in them were clear. It was the same woman I'd seen in the cloakroom in the Café Royal, possibly the same woman who had been talking to Alice at the charity run. Maggie showed me photos of her flat, of her closing the door behind Gabe. That door signified the end of my life as I had lived it. Slam. Silence. As final and fast as that.

'How long were they in there for?' I asked, my voice disembodied.

'About half an hour.'

I watched Gabe come out. I could see the woman grinning, a hand reaching out to pull at his lapel. He got into his car and drove away, back to work. I know where he was headed because I was in the office that day. I was in a meeting with him about Connaught Tower Two. I remember now that he was late to arrive. Not by much, maybe five minutes.

I was so angry I couldn't breathe.

I sat in Maggie's office, mute. I looked at Maggie and I hated her. I knew that was irrational and pointless, but I am a human being; a twisted mass of dangerous emotion. I wanted to shoot the messenger. I wanted to kill the messenger.

What I loathed, in an all-consuming rush that I had never expected to feel, was Maggie's success. It felt that it was at my expense. The qualities I first admired in her – the honesty, the brashness, the tell-it-like-it-is shtick – I now found repellent.

'Is this the woman you saw in the Café Royal?' Maggie asked.

I nodded. 'Who is she?' My voice didn't sound like my own.

Maggie got up and came and sat on the sofa next to me. Maybe she thought I would fall into her fleshy arms when I saw my husband and that woman together. That made me angrier still. She didn't know me. When I have been betrayed that is not what I do.

'I called you as soon as we had the photos, to confirm we are talking about the same woman. I've put Rory on the background checks. When Gabe drove away I knocked on her door, but she didn't answer. So far we don't know who she is.'

'I don't understand what you're saying.'

'I appreciate that this is difficult—'

'Don't say that. You have no idea at all.'

Maggie tried a different tack. 'No one is on the electoral roll for that address, there is no landline registered there.'

'Did you hear what they were talking about?'

'No,' Maggie replied.

'Did she get in the car?'

'No.'

I picked up one of the photos by its corner, as if it was radioactive. Their faces were inches apart. You fucking bastard you fucking bastard you fucking bastard, was a mantra spinning on repeat in my head but I was thinking about half an hour. What can be done, what can be said, what can be promised, in thirty minutes. How a life can unravel in such a short time.

I felt so overwhelmed by a surge of jealousy I couldn't breathe. I thought what I saw at the Café Royal would be the worst, but the cold calculated nature of this, here in this poky Paddington office, was worse. I wanted Maggie gone, I never wanted to see her again. I hated her for even knowing this shameful secret about me and my husband, I loathed her coolly surveying the wreck of my marriage. Marriage is hard, such hard, hard work. I looked at Maggie, she who had gaily told me that marriage and commitment had never panned out for her. She had been so glib, so pleased with herself, having substituted commitment and trust with temporary indulgences and passing fancies. She couldn't even begin to understand the bedrock that is laid down over the years of a marriage and how infidelity is a fracking team exploding right through the heart of it.

'I'm sorry,' she said. 'I think it's important to remember that this is not definitive evidence of an affair. He met her, but what they are doing is inconclusive.'

I saw Gabe's back retreating into her house, the door closing, the silence in the street. The tsunami that had broken over my marriage retreating down the beach and pausing, gathering strength to surge even more aggressively to obliterate everything in its path for a second time. Jesus, I was a glutton for punishment. I didn't have to commission these photos. I didn't have to *see* it. But that's the point, isn't it? It's human nature, the inability to turn off that screen, to look away from that car crash, to put down that photo, before it's too late. Way, way too late.

'There's something else,' Maggie said. 'Gabe took out a large amount of cash before he visited this woman. Is that usual behaviour?'

'Cash? How much?'

'It was a significant wodge, that's all I know.'

I stared at her, confounded. 'Is it a brothel?'

She paused for a moment and I fancied I saw respect on her face, that I had the guts to confront it. 'I doubt it. We were there for a considerable time. One delivery van and one car passed me. Brothels give themselves away because there's male traffic. For them to cover their costs there's high throughput. You can't disguise that unless you run it out of a nightclub or the back of a restaurant or from an area where most people couldn't care less.'

Maggie was interrupted by my phone ringing. It was Gabe. I hurled the phone across the room so hard Maggie had to duck.

CHAPTER 39

Alice

Three weeks and two days before

This afternoon it was Helene's turn to show me how things worked at GWM. I waited for a long time in her office because that was where we had arranged to meet, but I ended up kicking my heels because Helene was late. I was surprised, she knew as well as I did that in business it was important to always be on time. When she finally arrived, she looked flustered with high red spots on her cheeks, and I realised she had forgotten we were meeting.

'I can come back another day, Helene, if you prefer,' I tried to put a positive turn on it.

She was glancing around her office, distracted, but insisted I stayed. She sat down and put her hands on her clean and orderly desk. 'Let's start on the charity auction. What's the most important thing to do once an event has finished?'

'Plan the next one?'

Helene shook her head. 'Follow through. Now is not the time to let go. Even if the individual didn't donate on the night, we pursue, pursue and pursue until before they know it, we've got them in the palm of our hands. And they don't even know it.'

She had her fingers gripped around an imaginary stress

ball, her eyes fiery. 'So, from our list of every attendee, we start with a personalised card saying thanks.' She reached for a list in a neat pile on her neat desk, ran a fingernail over some calligraphy pens. 'So you can help Sara in my team with that. Leave Oblomov, anything addressed to Partridger and anything addressed to Members of Parliament to me personally,' she added. We filed out of Helene's office and towards Sara's desk. 'A good fundraiser makes people feel good, makes them feel wanted. Everybody wants to be wanted.'

Her movements were brittle and sharp, her voice had a tint of sarcasm to it. The look in Helene's eyes was strange. As if she had realised something she long held to be true wasn't any more. I wondered if Helene was having the menopause. Lily said her mum had gone completely bonkers with hormonal surges. I was about to ask her, but I was interrupted by a commotion further down the corridor. I walked towards Poppa's office and three men were stood up around Poppa's desk, Poppa holding a sheaf of papers in his hand. 'This is not good enough, don't you see it? It has to be perfect and we are already late!'

Soraya, Poppa's secretary, came hustling out of the room a moment later. She gave me a look that signalled bad day at the coalface and hurried away to her desk.

I sensed the tension in the office tightening, like a screw being turned. Something was going on with the Vauxhall development that wasn't working. I thought back to the notes I had found, the writing that was at this moment being scrubbed off our front wall. I needed to know what was happening. It was time to confront Poppa and get the truth, it was time to find out what Helene knew. I glanced at my stepmother. She was an onlooker to the argument but she had turned away and was on her phone and I couldn't see her face.

CHAPTER 40

Helene

Three weeks and two days before

I left Maggie's and went back to the office. I worked on autopilot, made my excuses and left early. I was surprisingly calm. I needed to be at home, to retreat to my place of safety. I almost cried with relief when I closed the front door behind me and threw my bag down. Now I could slide to the floor and dissolve.

I heard a noise upstairs.

Gabe and Alice were at work, the cleaner didn't come today. I stood very still, sensing in my bones that something was wrong; the very air in the house felt disturbed.

I climbed the stairs. A low noise I couldn't place was coming from my bedroom. A splash of water emanated from the en-suite bathroom; someone was humming. I walked towards that noise as if towards a siren singing from the rocks and pushed the door open all the way.

A woman with blonde hair piled messily on top of her head was lying in the bath, a sea of bubbles lapping at her neck. One curving foot with bright pink dots of nail colour was raised and resting on the taps. Our eyes met and she moved, standing fast so the water sluiced in an aggressive gurgle, foam draining off her limbs as she stepped out of the tub and in one movement plucked a black raincoat off the floor and began to wrap her wet limbs in it. It was the woman Maggie had shown me pictures of from Chelsea. I staggered back into the bedroom, horrified, but at the same time grotesquely fascinated by her nakedness. She stood defiantly in front of me, with no hint of embarrassment as she tied the belt in a tight, aggressive knot at her waist. She was tall, her boobs high and full, white streaks of bubble bath slicking down her tanned skin. I caught the flash of her blonde pubic hair, a mole on her stomach near her belly button.

'Get out,' I croaked, trying out the words for size. 'Get out,' I said louder, gaining in confidence, the depths of her transgression finally beginning to filter through to my voice.

She passed me in an instant, dark, watery footprints staining the carpet, and picked up a pair of heels I hadn't noticed before and headed into the corridor.

'Get out of my house, you fucking bitch!' I screamed at her as I ran towards her, crazy emotions flooding me.

She was at the bottom of the stairs and turned, looking up at me defiantly. 'I've got as much right to be here as you have,' she said before she opened the door and was gone.

I flew down the stairs and out the front of the house to see her jogging away up the street on bare feet, her shoes dangling from one hand.

I ran back into the steamy bathroom, a panting wreck, spying towels piled in heaps on the floor, the bathmat rumpled and sodden, the water in the tub still spinning from her presence. She had used my bath foam, it sat unstoppered on the side, half empty.

I picked up the bottle of bubble bath and hurled it to the floor in a rage. The glass shattered into a thousand ugly shards that scattered over the marble floor. Had she been in my house before? I turned and stared at the bed. They hadn't, had they? I slid down the wall to the bathroom floor as

another connection became clear. She had stolen my keys. I
hadn't lost them that day in the café – my initial fears, my
intuition, had been right. She had watched me, stalked me
and planned with vicious precision this invasion and humiliation. *I've got as much right to be here as you have.* I thumped
the floor. I didn't even feel the broken glass slice my finger.

I stumbled into the study, sat down and logged in to Gabe's
bank account. We had shared and personal accounts, but I
had access to all of it. We never had any secrets, or so he
had led me to believe. I wondered then how he had made
me think something so stupid. How had he convinced me
that our relationship was transparent? He talked and acted
it, and I was happy to be deceived. No, the truth was darker:
I wanted to be deceived, because I was stupid enough to
believe the fantasy. I thought I was above the grubby pain
of love betrayed.

And less than an hour later, I wondered why I had been
such a fool. Why I had treated Gabe so differently from how
I had treated every other man in my life, every other lover.

I began to forensically examine the accounts for the past
few months. The amount of money flowing out of our house-
hold was a river, and even though I knew that, I had never
examined the detail of it. I didn't care about the trail of blood
from my finger that began to meander around the letters on
the keyboard. After a while I began to see a pattern of cash
withdrawals from his personal account: five hundred pounds
here, a thousand there, other withdrawals for up to two
thousand pounds. I went back further, scrabbling round in
the boxes in the study and found Gabe's bank statements
from before he had transferred everything online. Eighteen
months ago, the large cash withdrawals weren't happening.

If he had been paying for her for a year and a half, he
must have been seeing her for longer. Gabe was just like all
the men I had ever known; none of them were faithful either.

This woman had come into my most personal space, had fouled my nest that I had worked so hard to make perfect. She had flaunted her flesh, had taunted me with her nakedness – here, she was saying, your husband likes this bush, he likes it this way, he likes these boobs, these very nipples here, he likes my long neck and he likes what sits inside my pretty head. She had trampled on every boundary and laid waste to my life, to everything I believed in and loved. And she had targeted my daughter. And Gabe had allowed it, he had taken pleasure from her. I wiped my bloodied hand across the last bank statement I had seen. What was I going to do now?

CHAPTER 41

Maggie

Three weeks and two days before

Two hours after Helene left my office I received the blunt recorded message that Helene wanted my work for her to end. It was over.

Rory was happy. 'Think positive,' he counselled. 'We got out of that potential mess in Vauxhall without getting burned. Gabe never rumbled us. We've got another success under our belt. Let's move on to the next case.' He went off to make a coffee, humming a pop tune under his breath.

An hour after that Simona found an envelope with the outstanding cash Helene owed us in the company mailbox. There was no message.

I phoned Helene and she answered straight away. I told her we'd received the money.

'I can't really talk, I'm at work,' she replied. Her voice was clipped and cold.

'Our clients are free to terminate the agreement at any time. But I'm always here if you need to talk or want us to investigate further.'

'I want you to destroy any information you're keeping in your files about my family,' she said.

I had to let her down gently. 'I'm afraid we can't do that,

we have to keep it for tax purposes. But it will be safely stored—'

'I don't believe you. I mean I don't believe you that it can't be got rid of.'

'I'm sorry, Helene, but that is the way we do it.' There was silence. 'Have you decided what you're going to do?'

'No.'

'Talk to him. I advise all my clients to talk it out. It's the only way. Go to counselling.'

She was surprised. 'You've changed your tune. I thought you were of the shock and awe school, Old Testament justice.'

'Sometimes. Hell, other times I just want people to be happy. It's difficult enough to find people with which to spend our days. If you ever need to talk, you know where to find me.'

She wasn't in the mood for goodbyes. She simply hung up.

And that was that. The Moreaus were out of my life.

I sat back in my chair and looked around my office, chief of my little domain, feeling empty. I sometimes had this sensation after a case had come to an end. Sentiments and attachments that had to be processed and put aside before we plunged into the next case and went back to hanging out in dark alleys and photographing silhouettes at windows.

We weren't going to start on Mrs Gupta's family mess until next week when her sister came back from a visit to Mumbai, so I gave Simona and Rory the rest of the day off. They cheered and there were smiles all round. I counted out Helene's money and logged it while Simona put on a sun hat and headed to a deckchair in Regent's Park with a good book and Rory said he was off to ogle men in swim shorts at a pool in Covent Garden. We were Londoners in the heat, hormones drifting on the hot air currents and mixing with the traffic fumes and the smell of rubbish.

When they'd gone, I watched the tramps weaving and the commuters hustling down Praed Street from the window for a while. I watched the new mothers, just discharged from St Mary's Hospital, hugging their precious bundles, the new fathers fumbling with prams and hovering anxiously around their partners as if they were too fragile to touch. I heard the cries of a *Big Issue* salesman. The hot afternoon wore on. I phoned Dwight, itchy for shits and giggles. He didn't answer or he dodged my calls.

I locked up, walked out past the queue of men waiting at the immigration lawyer's. I meandered directionless through central London, enjoying the summer heat. I was feeling dissatisfied, as if something about Helene and Gabe hadn't become clear to me. They were glamorous, they were alluring, I had liked observing them, but Helene had drawn a line under it all. She didn't want to know who the blonde-haired woman was. That was not unusual, nothing she had done was off beam. I wondered about the money. Was Gabe giving it to that woman, and if so, why?

And then I checked myself. I didn't need to know why, or when or how. I had found him out, I had been paid, it was over.

I don't know how it happened, but I ended up on Regent Street. There's one thing I like early evening when it's hot and the summer is in full swing and I'd just successfully completed another case. I needed a drink. The steps of the Langham felt like I was coming home; the bar, with its glittering rows of bottles and glasses, felt comfortingly familiar. I succumbed to the sensation of the drone of voices, a martini set on the little paper circle edged in blue, an olive and a smile, rising hopes and expectations. I phoned Dwight again, he didn't pick up.

I didn't use Tinder, I had never signed up to speed dating. I was old-fashioned, I liked a hotel bar. I wasn't looking for love, I was looking for thrills, and they are very different things.

I was halfway through my second martini when the bar door opened and Gabe walked in.

CHAPTER 42

Maggie

Three weeks and two days before

This time Gabe remembered who I was. He came straight over and held out his hand. 'Melissa.' He smiled at me. Maybe it was the hit of vodka from the drink, or the heat, or both, but I felt a surge of pure joy and anticipation run through me.

He pointed to the barman, like the man in the white shirt and black trousers was a secular priest performing his time-honoured rites. Gabe pointed to my glass and pointed to his own chest. Nothing else was said. He sat down.

A moment later we chinked drinks.

'How was your day?' he asked, a question that when he posed it was expansive and open to interpretation.

'Uneventful. Yours?'

He made a movement I couldn't interpret. 'Quiet.'

I had had no food, the drink was going to my head, the edges of my understanding were going fuzzy. 'How's the family?'

I watched his lips as he put the wide glass to them. 'Good.'

'I think I should say that your daughter wasn't very nice to me the last time I was in here. She warned me off you in the toilets.'

He looked shocked and then he rolled his eyes. 'She's very young. There's so much about adult relationships that she doesn't understand.'

I felt a shiver of transgression. 'So she's an idealist.'

'The last one left,' he said.

'Maybe you should let her in on the real world.'

He shook his head, took another long sip. 'That's what you don't understand. When it's your own flesh and blood, you want to wrap them in cotton wool forever.'

'So when the gentlemen callers come, you open the door with a pitchfork.'

'I'd give it to them two barrels.' He made a mock gesture of shooting someone with his two fingers outstretched.

'So there's been no one serious so far in her life?' I asked. He shook his head. 'She's got it all before her then.'

He smiled. 'I guess she has.'

'If there was one piece of advice about love that you could give her, what would it be?' I ventured.

'I could ask you the same thing. What advice would you, an older woman – sorry, a more mature woman – give to my eighteen-year-old?'

There were so many things I could say to that. An image of Colin, standing in court, flashed through me and nearly killed my good mood. I flicked the side of my glass and it rang with a high tone. 'I guess I would say seek out the good ones, avoid the mad, the bad and the violent. And pick the ones from loving families.'

He nodded. 'Probably easier said than done. Why aren't you married?' he asked.

I made an indecisive movement, halfway between a shrug and an apology. 'I couldn't stay faithful. I'm scared of commitment.' It wasn't a lie, but it was only half of the truth too. I took a long drink, realising I didn't care now to interpret his reaction because I was no longer working or getting paid for it. 'I can give advice, doesn't mean I can take it or live it.'

'What even is a loving family?' Gabe asked.

'I know what it isn't,' I said and failed to keep the bitterness out of my voice.

'Sounds like you have experience,' he said.

'Far too much,' I snapped, realising too late that I needed to dial it all down and keep it light. I called the barman over and began to try and order another drink but Gabe stopped me. 'I'm doing that,' he said forcefully, and two more martinis were before us.

'Cheers,' he said as we chinked glasses and nibbled olives. 'So, sounds like you have family difficulties,' he probed.

'My mum left me when I was seven. One day she just walked out and kept on going. I've never seen her since.' I took a long drink. 'I was made a ward of court and placed with a foster family.'

'Jesus,' Gabe said quietly.

'Yeah, quite the happy childhood I had.'

'I'm amazed you can be sarcastic about it.'

'It's the only way I can describe it,' I retorted.

He gave me a long look, absorbing the information. 'If you don't mind me saying, you seem to have done an admirable job in overcoming this . . .' he searched for a suitable word, 'disaster. You have a good job, you're a bright, entertaining person.' I said nothing. We sat in silence for a while. 'Have you ever forgiven her?' he asked.

'No.' My voice was a bark.

He swirled the drink around in his glass. 'Do you think not being able to forgive has altered the course of your life?'

'I think her running out on me has altered my life. Full stop.' I took another long slurp of martini. My hand was shaking. I rarely told anyone the story about my mother. I was too ashamed to accept that even at seven I had been as unlovable as that. I took a long look at Gabe, at the glass behind the bar refracting our images into a thousand distorted shapes and I thought about the damage tainted love inflicts. How it clings to a person through the years, how it burrows down into the very heart of our dark and twisted selves.

The barman came over. 'Would you guys like another round?'

We looked at each other. I knew I had to stop drinking. But knowing what was good for me and then doing it was not something I had ever been very adept at.

Gabe pushed his glass away and grinned at me. It was a beautiful lopsided grin that turned up at one corner. I wanted to tell him everything about my past, and I wanted to hear everything about his. I wanted to spend the rest of the night comparing stories and exchanging feelings and enjoying myself and watching him enjoy me in my turn.

I knew his gestures, I knew when he was having a good time and when he wasn't because I had studied him so carefully over four weeks, through long nights and quiet contemplative moments. I had seen him at restaurant tables when his eyes glazed over and his train of thought took him elsewhere, I had seen the indulgent pride he had for his daughter, I had seen him efficient with his secretary, I had observed him apprehensive with his lover. But I felt, with the clarity that only too many martinis can give you, that I had never seen him with such glittering eyes as he had in the Langham with me.

'What are we going to do now?' he asked.

I could think of many pleasurable things I could do with this cheat sitting next to me. Professional pride, morality, his wife, for a moment they were cast aside as nothing. It took all of my self-control to say goodbye, get my arse off that bar stool and out into the street. It was one of the biggest struggles I'd had with myself in years.

CHAPTER 43

Alice

Three weeks and two days before

I got home from work to find Helene in the kitchen with a bandaged hand and a bottle of wine already nearly finished. She wouldn't tell me how she hurt her hand, so I left her be, as Lily was coming round. The house stank of perfume, which was weird, but then Helene had been acting pretty weird lately.

Lily and I watched a film, and everything was kinda normal until Poppa came home around ten.

As soon as he came in the door, Helene rounded on him, screaming. 'That woman was here, in our house, your whore—' Poppa tried to say something but Helene was in full swing now. 'Don't lie to me! She stole my keys, didn't she? Like she wants to steal my husband! She can't find her own so she takes someone else's!'

Poppa's voice was much louder and angrier now. 'What are you talking about?'

Lily and I had sat up now, the film forgotten. We stared at each other, listening to their voices.

'I know who she is,' shouted Helene.

'What did you just say?' Poppa's voice was strangled.

'You're a lying bastard!'

I hurried out of the living room into the kitchen, Lily following behind me. Helene held a tight fury in her that made her hair lift and spit fly from her mouth.

I had never seen a row like this before. Poppa and Helene went snippy and snipey when they argued, with long meaningful silences that faded away over time. But this was jealousy in action, love splintering. I sensed such a great explosion coming I stood in awe of the emotional currents in the room.

'Get out,' Helene said to me sharply, turning Lily and me into shocked statues who couldn't comply. Poppa took the opportunity to hurry from the room instead. As he left I saw a look of hatred and contempt pass across Helene's face that sent a sliver of ice into my heart. No one who was married should look at a partner like that, I thought, it was too horrible. All Poppa has done is to love you. I fumed silently. I felt a flash of dislike for my stepmother.

'Did you say you lost your keys, Helene? Only they're here.' I picked them up off a kitchen shelf and placed them on the counter.

Helene stared at them with wild fury. 'That's the least of my worries,' she muttered under her breath, as she yanked at the door of the fridge and pulled a new bottle of wine out and unscrewed the top and tossed it aside. It rolled off the counter before bouncing noisily away on the tiles.

'It'll all pass in a few hours,' Lily said inappropriately. 'Can I have a glass of that, Mrs Moreau, my headache is banging.'

Helene stood still for a moment, then silently got a glass out of the cupboard and poured for Lily. Her hand was shaking with the effort of keeping her temper. Lily pulled out a stool and sat down. Helene tossed a packet of Japanese crackers contemptuously on to the island and Lily opened them and began munching. The sound of her teeth cracking the puffed-up pieces of rice was the only noise in the room. Lily was relaxed, even enjoying herself. She was used to a house full of bickering and reforming family and lives with the high drama of slamming doors and raised voices, threats of lawsuits and divorce ultimatums.

'Cheers,' Lily said to Helene and took a big gulp. I braced myself. I didn't think Lily appreciated how out of the ordinary Helene's behaviour was; that bigger explosions might be yet to come.

'My mum says men are like house cats,' Lily began. 'If you pet and feed them, they're less likely to show you their nails.'

'Claws,' I said.

Lily looked at me. 'What?'

'Cats have claws, not nails,' I snapped at Lily. Here she was, I thought meanly, a woman with one of the best educations the world has to offer, sitting in a kitchen with nothing to do.

'Chill out, Alice, arguing is just life, OK?' Lily said.

I gave her a dirty look and stomped out of the kitchen and found Poppa in the living room. 'What's going on?' I asked him. 'Who was in the house?' He didn't answer. 'Who is this woman Helene's talking about?' He closed his eyes and shook his head. 'Tell me, Poppa!'

'No.'

'Does this have something to do with the notes that were delivered here and at the office? I saw them, you know.'

He went white. The colour drained right out of him. 'I don't know what you're talking about,' he said, but he lacked the conviction to make it real.

'What notes?' Helene said. She had followed me into the living room. 'Has she been sending notes to you, Alice?'

'Who? What is going on?' I shouted.

'The graffiti on our wall, that's from her too, isn't it?' railed Helene. 'You'd better tell me the truth.' Her voice was full of threats unspoken.

The strength seemed to fail in Poppa's legs and he sat heavily on the nearest chair. He was gearing up for something, and for a terrible moment I wanted to block my ears to defend myself from what he was going to say. 'This is not what you think, it's not about sex, it's not what it looks like—'

'Oh no, you don't,' Helene shouted. 'You don't get to make us sit and listen like good little women. Just shut up.' Helene grabbed Poppa by the arm. 'Just get out. I want you out of this house!' There was confusion as Poppa stood and I tried to get him to sit down. 'Out of the way, Alice, this doesn't concern you.'

That put me in my place and I had something else to get angry about as Lily entered the room, wine glass in hand, Japanese cracker in the other, perfectly calm.

I hated Lily, hated Helene, hated the world.

Poppa was bundled out of the room by Helene. I heard his protests in the hall, Helene's high angry voice, and a moment later the front door banged.

Lily was still leaning against the living-room wall, not looking like she was in a hurry to go anywhere.

'Just get out, Lily!' I screamed.

She held her hands up, unconcerned. 'I'll catch ya later,' she said. She cocked her head towards the kitchen where Helene had gone. 'Give her some Valium, she needs to get some rest.'

I walked into the kitchen. 'Just give me some fucking space!' Helene yelled. I ran upstairs and past Poppa's bedroom. I saw thousands of beads of broken glass shimmering on the bathroom floor. I ran into my room and slammed the door as hard as I could, not once but five times. With each slam I was thinking, Helene doesn't get to throw him out. We belong here, not her. Whatever he's done, it's me and him, not me and her.

CHAPTER 44

Helene

Three weeks and one day before

All the old certainties of my life, of how I saw the world, were hanging by threads. My sanity was stretched thinner and thinner. In my last meeting with Maggie Malone, she had shown me those pictures of Gabe and asked me so casually what I was going to do, as if it was a choice between a skirt in blue or one in grey. She didn't care, but then again, why should she? If she had ever gotten emotionally entangled in her job she would be rocking in a white suit in a room with padded walls. Her job was to deliver the bad news and then get the hell out.

She hadn't experienced the invasion of that woman in my bathroom, lording it over me, signalling her triumph with her naked flesh. What made her tick? Was Gabe just the latest in a long line of saps whom she had snared? Or was she the dumb bitch who really thought she was in love? Both types were dangerous to my marriage. I knew, because I had been a mistress myself.

I have always known what men wanted. Ever since I was young, I had that thing that drove them crazy – I could stoke desire in them that obliterated everything else. Passion that made them forget they were married, forget they had children, that what they wanted to do to me could ruin their lives.

It was everywhere. Walking down a street, sitting at a café table, the eyes of men would fall on me, and for a few moments their humdrum, day-to-day concerns could be forgotten and I had them in my hands, in my power.

I didn't care about the wives I cheated, I didn't give them a second thought. They weren't real. There was only one rule I lived by, never get emotionally attached. And I never did. I was a master at being a mistress.

I got off on the power of powerful men. I learned how to dress, how to act, how to maintain a façade. It was trial and error in the early days, but practice made perfect. And if you work hard at something, you expect to get paid. Not the sleazy transactions of the hooker, that's not what I was. I showed those men a good time and in return they showered me with gifts to prove how much they valued me – jewellery, clothes, weekend-away breaks, a nice flat, a cookery course. And I would sell on most of those things, and if I couldn't, I would convert them into something far more precious – class. The money I earned I put to good use, and after years of practising I became perfect.

I loved being a mistress, a mistress to powerful men even more. The game playing, the anticipation and the risks made the hotel rooms more beautiful, the beds softer, the meals tastier. It was all such a turn-on – I was the one they betrayed their wives for, even though they had made vows to them, *even though* they loved them. That's how irresistible I was.

And now, many years later, I was old and vulnerable and on the other side of the hard bargain. And I saw with brutal clarity the pain that I had caused those wives, the humiliation I had wrought. Maybe I had got my just desserts.

Maggie didn't have the woman's name, but she had an address. She had advised me not to go to that Chelsea flat, she had urged me to talk to Gabe. But I imagined over and over the intense joy of the moment of surprise, when she would realise I wasn't as dumb as she had thought, that I wasn't someone to underestimate in such a dismissive and casual way, that flaunting her naked body in my bathroom would not stand.

She was going to pay for that. I now had the upper hand after all these weeks of torment and it gave me a perverse sense of power and satisfaction. I wasn't going down without a fight, and I knew how to fight. That's what I disliked about Gabe – deep down I had always suspected that he thought me fragile or weak. He was always the strong one, the one that had overcome death and tragedy and ploughed on, keeping a smile on his face and his family together.

Well, wives can have secrets from their husbands in return. Tit for tat, Gabe Moreau. He had no idea what I had walked away from in a different life; he had no idea that he didn't know the real me at all. I hadn't accepted the shitty cards I was dealt. With the right work and application it had been possible to leave it all behind. But people who manage to do that are people who fight.

I ripped Maggie's photos of Gabe and that woman in half, right through the two of them. The slag's arm ended up severed from her body.

I left the café and took a taxi to Chelsea, got out a five-minute walk from the bitch's house. I stood in her darkening street and then I approached and knocked on her door.

CHAPTER 45

Maggie

Three weeks and one day before

The next day was strange. The Blue and White was under-employed; we wasted our time in the office building paper airplanes and throwing them out of the window, Simona defrosted the office fridge and found a Pret ready meal that was two years old. We spent an hour discussing whether to recover the old sofa. I really wanted to do it in velvet, which Rory thought was hideous.

'What's wrong with you?' Rory asked at one point, as he noticed me listlessly staring out of the window at nothing.

I got defensive. 'What? Nothing's wrong.'

'Liar,' he said. There was a companionable silence. 'What does a wife who suffers from insomnia say to her property developer husband when they're lying in bed together?' he said.

'I don't know, Rory, what does she say?'

'Darling, tell me about your work.'

Neither Simona nor I could raise a titter.

'You two are no fun at all,' Rory complained.

I got up and wandered over to the window, stared out at the cranes above Paddington. 'Does something strike you as odd about the Moreau case? It feels unresolved.'

'What do you mean?' Simona asked.

'Helene sacked us just when it was getting interesting.'

Rory gave me a dismissive look. 'Thank God for that, I say, we were getting into complicated territory. It ended just at the right time – any longer and he would have begun to turn your head!'

I coloured and said nothing, but Rory had seen. 'Jesus, Maggie! He really did!'

He was interrupted by the phone ringing and Simona had a short conversation that involved a lot of 'of course's and 'no problem at all's. She hung up and looked pleased. 'We've got a new client on her way. A mother who's worried about her teenage daughter's boyfriend.'

Rory was still staring at me and I squirmed under his gaze. 'Well, that's a first,' he said. 'You need to get yourself a lover, pronto, Maggie, or at least a shag—'

'That's enough, Rory!'

He held his hands up in mock defeat.

'What is going on?' Simona asked, the phone dangling uselessly in her hand.

'Maggie's finally shown a weak spot in that hard shell of hers—'

'For fuck's sake, Rory, you've got it all wrong!' I yanked at my bag and pulled it over my shoulder. 'I'm going to get some air, you see this new client.'

But Rory wouldn't let it go. 'It's a good thing, Maggie, to care about someone, it'll make you a nicer person—'

'What?'

He knew he had gone too far. 'I don't mean you're not nice, but this job, it corrodes the soul, you need to reach out to someone maybe, show yourself—'

'Fuck off!' I slammed the door behind me so hard the men in the corridor outside the lawyer's shrank back against the wall.

As I stomped down the stairs I pulled out my phone and called Dwight. I needed a distraction, and I knew I was using him, but I was being selfish and I didn't care. But he still didn't answer.

CHAPTER 46

Maggie

Three weeks and one day before

I slunk back into the office two hours later, realising I was being childish. We made up in the only way a gay Irish bloke, a studious bookworm and a working-class Cockney do with the day off and the sun out – we went and took up residence in a pub garden and got the drinks in and packets of Walkers and one of pork scratchings and we drank all afternoon at a picnic table in the sun, screeching with laughter and talking sex and telling tall tales.

Many hours later, in the early evening, I fell out of the pub and began to amble towards home. My recent bad mood had lifted and I was looking forward to the new case starting next week. I knew Mrs Gupta would take me somewhere different from mansions and skyscrapers, black official cars and celebrities. That was part of the joy of the job, you never knew where you would end up, but I was looking forward to eating a lot of chicken dopiazas.

My stomach was rumbling for a Ruby Murray when I rounded a corner in Marylebone and stopped dead. Gabe and Lily were walking away from me. I retreated back along the pavement in case either of them turned round. I looked around for Alice; she was nowhere to be seen. Lily was standing close to Gabe, talking intently to him.

It was ten to seven, he had most likely come out of work and met her. Today was one of the days Helene didn't come in to the office.

The joy of my afternoon in the pub vanished. I didn't like what I saw. At one point Gabe glanced behind him, he seemed nervous and watchful as she was artlessly gabbering away at him, her hands a pantomime of gesticulation. I felt a slow anger burning inside and a fear that I had been outsmarted.

I began to follow them. They turned a couple more corners and walked up the steps of a building with iron railings and rang a bell. A moment later they went in together.

The townhouse had a brass control panel with eight buttons. It had long ago been converted into small offices – lawyers, consultants, private medical practices, probably some private flats on the upper storeys. I retreated to a downstairs yard by the steps and waited. Had I really overlooked the obvious? Was Gabe in fact having an affair with Lily, his daughter's friend? It fitted, I reasoned, and the longer I thought about it, it fitted all too well. Teenage friendships were volatile things with deep and treacherous cross-currents that were often impossible for adults to spot. Affairs are about opportunity – Gabe had plenty of moments to admire the svelte and enthusiastic Lily, she had a personality that revelled in attention and breaking taboos.

I spent a long time in that smelly spot near the bins wondering what the two of them were doing inside that building. A hangover began to clamour to be heard against the inside of my skull. It was a long forty-five minutes before the door opened and Lily tripped down the steps, followed by Gabe and another man. She was looking very pleased with herself, but Gabe, now that I got a longer look at him, seemed tired and drained. The man shook Gabe's hand. 'Thanks so much again,' he said.

'It was no problem,' Gabe replied quickly.

'See, I told you that it would be a breeze with Mr Moreau,' Lily said to the man, and I realised it was her father.

'Well, any time you need something like that translated, just give me a call,' Gabe said, looking keen to be gone.

'You must come and see the place sometime,' Lily's father said, 'the sailing's amazing.'

'I really hope you enjoy the house,' Gabe said.

'Have you ever tried Croatian wine?' Lily's father continued.

Gabe smiled. 'It's as good as anything grown in Italy.'

The three of them walked away up the street, still discussing the merits of red and white wine.

I leaned back against the wall. I had been stuck in a yard full of rubbish, my mind whirling with lurid scenarios, while Gabe had been helping Lily's dad with what sounded like a contract on a holiday home. I was more relieved than I expected, suddenly seeing their interaction as innocent.

I watched them all shake hands further up the street and Lily and her dad walked away. Once they were out of sight Gabe leaned back heavily on some railings and pulled out a packet of cigarettes, lit one and inhaled deeply. This was odd, I'd never seen him smoking before. Gabe cut back down the street and passed above me.

I climbed the stairs and began to follow him. I liked following Gabe Moreau. I'd be a liar if I didn't say that I liked watching him. The feelings I had experienced the previous evening when we had a drink together in the Langham came back in a pleasing rush, but I began to sense that something was wrong. He was distracted; he stepped out into the road without looking and was beaten back by the blare of a car horn. He weaved uncertainly down the street. At one point he stopped and began to walk the other way, then seemed to change his mind and continued. He was muttering to himself. Gabe walked on to near Baker Street and hailed a cab and headed south. I followed. He went to Connaught Tower. The sun was setting in the west, a vast hot globe of heat dipping into the sour, stinking city. The taxi let him out and he walked slowly up a grass verge and unlocked the construction door into the Connaught Tower site.

He turned round.

I was not quite behind a wall I had been heading for and he saw me. Maybe it was because I had been in that grey area where I wasn't being paid and I wasn't on a job, that I got lazy. He stared at me in confusion. I swore under my breath and began to raise my hand towards him, preparing to brazen it out. He had a stricken look and he muttered something I couldn't catch. He disappeared into the building.

I hesitated for a moment, knowing I had a situation that was fast escalating away from me. I made a decision and followed him in. It was dark and gloomy in the foyer, the ground-floor windows were blocked by construction hoardings. I could make out the fountain taking shape in the middle of the floor, the pipework poking skywards ready for a cement base to be poured.

The empty lift shaft was on the far side of the fountain next to the stairs. Gabe was nowhere to be seen and I reckoned he was walking up the stairs to the fifth floor. I hurried to follow him, hearing the faintest echo of the building, concrete expanding or contracting, above me. I climbed the first flight of stairs before indecision began to swamp me. Should I meet him and brazen it out? Come clean about what I was doing, about Helene's role? I dithered for a few moments, then changed my mind and turned round. I came back out of the tower and hustled past a block of flats so I would be able to see him on the fifth floor. As I came round the corner I saw something that for an instant looked like an old coat falling down the side of Connaught Tower. It was only the shattering impact on the scrubby grass below that made me realise it was not a piece of clothing but someone. I ran towards the crumpled heap, each step bringing the details into sharper focus – the dark trousers, the splayed and contorted legs, a blue Oxford shirt, stained with blood.

CHAPTER 47

Alice

Three weeks and one day before

The police came round in a pair, to tell us the news. Helene opened the door. I came out of my bedroom because I heard strange noises in the hall, the tinny gurgle of radios spouting jargon. They insisted we all went into the living room.

When they told us what had happened to Poppa, I began to scream over and over, 'How did this happen?' I had seen Poppa only yesterday, before Helene chucked him out of the house.

Helene collapsed on the floor, mute. One officer tried to get her to stand up, the other one asked me if there was someone I wanted to phone.

The police said that an exact sequence of events was still unclear. They reassured us of a full investigation. First, they needed to talk about practical things – someone needed to come and identify the body. I could feel hysterics gathering in me. 'We will do our utmost to find out how he fell, Ms Moreau,' the policewoman said.

'What?' I asked, standing tall, my fists balled. 'Are you suggesting my dad jumped?'

The police officers glanced at each other. 'We don't know

what happened exactly at this stage, Ms Moreau. We have to pursue every avenue to find an accurate sequence of events, and that is just one possibility we are looking into—'

I started shouting then, 'No, no, never, don't you dare say that to me, he didn't jump, he would never do that.'

The police were calm, as they are trained to be. 'We know this must be tremendously difficult for you—'

'He must have fallen, or been pushed! Maybe he was pushed off!'

Helene had her hands over her face as she sat slumped on the carpet.

Then we heard for the first time someone else had been up in Connaught Tower with Poppa.

'Who was with him?' I shouted.

'We're still checking the details, but it was a woman who says she was working for Mrs Moreau, a—'

Helene dropped her hands. She raised her face to the ceiling. Her tears were all dried up, her eyes ablaze. She had a look on her face, a darkness that I had never seen before. Even in my moment of utter despair and bewilderment, that look scared me.

'Maggie fucking Malone!' she growled.

'Who's Maggie Malone?' I shouted.

CHAPTER 48

Maggie

Three weeks before

'This is a recording taken at Kennington Police Station on Friday, July 22nd, 2016. The time is 12.30 p.m. Present are Detective Inspector Catherine Patricia Owen and Maggie Malone. Maggie, you are under police caution, do you understand? Ms Malone has nodded and has declined to have legal representation at this time—'

'Goddammit, I'm not a moron.'

'Maggie, can you please calm down.'

'I don't have to calm down. I don't understand why I'm here.'

'We need to clarify some things about the incident yesterday at Connaught Tower in Vauxhall.'

'We sure do.'

DI Owen began to lay it all out. 'So, according to your statement which you gave last night, on the evening of July 21st you followed Gabe Moreau to Connaught Tower and you followed him into the ground floor of the building.'

'Yes.'

'Why did you follow Mr Moreau to this building?'

'Because I had been hired to find out what he was doing, where he was going, that type of thing. It's not illegal.'

'OK. What happened then?'

'I wanted to know if he was meeting someone there.'

'And did he?'

'Not that I saw, but I was only on the ground and first floor, I knew he would probably be going up to the fifth floor. There might have been someone up there waiting for him.'

'How did you know he would go to the fifth floor?'

'He has a ritual, he goes up to that floor and stares out at dusk, into the setting sun.'

'You know his habits quite well.'

'I know what he does better than his wife, probably.'

'That's an interesting way of putting it.'

'Jesus! Stop trying to twist everything I say. If I know this about him, lots of people probably do.'

'Did you know him socially?'

'Not really. I mean no.' DI Owen paused. Everything I said made me look guilty and that made me madder.

'I don't understand what you mean, did you know him to talk to him?'

'I had a drink with him once, well, two or three times, in a bar near his office. It was part of the job.'

DI Owen checked a file that sat in front of her on the table and frowned a little. 'Explain your job to me.'

'I was hired by Mrs Moreau because she was suspicious her husband was cheating on her. One way to test this is to put a woman in his eyeline and see how he responds.'

'I don't understand.'

Because you're a fucking moron, I thought to myself. 'It's called honeytrapping. If he flirts or asks to see you again, it establishes a pattern of behaviour, which shows he's probably being unfaithful.'

'Did your honeytrap work?' she asked.

'No. Jesus! I said all this to the guys at the scene last night!

I called the ambulance and the police as soon as he fell. I've repeated my statement eight fucking times!'

'You need to calm right down, Ms Malone. Let's go back a moment to really get a sequence of events. You followed him into the ground floor of the building.'

'Yes.'

'How did you get in?'

'I followed Gabe in. He hadn't locked the door behind him.'

'So you were trespassing on private property.' She looked at me but I didn't answer. 'Then what happened?'

'I saw he wasn't in the foyer, so I began to climb the stairs, I thought I heard something . . .' I tailed off, unsure what it was I couldn't catch hold of. I shook my head. 'Then I changed my mind and came back down the stairs—'

'Why did you change your mind?'

'I don't know! I think he had seen me following him and I was unsure whether to speak to him and come clean or not. Then I went past a building so I would be able to see him from by the flats. I heard the impact of him hitting the ground.'

'So you didn't see him fall?'

'No, not all the way. I rushed over and tried to help him. Other people turned up pretty soon and we began to—'

'OK. What was your state of mind in Connaught Tower?'

'What do you mean?'

'Were you angry?'

'Everyone's angry in this town! Give me a fucking break!'

'Can you please answer the question. Were you in an angry state of mind?'

'No.'

'Had you been drinking, Maggie?'

'I'd had a few.'

'How many is a few?'

'More than one, less than eight.'

'Does drinking make you angry, Maggie?'

'What's your point?'

'Were you up on the fifth floor of Connaught Tower with Gabe Moreau?'

'No!'

'The thing is, Maggie, there are three possible outcomes here. Gabe either fell accidentally, jumped, or was pushed – and make no mistake, we're going to find out which.'

'I never pushed him!'

'The problem is we're getting some quite disturbing reports about you.'

'Of course you are – because I get results!'

'Mrs Moreau is understandably very upset at present. But she said quite clearly she thought you had developed an unhealthy obsession with her husband. That you weren't professional in your dealings with her. That you had become . . . stalkerish—'

'*What?*'

'She said that you felt spurned when your honeytrap on Gabe Moreau failed, because you claim, and I quote, "I have a hundred per cent success rate with them. They work every time." And your employee, Rory Brown, said that you often said how attractive Gabe was. The big fish you wanted to catch, he said.'

'That's just a silly turn of phrase, said over a drink!'

'And that night at Connaught Tower, you were no longer working for Mrs Moreau, were you? She had terminated her arrangement with you before that. So what were you doing following him there?'

'I just bumped into him and thought—' I had to stop myself when I saw her face. I sounded like a deranged fool.

Detective Owen let the silence stretch. She was trying to make me feel uncomfortable, and it was working. 'Exactly how many times did you have a drink with Gabe Moreau? His wife thinks you had a couple, but she said she agreed to only one.'

'This is irrelevant! You want to know what happened to Gabe, get the CCTV camera footage, that'll show you—'

'Interesting you mention those, because the system was deactivated.' She looked at me again. 'Were you having an affair with Gabe Moreau?'

'No.'

'Did he spurn you and that made you mad? Did you think you would teach him a lesson?'

'For fuck's sake!'

'I don't think you're taking this seriously enough, Maggie. A man has died, potentially in suspicious circumstances, and we are going to get the truth. I will ask you one more time—'

'I never had an affair with Gabe Moreau!'

'Did Gabe cry out?'

'What?'

'When he fell, did he make a sound?'

'Not that I heard.'

'But he died in your arms, didn't he?'

I wanted to spit I was so angry. 'He died shortly after he landed. His spine was crushed, both legs broken. He couldn't breathe.' Let her picture it, let it sink in. I wanted to punish her for this questioning, for what terrible scenes she was forcing me to recall.

'Did he say anything to you before he died?'

I hesitated, but only for a moment. 'No.'

'We have a witness saying that he was talking to you before he died.'

'That's a lie.' I stood up because I was really about to lose it. 'Anything else?'

DI Owen looked at me calmly. She was a good interviewer, fully in control and I wasn't. 'Are the bad habits coming back, Maggie? Is Gabe another Colin Torday?' I slammed the desk with my palm. I shouldn't have done it, I know, but sometimes a woman just can't help it. DI Owen didn't flinch, but a tight smile of triumph spread across her face. 'You've still got your temper, Maggie. Even after all these years.'

'Can I go?'

'That's all for now. We just need to take DNA and finger-prints from you before you go—'

She had prodded me too many times and I lacked the self-restraint to stay calm. 'You know I'm already in the system. Everybody fucking knows that! Now go fuck yourselves.'

I slammed my chair back and marched out of the room. If I had expected to feel triumphant, like I had stuck it to the man, I didn't. As I left the station I heard the impact, the dull shudder of flesh and bone and sinew hitting dried mud replaying in my mind, over and over. I remembered his eyes as I cradled him, his desperate need in his final moments as the heat and the liquids drained from him. The tears came then, my anger drowned out. They only stopped when three reporters rushed me as I came out of the station.

CHAPTER 49

Alice

Two weeks and four days before

I went to Connaught Tower this afternoon. I had to see, to try and believe it had really happened. I wanted the world to freeze just as it was, for everything to be captured at the exact moment it had fallen apart, in respect and mourning for Poppa, and never unthaw again. But of course commerce never stops. Work at GWM paused for a day, but was back at full throttle. There were deadlines to meet, people that had to be paid. But as I passed through the Connaught Tower foyer the builders stopped what they were doing and doffed their hard hats to me. They looked ashamed. I walked the five floors up, emerged into silence, the distant hum of the city punctuated by bangs that sounded like gunfire.

The police tape was still up across the area by the window but I stepped over it; the detectives had done their work now. I could see the view that Poppa saw. What he last looked out upon. I walked to the edge of the floor, stood by the large space where plate-glass windows would soon seal the house-holders in. I was facing west, but the day was young and I was in shade and the wind felt cold. I reached out into air, feeling dizzy.

Poppa, Milo, Momma. Everyone I loved was snatched from me. My love was a curse that made people die in pain.

Last night, scratchy with lost sleep and wandering zombie-like round the house, I ended up in the study and found a postcard that had never been sent. Its jaunty 'Greetings from Devon' reminded me of a sunny day on Putsborough Beach when I was barely ten years old, Poppa's prized video camera in my hands as I walked backwards through the waves, filming him. I could still hear his voice, directing, encouraging, imploring: 'Alice! Get further away, the perspective's better!' But I didn't want to ever be further away from him, I always wanted to be closer, closer and closer. I loved my darling poppa. He was mine and mine alone. He would never leave me, someone took him from me. Someone else did this.

I felt the hole left by him as a disembowelling. A nuclear wind howled through me. I saw the streets and buildings and the grey curve of the river of the city where our family had made its home and I stepped forward and looked over at the ground. Poppa is already so far away from me, hurtling at supersonic speed into the past.

I turned round because someone was calling my name. Helene was walking towards me, arms outstretched. 'I think you should come away,' she said.

To where, I wanted to scream, to where?

CHAPTER 50

Maggie

Two weeks before

I tried phoning Helene many times, but she didn't answer. I took to writing her letters, trying to put my feelings of regret into words.

The letters came back unopened.

So this is how it ends, I thought. Eventually Rory told me to stop. Our cases don't always end well. I needed to toughen up. It was a hard lesson to learn. Because you watch someone's life, because you hear their pain and suspicion, doesn't mean you know anything about them. I had forgotten this in the Moreaus' case.

I tried to go round to Helene's house with a bunch of flowers. Simona told me to stay away, in fact she did more than that, grabbing the bouquet from me and forcing me back into the chair. 'Imagine if you're photographed, it just makes it all worse, we're trying to repair the damage, Maggie! Until they declare what happened to Gabe Moreau you need to stay out of sight and far away from their home.'

I argued with her, his death was not my fault, but she hit right back. 'No, but Helene is grieving and people in pain need to be respected.' Simona was right, but I didn't like the fact she was right.

On the day of Gabe's funeral I stood for a second time in the graveyard where I'd followed him earlier in the summer, watching the throng of people through the trees. Gabe was buried, not cremated. Helene wore a veil. I glimpsed a flash of Alice's red hair underneath a beret. At one point in the service someone howled. I didn't know if Helene had ever confronted Gabe about the woman in Chelsea, or if their last interactions as a married couple had been an argument. I wondered how Helene and Alice's relationship would be now, the man who connected them gone in such a brutal and sudden way.

I didn't see the woman from Chelsea.

CHAPTER 51

Helene

Two weeks before

Back at the house after the funeral service I retreated to the bedroom. I could hear the guests arriving downstairs, the hub and swell of them, the smell of lunch drifting up the stairs and into the bedroom, the cloying scent of lilies. So many people had come to show how much they loved and respected Gabe.

I took out my earrings with shaking hands and put them on the dresser. They were heavy and the day was stifling. I somehow had to get back down those stairs, endure the afternoon. Face the queue that would form as I shook hands and hugged over-perfumed women and red-faced old men.

Young girls think life is a train ride that stops at the following stations: Love, Sex, Marriage. But the final destination is Happiness, where the engine is uncoupled and you idle away your life, never wanting or needing to leave. I was that young girl once, I dreamed that if I was very good and obedient my life would take that journey. But my train has been driven straight off a cliff. I have been destroyed. My entire life was fiction.

He killed himself when we had decades longer together. He abandoned Alice when she was only eighteen.

I felt my knees going. I couldn't sit down, otherwise I was never going to get back up again. I gripped the side of the dresser so hard I looked like a woman in labour.

I had been in love with a man who I knew not at all. He had done something so awful I couldn't begin to contemplate it. Every gesture, every conversation, looping back days, months and years, I couldn't rely on any of it. I never saw him as capable of throwing himself off that tower. I had no indication he would or ever could do that. Every time he smiled at me, every time he laughed, it was all a lie because underneath he was an oozing mess of emotional pain, in such a dark place that he couldn't stand the effort of living.

The door opened without anyone knocking. Irina Oblomov was striding across the bedroom towards me. 'What are you doing in here alone? No wife is alone at a time like this.' She held me by both arms and pulled me upright and forced me to look in the full-length mirror. 'You know what Gabe said to me at your charity event? He said, "My wife is a force of nature."' Irina actually shook me. 'That is what you are. Strong as iron. A lioness. Yes?'

She was staring back at me in the mirror. We looked comical next to each other, her short and fleshy body in its stiff mourning twin set, her short hair set just so, my dank blonde tresses accentuating my hollow cheeks. I was too shocked to know what to do; I was mute. 'You are more strong than you can ever believe,' Irina continued. 'Today you show that strength. Tears are for other days. Not today.' I just stared; all will to speak had left me. 'Love has given you strength to endure today. Yes?'

I nodded, but I couldn't move. Irina put a perfumed hand on my face, still standing behind me as I looked in the mirror. 'You are a woman. A woman! You can survive anything.' She nodded, full of conviction. 'You can survive even this. Yes?'

Some of her strength moved me. Her conviction was infectious. I took a deep breath and stood up taller.

'Say it,' Irina intoned.

'I can survive it. I am a woman and I can do it.' Irina was right, I felt better.

'You will do anything for your family, yes? To see it safe, to see its reputation kept, you will do *anything*.'

She shook me forcefully, my body moving left and right like one of Alice's old rag dolls.

'Resist me.' She shook me again and this time I stood stronger. 'You see, there is nothing stronger than a woman in grief.'

I took a long, deep breath. I stared at my reflection and repeated her words, this time with conviction. 'There is nothing stronger than a woman in grief.'

Irina was right. I would do anything to save my reputation, that of my family and my daughter. Irina moved me towards the door.

'Wait!' I commanded. 'My earrings.'

'Good girl,' Irina said. 'You can and you will look magnificent.' She picked them up and put them in my ears. 'You do two things downstairs.'

'I do?'

'Don't eat and don't drink. Let's go.'

And the wife of Gabe's business rival followed me down the stairs.

I spent the afternoon listening to many kind things that people said, to many expressions of love and sorrow. None of it helped. Not even a little bit. Because some things that you hear are so shocking you can never get them out of your head. Maggie was there with Gabe when he jumped. She held him while he died. *She* was there with him at the end, not me.

It was the greatest transgression I had ever known. It

felt a thousand times worse than him cheating with that woman.

The truth of what really happened that night at Connaught Tower had not been told. Maggie Malone was a fucking liar.

CHAPTER 52

Alice

Twelve days before

Grief is being marooned in a tiny, leaking boat on a storm-tossed sea. The waves are a hundred feet high, the coast many miles away. The disorientation is fear and it left me almost unable to breathe.

But today I woke and for a blessed moment the waves were a little further apart.

I struggled downstairs to find Helene in her rabbit-ear slippers sitting at the island, smoking. I never knew she smoked. Her face was a hard line, her hair straggly. She nodded hello. 'Have you slept?' I asked, but I knew the answer. She shook her head, tapped her fag. I sat down next to her. 'Tell me everything about Maggie Malone.' In nearly a week it was the first time we had been alone at a moment when I had felt able to ask about this other woman, the woman who was with Poppa, at the end.

Helene ran her tongue around her teeth, as if cleaning a bad taste off them. She ground out her fag.

'I never wanted you to know any of this, Alice.' Her eyes were dead, her face emotionless. 'And I'm sorry. I suspected Gabe was having an affair, so I hired Malone to find out.'

I was so shocked I could hardly breathe. 'That isn't possible. Poppa would never do that – he loves you!'

Helene closed her eyes for a long moment, as if against the sun on a hot day.

'Remember that night Gabe and I went to the Café Royal? I saw him in a cloakroom with a woman, and I didn't like what I saw.'

'What did you see? You must not have understood!'

She looked irritated. 'Alice, that woman stole my keys and broke into our house. She took a dip in my tub, she was *right here*, she accosted you at the fun run.'

I said nothing, anger tapping an insistent beat against my skull. There was no woman at the fun run, there were hundreds of women. One thing I knew for sure: Helene just didn't like to lose. My stepmother had always had an over-active imagination, planning brilliant schemes and plans. She was a drama queen. Who's to say what she saw in the Café Royal was even real? And the bathtub tale feels like attention seeking of the first order – I found her keys on the side, if she would remember.

'Who was this woman, then?'

'Malone found out she lived in Chelsea, she got photographs of your father and her together. I never got a name.'

'Did you talk to her?'

Helene shook her head, but she didn't look me in the eye. 'I went to her flat once but there was no answer. After I saw the photos, I . . . I panicked, and sacked Maggie.' Helene lit another cigarette, fumbling nervously with the ashtray and the box, pulling the foil apart with shaking fingers. 'What I was paying her to do seemed so sordid and wrong. I didn't want to know who she actually was.'

'Show me the pictures.'

'I don't have them, I destroyed them. I couldn't have that stuff here in the house, polluting it!'

I sat very still in our kitchen. A strange sensation began to dawn. Helene was lying. 'Why was Malone with Poppa at Connaught Tower if she wasn't working any more for you?'

Helene shook her head. 'I don't know. The answers she's given the police are not complete.' She looked at me, desperate. 'Why did he do it, Alice? Why did he choose *this* way?'

The emotional breakers battering my beach retreated and a hard pebble of resentment shone through the sand. The police had still not concluded what really happened at Connaught Tower that night. They were still investigating Poppa's death. Yet here was Helene, so ready to believe the worst – that he threw himself off. That he would abandon me after everything he'd been through, after all he had overcome. 'He didn't. He would never do that. At best it was an accident.'

Helene took a deep breath. 'We can't help each other unless we're honest. We can't begin to move forward unless we accept that . . . unless we face it. That ultimately it was a choice he made.' She took a drag on her cigarette. 'I loved your father so much.' She didn't say his name, she had taken to calling him my father. I didn't like it.

Did she? When I think back over the last six years, is that what I saw? Was that love? He had loved me, I know that. I absolutely know that.

'Do you think he loved this other woman?' Helene asked.

Her voice was small and pathetic, and my pebble of resentment grew bigger. I got angry at Helene's self-obsession. She looked different – older and weaker. I hated weak women. She didn't understand anything about the family she married into – about Poppa or me. I wanted to scream it at her smeary face – *Don't you get it?* My mum died in fear and pain at my poppa's hands. Yet I loved him totally and unwaveringly, because Poppa was a magnet for unwavering love and loyalty.

Helene had it so wrong. The question she should have been asking was how much did this mystery woman love Poppa. And I realised that I was desperate to meet this woman, to have her talk to me about Poppa, to hear how much she loved and admired him. How could it be otherwise?

I picked up my phone and typed Maggie's name into Google and looked again at the photo of the woman who had been flirting with Poppa in the Langham Hotel. I had even warned the tart off in the toilets. Something sour invaded my mouth.

I didn't trust Helene. Or this Maggie Malone.

CHAPTER 53

Helene

Twelve days before

From feeling assaulted and exposed on all sides, I now felt safe. And safety allowed me to move into a new phase where anger began to consume my very flesh. Anger allowed me clarity to see where my duty lay. I was focused on what I had to do, which was care for Alice. I was unsure what family was, before Gabe made his unimaginable choice. I thought that that woman could split us into single people, like metal through wood, but I now knew I was wrong. We were a family, the strongest unit.

I had to bear some responsibility. Milo's death rocked Gabe, but I hired Maggie, it was me who put that in motion. The police said that Maggie admitted that she was seen by Gabe before he entered Connaught Tower. He would have put it all together then – understanding who and what kind of person Maggie was, and that I would have been the one that had hired her. He had been caught; his lover had emerged from the shadows and into his very house, but I had already discovered much about her. Standing outside Connaught Tower, Gabe would have known our beautiful story had ended. He would have realised that he had destroyed it.

We can overcome anything once. Gabe had managed it,

all those years ago when Clara died at his hands, but he had ruined everything that was good in his life a second time. There was no coming back from that. So it is up to me to struggle on with the remnants of his family.

That evening I felt strong enough to take a look at the box of Gabe's effects that the police had given us. I saw office keys and his watch, his mobile phone and a crumpled business card. Some bloodstained pieces of clothing in their clear plastic bags made me start to put the whole box aside but the clear packages shifted and I saw a second mobile phone.

I pulled it out, held it in my hand. It was a cheap burner model, still charged, and I turned it on. It contained only one number that had been called and received. I looked at the incoming texts.

The first said 'You can't let me go x'. The second said 'Alice need never know xx', and the last, 'I deserve more x'.

Gabe hadn't answered any of the texts. I called the number. It was disconnected. Another thought came to me about Gabe's phone and those texts. They had never mentioned me. It was as if I didn't feature in Gabe or Alice's life at all.

CHAPTER 54

Helene

Eleven days before

I took my rage at Gabe and what he had done into GWM. I wore my widow's weeds when I met the company directors in the conference room. My clothes gave the men bad juju and I was pleased.

The meeting didn't go how they expected.

The company lawyer had phoned the week before, and had then visited the house. There were things about the structure of GWM that were unusual. Gabe was the majority shareholder and chief executive; upon his death his share passed to me. So I now owned fifty-nine per cent of the company. He asked me if I even knew about this.

The man was a fucking moron.

The directors and management team of GWM were keen to meet as early as possible. They were desperate to wrest that share from me.

But I was up for the fight. Since Gabe's death I had been on a journey from blubbering, self-pitying wreck to a creature full of rage that reared and bit wherever she fancied. The day I went into GWM I hadn't slept, I was spectral and consumed by a limitless energy. I wanted to bring GWM back to life, to carry on Gabe's work under the umbrella of a bigger, better, more adept firm. I was there to tell the board just that.

In the conference room the chief operating officer outlined the options for me. They could appoint a new boss to run the company on my behalf, or I could sell all or part of the company I owned at a mutually acceptable price.

I told them I wanted to run it.

'With respect, Helene, that's not possible,' one of them said.

'Why not?'

'This company has fifty-seven employees, and hundreds more contractors and unfinished projects worth seventy-five million, many at a critical stage. You have done valuable but small-scale work on social responsibility.'

I turned to the lawyer. 'Legally, I am in control of this company.'

He had turned white, his lips an anus of stress. 'Yes.'

'Then I am going to run GWM Holdings, starting today.'

The operating officer had heard enough. 'This is outrageous!'

The head of marketing took over. 'I agree that this is fanciful. Hundreds of jobs depend on us and the decisions we take, which you simply don't appreciate. If you take over we'll be made a laughing stock!'

I turned to the lawyer. 'I want you to agree severance terms with these two; I'm recruiting new personnel starting today.'

A glass of water by the arm of the marketing boss spun across the table as he knocked it over. He put his fists gorilla -like on the table. 'You don't have the right!'

'I have every right.'

'You're not bringing this company down!'

'Gabe would want me to run it. Is this about you, or is this about the company? Because I only want one of those things.'

The operating officer took a different path, and began pleading. 'Helene, we have been friends for many years—'

'No, we haven't.'

'Please reconsider for a period of time—'

'The lawyers are going to be over this like flies on shit,' the marketing director thundered.

'Good. It'll clear the mess away quicker.'

There was uproar as the marketing man stood and slammed his way out of the room and somebody else went with him and there was a lot of empty talk and pointless gestures. I got up from my seat and went to look out of the conference-room window at Regent Street, at the energy and bustle in the street below. A moment later I turned back round to the shocked faces in the room. 'So, gentlemen, we've got work to do.'

'Helene, please take some time to think this through,' the lawyer counselled. 'This is grief talking! There are so many challenges, it will be very difficult to sustain the level of intensity needed to run a business of this size—'

'And that's because I'm so busy doing what, exactly? Shopping? Decorating? I've heard enough.' I'd been thinking about many things since Gabe died, since I became a widow, unencumbered but for an eighteen-year-old stepdaughter. It was the perfect solution. I would work, I would pour all my energy, brains and ambition into the company I now owned.

'OK, so what . . .' the finance officer spluttered and began again. 'So what are your plans for the company, what ideas have you got, how are we going to address the problem of our debt?'

'There is one thing we are going to address today. The provision for social housing in Connaught Towers One and Two. It's going to be changed.'

I saw the men in the room glance at each other, adapting to new information as it came at them.

I walked to the door and opened it and asked Soraya to assemble the entire company. News that something was up travelled fast and moments later everyone was crowded in the lobby. I stood on a chair and addressed the room.

'I'm Helene Moreau. As of today, I'm the head of GWM. We've all had a shock, since Gabe died, but we can and we must recover. Gabe is gone, and we mourn him and we miss him. But you work for me now. I am the boss of this company. If you're unhappy about that, you can be on your way. If you stay and you've got a good idea, come see me.' There were three seconds of uncomfortable silence, with men and women gawping. 'I have one plan. I'm going to make this the most high-profile property company in London within five years. Get on board or get out now.'

The silence was a wall, but then someone began clapping, and the applause spread until it became a wave that swamped everyone and every corner of the office.

CHAPTER 55

Maggie

Ten days before

I knew when I'd been conned. And nobody conned Maggie Malone.

It was Rory who shared the online news report with me, reading it out from his phone. There was a photo he showed me too, of Helene Moreau surrounded by the board of GWM, whose name wasn't going to be changed – how charming – now that she was the head of the company. She was still wearing black, she wasn't smiling, her self-possession radiating out in a hundred thousand pixels. There was a lot of talk about tragedy and unexpected loss and mourning and moving on and a new stage and so much bullshit I wanted to scream.

Rory tried to get me to calm down but I wasn't listening. 'Don't presume, Maggie, we've only read a news report,' Rory counselled.

The situation stank.

I got out of my seat and paced the office and no amount of shouting from Rory could get me to calm down. I drove round to Helene's house and parked up. I went straight up and knocked on the door.

I was ready for a confrontation but there was no answer. I tried several more times, but no one was in. I retreated from Helene's front step and walked past the three houses to the corner. I noticed that the graffiti had been scrubbed off their garden wall. I walked round the corner house and ended up by the entrance to the alley that led down the backs of the houses.

I walked down the alley, the crunch of gravel underfoot, the roses and vines of carefully cultivated urban gardens spilling over fencing and walls. I looked over Helene's fence at the patio doors at the back of the house but the sun was at the wrong angle and I couldn't see in. The alley ended in a high fence with a locked gate. I pulled myself up and managed to see a large untended garden belonging to a small block of flats. I jumped back down again and stood for a moment looking around. I pulled aside a mass of ivy that hung over part of the fence. Everything looked normal, until suddenly I realised it didn't.

I looked closer at part of the fence next to the gate. I pushed it and three slats fell away like a little door. I pulled myself through into the garden belonging to the flats and had a clear path round the side of the building into a road that ran at right angles to the Moreaus' own.

I have many times in my life had cause to hate myself, but here was a new low. I had overlooked the obvious. All the hours Rory, Simona and I had sat and watched the front door and side alley of the Moreaus' house, Gabe, Helene or even Alice could have been slipping out unnoticed via the flats. Yet I had given everyone in this house an alibi for Milo's murder.

I phoned Rory. 'I'm standing outside the third exit from the Moreau house. There's a hidden way out of the alley.'

Rory used a string of expletives that would have made a navvie blush. 'I checked that alley carefully. There was no way anyone could climb those fences without making a hell of a racket—'

'Whoever did it was clever. It was well hidden.'

'We have to tell the police.'

'I'm on it.'

CHAPTER 56

Maggie

Ten days before

I met Dwight in a room at Kennington Police Station, housed in a tired Sixties office block south of the river. As I ranted at him he did his best to look interested.

'I'm telling you Gabe was enjoying life, he didn't jump. I watched him for more than a month, day and night, I shared drinks with him, spent a whole evening with him—'

'Is that so?' Dwight crossed his arms, pushed his bum back on to his desk. That had come out wrong, but that wasn't the issue that was most important at that moment. I wondered if I saw hurt on his features, hope raised and dashed.

'Helene taking over the company proves it,' I added.

'I'm telling you the initial forensics on Gabe Moreau's death are inconclusive,' Dwight countered. 'The dust all over the floors up at Connaught Tower is full of footprints that don't make any sense as yet, but we have a trail of Moreau's footprints in a pattern pacing back and forth by the window—'

'He was being threatened – there was a threatening message on the wall of their house.'

'Yes, and we are working through that. The angle of how Gabe's body fell is also being examined, but you said yourself there was no noise of a struggle.'

'The CCTV was turned off.'

'We have interviewed the contractor who cut the line by mistake a day before Gabe's death—'

I was astonished at his calmness. 'Are you listening to me? I'm hired to follow Gabe Moreau two weeks before a local campaigner is murdered. I'm conveniently there to give the whole family an alibi, except I've discovered there's another hidden exit from the house. His wife sat there in my office and told me she wanted to kill him!'

'You tell me every client of yours wants to kill their spouse. Hell, I wanted to kill mine! The science will prove what happened. And by the way, I heard about how you stormed out of here the other day when officers were simply trying to ask you some questions – let the guys do their jobs!'

'Helene's got motive to kill him. She could be punishing him for having an affair and using me to cover her tracks. She met and married him within six months, now six years later she's got rid of him and is running the entire company! The woman's a fucking psychopath in designer clothing!'

'Maggie—'

But I was in full flow now, moving round his office in an agitated manner. 'Don't you think it's weird that a grassroots hero opposing the building of new flats and the boss of the company that's going to be building those flats are both dead? They must be connected, only an idiot could think otherwise! Milo knew the whole family and they have no alibi—'

'Come on, Maggie, you sound like this is the 1950s! Alibis? Get real – most murders are solved these days using physical evidence, DNA traces, hair, blood, you know this.'

'But you don't have any physical evidence, do you!'

'Milo and Gabe, we believe at the moment, are separate issues.' He sounded tired. 'Milo was murdered with extreme violence in his own home—'

'You're going nowhere fast with that investigation, aren't you?'

'Wrong. We are pursuing multiple leads on that case at the moment—'

'What leads?'

'We have chatter that he may have been involved in the selling of reds and blues—'

'Drugs?'

'Yes, Class As. Maybe that's why the girlfriend was so low profile.'

'You still can't find her? What about their texts, phone messages?'

'Her number's a burner phone, messages reveal nothing.'

'Well, ask his friends, someone must have—'

'Maggie, I know how to run a murder investigation!' He walked round his desk and sat heavily in his chair again. 'Gabe's case is tragic for different reasons. He was a middle-aged man who probably had many reasons to be depressed or want it to end—'

'I was there. He died in my arms. Do you know what the injuries are like on a man who jumps five storeys on to sun-baked earth? Gabe Moreau did not kill himself. He had a daughter who he loved – he never stopped talking about her. She had lost her mother already! What kind of father compounds that?'

'That's the problem with suicide. It leaves so many things unresolved. You can shake your head all you like, but that's the truth and you know it. It's the biggest what-if you'll find, however much it frustrates you. Sometimes people pedal for so long and so hard, looking good on the surface, looking on top to the outside world, and then they just can't do it any more. Think about what he survived – his family was blown to bits in Yugoslavia, weren't they? He came here with nothing? That's as fundamental as it gets. While he seemed to have overcome, I bet that stays with you; I've heard about it before with those who've endured horrific events, that years later when everything should be fine, it overwhelms them.' Dwight paused, then leaned forward and urged me to listen. 'If you want my advice, Maggie, take a step back.'

'I'm not going to let this lie. I'm going to find out what really happened.'

'How are you going to do that?'

'I'm going to crawl over every little piece of evidence, I'm going to go so far back into that family's history that the past will open like—'

Dwight got very angry then. 'You're going to stop this, right now. You jeopardise this police investigation into Milo's murder, which is high profile enough as it is, and whatever happened to Gabe Moreau, *and we don't know yet,* there will be very serious consequences. And I implore you to leave the Moreau family alone. I will feed back your information about the lack of an alibi for the family on the night of the murder, but remember you've got history of getting too closely connected to people.'

I sat down sharply on a chair. Dwight probably thought he was giving me a straight answer, but it felt like a really low blow. And boy, it hurt something chronic.

Dwight must have seen my face as he began to backtrack. 'Sorry, Maggie, you know I didn't mean it like that, what you did in the past doesn't count for anything now.'

I felt sweat spring out all across my body.

Did Helene know about Colin Torday, a name that still resonated as strongly now as it had more than twenty years ago? If she did, what was I up against? Her cool, controlled exterior, the precise, smooth movements, did they hide a calculating killer underneath?

'That's exactly how you meant it,' I said to Dwight. '*Don't you think that's another reason why she hired me!* She picked me very carefully indeed.'

We remained stuck in toxic silence for a moment or two, the promise and flights of fancy of our recent nights together all destroyed. It was the story of my life.

'So who was Gabe's mistress? You'll be doing the police a favour if you pass on the details—'

'Don't worry, I'm going to find out.'

'Maggie, don't—'

But I was out the door and slamming it before I heard him finish.

CHAPTER 57

Alice

Nine days before

Detective Dwight Reed came round to the office for our next interview. I was proud that my co-workers stopped and gawped as they tracked his journey down the corridors to my office; the water-cooler dwellers now had something weighty to talk about! I had been shadowing a group in the design team the last couple of days; they treated me as if I was a precious piece of china that they were about to break at any moment, they looked terrified of where my emotions must be taking me, but I would rather be busy than sitting around at home. People were very kind in those early days following Poppa's death. The staff didn't know what to make of Helene taking over – she had announced that the company was going to go in a fresh direction but few details had been released about her plans and gossip and rumour were rife. I wondered if power was going to go to her head.

I led Dwight into a private meeting room. The interview didn't go how I expected. He was colder on this second interview, something between us had shifted.

He asked me new questions about Milo. 'Did he ever mention anything about blues and reds to you?'

I shook my head. 'What does that mean?'

'He ever talk about drugs, or drug dealers, anything like that?'

'No.'

He got out several photos of feral-looking men and asked me if I knew or had ever met any of them, had seen them ever with Milo, but they were strangers to me.

'Did you know that the fence in the alley of a neighbouring property to yours is broken and that there is a way of getting to a side street unseen?'

'Why is that relevant to anything?'

'Have you ever used it?'

'I had no idea you could get out through there.'

'You absolutely sure about that?'

I felt angry and uncomfortable with his tone. It reminded me of how I had been made to feel at times in my police interviews regarding my old teacher, Mr Dewhurst. But I was very strong, as I had been then. I knew where the truth lay in that story and I drew on that strength now, years later. I remembered the cold, appraising looks of the police back then, trying to see if they could spot a liar, a child fantasist.

It was time to turn the heat in another direction. 'My poppa was being threatened before he died.' Dwight looked up at me sharply. 'Someone was sending him messages at home and at work.'

'What kind of messages?'

I opened my phone and showed him the two notes I had found. 'There were probably others.'

'Do you have the originals?'

I shook my head. 'One might still be at the office.'

'I'm here on the Milo case, but you need to tell the team working on what happened to your dad about these immediately,' Dwight said. I nodded.

A few moments later Dwight got up and our conversation was over. We left the office and he turned towards the lobby. 'You don't want to speak to Helene?' I asked.

His answer surprised me. 'I already did. She came down to the station earlier today.'

CHAPTER 58

Helene

Nine days before

Inspector Reed had phoned and asked if he could talk to me again about Milo, and considering my family's latest tragedy, was happy to come round, but I was so desperate to get out of that cursed house, which whispered of Gabe at every turn, I practically ran to the station.

He was colder towards me than previously, which set my antennae twitching. Something about blues and reds, which made no sense to me, but made me worry they were making out Milo was a drug dealer. I didn't buy it, but then, what did I know? He asked me whether Milo had ever mentioned a girlfriend or a woman he was seeing to me. I stumbled in my reply, wondering if Alice had been lying to me. Had she been seeing him for longer than she claimed? No, it wasn't possible. DI Reed noticed my discomfort and I coloured. That made me angry.

'Seems to me you know next to nothing about his murder after a whole month. Was he killed in a crime of passion or was he a drug dealer? It's unlikely to be both. You need to work harder, Detective Reed.'

Then it was his turn to flush with anger. He told me there was a third way out of our house via the back fence into a neighbouring road. A secret route, apparently. I scoffed; it was more likely a fence piece broken by the grandchildren from next door and badly patched up to escape a scolding. But I knew who had told the police about it: Maggie. She had used the back alley to spy on my family. The idea that she had been grubbing around on my property, trampling over my boundaries, made me twitchy with anger.

DI Reed's insinuations didn't stop there. 'I understand you're running GWM,' he said.

'Yes. I've taken over day-to-day control of the company. It's not a surprise, it's how the company was structured. It's a family enterprise.'

'A lot to take on, considering what's happened.'

'I need to be busy. I'd go mad with anger, otherwise.' I stood up. This was a waste of time and I had a lot to do.

'I haven't finished,' Dwight said.

'Yes, you have.' I turned to the door. 'I'm in here again because of Maggie Malone's meddling. That's not going to happen again. Stop trying to look for things that aren't there. If you want to talk to me again, call my lawyer.'

I walked out of the room. This had gone far enough. Maggie was raised to relish a fight – well, I fumed, she was going to get one. I took out my phone and made a call.

CHAPTER 59

Maggie

Nine days before

There was discord at the Blue and White. We were all pulling in different directions. Rory and Simone had been taking turns to tail the teenager whose mother was worried she was hanging with the wrong crowd while I had spent long hours out of the office snooping around in Chelsea trying to track down Gabe's lover. Rory and Simona had more success than me – Rory found out within five hours that our pretty teenage Juliette was smoking dope by a boarded-up electrical shop that backs on to a park. He took pictures of Juliette's slim young arms around the neck of a skinny man about ten years older than her with a goatee and too many piercings. He had the wasted, twitchy look of a long-time consumer of something illegal and by the fawning way Juliette gazed at him, it wouldn't be long before she'd do something stupid with a needle to try and get closer to him.

I knew that money couldn't insulate you from passions that were counterproductive. All that hard work that Juliette's mother had put in over the years, the money she had spent on private school and summer holiday clubs, and she couldn't stop her daughter from revelling in the nasty. Soon I would be phoning her mother and confirming her worst fears and relating another sorry tale of love gone wrong.

I told no one that I was sleeping badly. Gabe's death had left me with a heavy weight of guilt and self-recrimination. Did his fall have anything to do with him seeing me? Had there been someone up in the tower waiting for him that evening, and if so, who? I felt out of sorts and ill at ease.

And worst of all, Gabe's case had resurrected feelings I had carried with me since I was nineteen, since Colin Torday came into my life. It made me more determined to find out who this woman in Chelsea was, and what had happened to Gabe in Connaught Tower. If I connected Milo and Gabe's deaths, even better.

I left Rory and Simona to man the office while I spent the long hours outside the home of Gabe's mystery woman. No one ever answered the door. I roused the few neighbours who occupied surrounding flats; no one could tell me anything about the occupant of number 12 on the middle floor. I showed her photo, they shrugged and closed their doors, I accosted the street cleaner and received only a shake of the head. No lights ever came on on the middle floor.

Finally, after getting variously hot, bored and aching, a guy in his thirties drove up with a surfboard on the roof and got out and approached the building. He was happy to talk. He lived on the ground floor, and hadn't seen the woman upstairs for ages. Hadn't heard her, either, when I asked him about that. Instinctively we both looked up at the windows, where the blinds were not lowered.

'What else can you tell me about her?' I asked.

'I never spoke to her,' he said. His English was impeccable, with a French accent. I guessed him to be a banker who had enjoyed a few days on a Cornish beach.

'Ever see anyone visit her?'

He shook his head, his surfboard tucked under one arm now, keen to go and get on with his evening.

'She drove a car.'

'I don't suppose you can remember . . .'

He looked around, disinterested. 'It's not here. She drove a Porsche 911, silver, vintage.'

There was one thing you can say about bankers, I thought, they were competitive little fuckers around cars. 'I don't suppose you know the registration, do you?' He gave a Gallic shrug. Of course he didn't. No one remembered details like that.

'It was an L reg.' He walked into his flat.

In the days had been coming to her street I had never seen her car. I looked back at the dark windows. She was no longer here, or something far more unpleasant had happened. I needed to get in there, and fast.

CHAPTER 60

Alice

Nine days before

After Dwight left I stayed late at the office. I watched as everyone else put on their sunglasses and picked up their bags and headed out into the evening sunshine. I was immune to their pleasure, inoculated against the joys of summer. They said their nervous and deferential goodbyes to me and finally I was left alone. It was better here than home. I couldn't stand being at home then.

When the last person had headed for the exit, I went into Poppa's office. It was filled with wilting bouquets of flowers no one had dared move and stank of old flower water. I took out his set of keys that had come back to the family in the box of his effects. I unlocked the filing cabinet and began rooting through everything in there, photographing what was important.

I didn't find the scribbled warning note. Someone, maybe Poppa himself, or Soraya in an act of secretarial loyalty, had destroyed it.

But I found another.

It was a scrawled note in blue biro on a piece of paper, a mock-up of a last will and testament. 'With my dying breath I offer GWM to Arkady Oblomov for the fair market price prevailing in our western capitalist system. Nastrovya!' And a smiling emoji. It was dated nine months previously. There was the faint curve of the base of a sticky wine glass staining the corner of the paper. I imagined Poppa and Arkady in a bar thick with vaping smoke and empty bottles of red. Showman Arkady making a joke, writing out this declaration that Poppa was supposed to sign. I imagined Poppa's eyes crinkling, throwing back his head and laughing, ordering another round. But I imagined he would have been sober underneath.

But it was serious enough for Poppa to keep it. I wondered how much of a joke it really was. How keen was a man's need to have what he desires? Stay away, Arkady, I thought, from what Poppa built from nothing.

I spent several hours in Poppa's office and I didn't hear Helene arrive.

'What are you looking for, Alice?'

Her voice made me jump; I dropped the file I was holding. Helene had taken to wearing widow's weeds – even in the heat of the summer her thin arms were encased in black, her legs covered with dark tights. They made her look stiff and vacant, like photos of that weird wife of President Reagan.

'I'm looking at all aspects of the GWM business. I have to keep busy.'

'That's very commendable. How did you get into the filing cabinet?'

'I have Poppa's keys.'

Her eyes slid to the heavy bunch on the desk. For a moment I thought she was going to grab them, but she stood by the door.

'I think you need to leave.'

I felt my hands clench into little fists.

Poppa and Helene always treated me like a little kid. After what happened with Mr Dewhurst, Helene in particular felt that she was *owed*. Well, that was a long time ago now, years. That scandal has died and isn't coming back. We won. And then I wondered why Helene was there late at night at the offices all alone, but before I could ask her, she said something.

'Did your police interview go OK?'

I nodded.

'You don't have to worry about Malone bothering us any more. I've taken care of her.'

Her voice was so cold and detached that for the first time I was scared of my stepmother.

CHAPTER 61

Helene

Nine days before

I found Alice snooping around in Gabe's office that evening. There were several explanations, none of them welcome. The most obvious conclusion was that she hadn't accepted his death and was desperate to find someone, other than him, to blame. I began to wonder if I was the nearest thing.

Was she going to punish me in some way for hiring Maggie, for doubting Gabe's love? It's hard for a daddy's girl to accept that their parent is less than perfect; that they were a conflicted, oozing mess of pain and compromise and bad decisions. Grief warps people, and this might have thrown her off.

I was worried about that. My family was out of balance. Alice and I were teetering round a gaping Gabe-shaped hole, and one or both of us was in danger of falling in.

Gabe's death meant a changing relationship between me and Alice was inevitable. While she had accepted me taking over the business, she could just as well change her mind and cause trouble.

I walked into the office. 'What are you looking for, Alice?'

'Nothing.' Her reply was mumbled and she was nervous. She folded closed a large file of papers that were open on

Gabe's desk and put them back in the filing cabinet. The tension of things unsaid tightened around us.

It was time to win her over. I was good at soothing out knotted shoulders, bringing people back to places they would prefer to be. I had done it with men all my life. A little girl wouldn't be so difficult. Her grief had knocked her off her feet and sent her scurrying into this office to hunt for a why and a who. It was time to put an end to these blossoming conspiracy theories.

'Why don't you come home with me? We can get some food. You don't want to be in this office all by yourself.' She didn't budge. Her little chin jutted forward, her righteousness and stubbornness coming out. She looked so like Gabe at that moment it took my breath away, tipped me closer to the edge of the hole. 'You're not going to find any answers to his death in that filing cabinet. Now is the time to pull together as a family, not apart.'

'This was Poppa's office. It's not yours. It should be mine.' She slammed the filing cabinet closed so hard it shrieked on its rails.

It was so like Alice to think like this, to stamp her feet and shout to try and get what she wanted.

My voice was soft, I knew I needed to remain calm and I passed the test. She was too immature to remember how her father and I helped her over the first big emotional crisis of her teenage years. Some notes were discovered from Alice's teacher Mr Dewhurst to her. Love notes. She had written others back to him. She was being groomed. She was fourteen years old. Gabe was incandescent, he wanted to flatten the man. I had to physically hold him back from racing out the door and accelerating the car through that dirty old pervert's front room. I urged him to let the authorities deal with it. I called the police, they contacted the school and they took it from there. I felt sorry for Gabe, so sorry. He blamed himself, he felt he had failed, that his primary job had been to protect her, and she had ended up walking into the clutches of an unscrupulous man who had abused his position of trust. I suppose the outcome was a triumph. Dewhurst lost his job, would never get a reference or work with young people again. We tried to keep the disruption to Alice to a minimum and we succeeded. She didn't even have to change schools.

I was worried then about how she would react, but she was brilliant. She has a limitless capacity to see the positive in even the worst situations.

My heart softened towards this damaged little creature. 'One day, Alice, I have no doubt that GMW will be yours. When you're a little older.'

She pouted at me, but said nothing. The knocks that life had given her had made her strong. She would outlive me, I thought.

CHAPTER 62

Maggie

Eight days before

It was Rory who finally came up trumps on the Chelsea flat. He had made a succession of calls to local estate agents and found out that a flat in the Queen's Gate development had just come on the rental market. It was the middle floor of number 12.

Presumably Jezza from Foxtons hadn't encountered a dead body when he'd got hold of the keys and when I spoke to him, keen to live in Queen's Gate for its quiet location, he hurried me along, boasting that the flat would be gone that day. In London's overheated rental hell zone, I had no reason to disbelieve him. I told him I'd meet him in an hour.

Jezza was in a hurry, but so was I. He had left his liveried mini running when I turned up at the flat, in case he needed to rev away up the street if I didn't show. He stepped out of the car and aggressively shook my hand and we were inside the corridor moments later.

'This is the first day this place has been on the market. I have more viewings later. It's a great opportunity,' Jezza said, full of conviction. 'It's a very international clientele in this part of Chelsea.' He smiled; he had bleached his teeth. They made his eyes look cold and his brain look small. He was eyeing me up, checking my watch and the quality of my shoes. He didn't have time for time-wasters, any more than anyone else did. 'There's a direct route into the City obviously, great connections,' he continued.

I once caught out an estate agent with his lover. They would fuck in empty houses that he would later show to clients. I wondered if Jezza was going to bring his girlfriend here. I looked around the poorly cleaned kitchen. I doubted it. The place was a passion killer.

'Do you know when the last tenant left?'

'Just last week.'

I opened a kitchen cabinet, saw a couple of mismatched glasses and an espresso cup. Other cupboards were clean and empty. I glanced into a small living room and headed into the bedroom.

The double bed was stripped, faint stains of old passion blooming on the mattress. A chest of drawers occupied a corner, its drawers standing open. I walked over and glanced inside, but they had been cleared. Jezza's phone rang and he moved back into the kitchen to take it. I bent down and peered quickly under the bed, but there was nothing there except a couple of fluttering clothes moths feasting on the carpet and balls of dust, but something caught my eye under the chest of drawers. A moment later an empty packet of prescription pills was in my hand. I pushed it into my pocket and opened the door to the cramped en-suite bathroom. The cabinet above the sink was empty but in the pedal bin was a used bottle of hair dye and the packaging. Whoever had lived here was now Conker by L'Oréal.

'Who's the landlord?' I asked Jezza who, call finished, had come back into the room and was ready to lead me to the exit.

'We manage the flat for the property company, so there's no need for you to worry—'

'I'm very interested in the flat. I'd like to know who the landlord is.'

Jezza sensed a deal being close to closing, and he did what all good salesmen do, he gave me what I wanted to hear. 'They are very good landlords.' He smiled his bleachy-toothed smile as he opened the flat door.

'But what are they called, Jezza?'

'Mount Southern Holdings. Shall I have a contract drawn up and emailed over to you?'

'I have to see one other place,' I said as we reached the street. Jezza's face fell a fraction. He had been in the business long enough to know I wasn't a sure thing. We shook hands in double-quick time and a minute later Jezza roared away at speed from the cul-de-sac, off to hunt for more lucrative options.

When he'd gone I pulled out the pill packet. There was a name printed on the label – Miss L Warriner – and the address of a pharmacy in Peckham, south-east London. I stared back at her flat, thinking about Jezza's sell. *There's a direct route into the City obviously, great connections.*

I was thinking about connections, all over London, millions of individual journeys taken every day, yet the least travelled route? Chelsea to the Old Kent Road, the Old Kent Road to Chelsea. Here was a woman with an SW1 address, supposedly the lover of a rich and glamorous man, who until recently had probably been living in Peckham, and dyed her hair with cheap dye from a high street chemist.

Who was Miss L Warriner?

CHAPTER 63

Maggie

Eight days before

I travelled back to the office intending to take a second look at the photos we'd taken of Gabe and Warriner in the street in Chelsea. It was early evening by the time I got back to Paddington and I found Dwight waiting outside, basking in the last rays of the sun. He must have forgiven me for giving him the hairdryer treatment the other day. I felt the sharp tang of anticipation and desire.

'I've got some questions for you,' he said.

'Fire away,' I said. 'But you have to buy me a drink first.' We stood looking at each other, my mind flooded with images of the last time we were together. 'I have a great selection at my flat,' I added. Come on, Dwight, I thought, the best way to get over an argument is to kiss and make up.

Two hours later Dwight and I were in my bed, and I felt more at peace than I had done since Gabe's death. My head was resting on his broad chest, the sounds of car horns and couples bickering in the street were a soft and pleasing backdrop.

'When you had your drinks with Gabe, what did you talk about?' Dwight asked.

I sat up and plumped a pillow behind my head and reached

over for my glass of red wine. 'What do you want to know?'

'Did he talk about work?'

'He talked about his family mainly. He talked about his childhood.'

'Did he ever mention drugs to you?'

'Drugs?' I shook my head.

'Did you ever do drugs with him?'

I leaned over the bed and pulled a T-shirt off the floor and put it on. I found Dwight's questions exposing and I needed to cover myself. 'No. But you think Gabe and Milo's deaths are related, don't you?' Dwight paused and that got me excited. 'You do, don't you? I *knew* it.'

Dwight sighed. 'No, actually, Maggie, we don't, but the case is proving difficult. That drug dealer we arrested in the wake of Milo's murder was a dead end. It wasn't him. He had been seen on the estate earlier that night, but he was captured on CCTV robbing a convenience store in Tooting at the time of the murder.'

'So you're back to square one.'

'Not at all,' Dwight said defensively. 'We've got all sorts of leads and information we're pursuing.'

'Yeah, and Gabe threw himself off that tower, I suppose,' I retorted sarcastically.

Dwight gave me a strange look, pained and vulnerable at the same time. He put his wine down and began to get dressed.

'Milo's got a friend from when they were kids, he lives nearby, a black guy named Larry. He told us Milo was going on about blues or reds.'

'What are they?'

'Well, blue is slang for heroin, and methamphetamine.'

'Reds and blues are depressants, aren't they?'

Dwight nodded. 'Red is slang for any drug you want to name, but in Vauxhall, crack is called reds.'

'In the Matrix, you can take the blue or red pill, can't you? The red pill shows you the truth, shows you it's cowardly to live a lie.'

'I guess,' added Dwight.

'Well, there's a lie going on somewhere over Milo's death – and Gabe's.'

'We found the usual recreational crap in his house, roaches in the bins, that type of thing. The guy certainly liked a party. He helped organise raves all over that estate in the abandoned buildings there.'

'But you don't have him as a drug dealer, do you?'

'No, I don't, to be honest.'

'The answer is somewhere in Gabe's company, I'm sure of it. One night when I followed the Moreaus home there was graffiti on their house. "You can't hide" scrawled in red paint.'

'I know, the daughter Alice told us. She'd also found threatening notes, addressed to her dad.'

I sat bolt upright now. 'See! I told you! What did they say?'

'Inconclusive. They could have been from the mistress, or from someone else, it's unclear at this stage.'

'This is proof, don't you see? – Milo and Gabe were killed for the same reasons—'

'Maggie—'

'It's something to do with that property deal, I'd bet my life on it – Milo knew too much and was murdered and Gabe came second—'

'Maggie!' His tone brought me up short. 'Stop it. This is pure speculation, based on nothing more than a hunch. The last time I saw you, you thought Helene had pushed Gabe off.'

I was about to let rip at him but struggled to stay silent instead. 'There's one thing I know,' I said eventually, 'over affairs of the heart, I'm always right.'

He paused, looking unhappy. 'Problem is, Maggie, believing Gabe was murdered gets you off the hook. But according to the police, at this stage, it's just as likely he saw you, realised you had been following and reporting back to his wife, and took matters into his own hands. It's just as likely your mistake led to his death as any conspiracy theory.'

'Bullshit!' I was furious, but Dwight didn't back down. He stood up to go. I got up and tried to pull him back down on to the bed. He looked at me and shook his head. 'This game is old, Maggie.'

'I checked out Gabe's lover. She's done a bunk from the flat in Chelsea.'

'So?'

'Pretty fast after he died, no? Why did she do that?'

'I don't know, Maggie!'

'Listen, Dwight, this is important. Maybe she wasn't his lover, maybe Helene knew that all along. Maybe she hired me to make it *look* like that woman was Gabe's lover, when there's something else entirely going on. Maybe it's a blackmail deal and Helene hired me as a cover for something we don't know about. Something so bad that it could lead to his death—' I stopped, Dwight was studying his phone. 'Are you listening to me?'

Dwight looked up. 'You know what, Maggie? Hunt down this lover/non-lover if you want. Waste your time on this family that doesn't want you involved if that gets you off. But where's your life going, Maggie? What's the plan?'

'I don't have a plan. I just like going with the flow.'

It didn't wash. 'We all have fears, Maggie. Being afraid isn't a weakness. Don't feel scared that you can feel.' I made a scoffing sound that irritated him. 'You know what? I want to build something.' He pulled on his shoes. 'Ask yourself, Maggie, do you still want to be here like this next year, in five years? All these casual maybe/maybe-not games?'

I knelt on the bed and came up behind him, wrapped my arms around his chest, keen to use my powers to get him to slide back under the sheets. 'Come on, let's not fight.'

He pushed me away. 'Just because you always see the bad end of relationships doesn't mean they are not worth having.'

'Come back to bed,' I whispered.

But Dwight wasn't through. 'When you swim through the kind of shit I do in my job, Maggie, you need the comfort of another human being to be able to bear it. I mean in here.' He tapped the side of his head. 'You need a mental connection. You need to make a leap of faith. You are at the most vulnerable you'll ever be, but that's not a bad thing.'

I shoved him roughly away. 'I think you'd better go, Dwight.'

It was as if I had slapped him. He stood up suddenly and pulled the last of his clothes on. 'Jesus, you've got a screw loose, Maggie.' He slammed the door as a final fuck you.

I slumped back down on the bed, a bad mood obliterating every soothing sensation and feeling of the last few hours. I hadn't given Dwight what he wanted to hear, because I couldn't and I would never be able to. When you had a past like mine, all the usual words that make life worth living – comfort, love, partner, commitment – are negatives, not positives. But I couldn't tell him that. Not now, not ever.

And like so many times before, I fell asleep alone, the name Colin Torday on my mind and the warmth of a just-departed human being cooling in the sheets.

CHAPTER 64

Maggie

Seven days before

By the following morning I had blocked my argument with Dwight from my mind and chose to remember the sharp pleasures of being with him, being under him. Dwight gave me the means to rock on; it was summer and I was satisfied. I'd already checked some databases for Gabe's mystery woman and I was sure that with a name and an address we'd find her pretty soon. As the water drummed on my head from the shower, I was working out how quickly we'd see what had really been going on in Gabe Moreau's life, maybe what really happened on the fifth floor of Connaught Tower.

I was doing the old back rub with a towel when I saw the phone dancing on the bedside table. Odd, Simona never rang, she only texted. I ignored it until she rang again. Once I'd thrown the towel over the radiator I answered it.

She asked me if I'd seen the *Daily Mail* online. She said we had a problem. Then she got flustered and said that I had a problem.

I opened the site.

Troubling case of the death of a millionaire businessman and the snooper hounding him

There are calls today for private detectives to be regulated after the troubling and still unresolved death of millionaire property developer Gabe Moreau.

Gabe Moreau was a charismatic and handsome self-made millionaire who was a regular on London's charity fundraising circuit. Having come to the UK as a refugee from war-torn Croatia, he had overcome the tragic death of his first wife when the car they were travelling in plunged into a river, and gone on to build a multi-million pound property empire in the capital. Two weeks ago Gabe Moreau fell to his death from Connaught Tower, a skyscraper of luxury apartments that his company GWM was building in Vauxhall, London. The controversial development on a site by the Thames formerly known for its crime and social problems had been at the centre of protests over the loss of low-cost social homes in the capital. Investigations into Gabe Moreau's death are ongoing, but it has now been revealed that with Moreau in the skyscraper at the time of his death was Maggie Malone, a private investigator once hired by Moreau's wife Helene to look into whether he was having an affair.

Maggie Malone, 42, runs the Blue and White, a private investigation agency that according to her website 'does the hard work exposing cheats so you don't have to'. But the self-proclaimed top private detective hides a controversial past. In 1994, Malone was convicted of stalking her former boyfriend Colin Torday, given a restraining order and ordered to do one hundred hours community service.

'I hired Malone at a moment of deep personal pain,' Helene explained. 'Every marriage has its strains and I worried Gabe was having an affair. A wife has a right to know what her husband is doing,' Helene added. 'But it's certainly not right that the woman I hired to do a specific job developed an obsession with my husband that may have contributed to, or directly caused, a tragedy. I had terminated my relationship with Malone but unknown to me she was still following my husband long afterwards. That's stalking, pure and simple, and invasion of privacy. I believe that Maggie Malone is an unstable woman who should under no circumstances be undertaking this kind of work. She is not mentally suited to it.'

More troubling still, according to police sources Malone has not been forthcoming with investigators as to what she was doing with Moreau in Connaught Tower or indeed what relationship she had developed with him.

The growing private investigations industry has been attacked for poor results, underhand tactics and invasion of privacy, yet legally there is very little to stop anyone setting themselves up in the business. This troubling case asks some unanswered questions: why was a woman convicted of stalking her boyfriend twenty years ago allowed – essentially – to get paid to stalk other men today?

A Metropolitan Police spokesman said: 'We won't comment on an ongoing investigation into Gabe Moreau's death, but we have made representations to Parliament for the regulation of the private detective industry.'

A spokeswoman from Homes are for Living In, a pressure group campaigning for more low-cost housing in London, said: 'Thousands of ordinary Londoners are being driven from the capital as their council homes are replaced by luxury developments that are of no benefit to local communities. Sadly, that process is underway in Vauxhall, as in many other parts of our great city.

There was a photo of Gabe in a restaurant on holiday, happy and relaxed, Helene looking gorgeous and content beside him. There was a photo of me, taken off the website, unsmiling and confrontational, arms crossed.

When I got to the office, Rory and Simona met me at the door looking like they were about to announce someone had died. Rory put a cup of coffee down in front of me. 'Well, this is a pile of shit,' he said quietly.

That was an understatement. Rory and Simona had trusted and believed in me, had given years of their life to helping me grow the Blue and White. While I had never lied about my past, I'd never told them about it either. It wasn't exactly something that came up easily in conversation. I had tried to move on from it, I had tried to live better, and as the years had passed, it had faded but never disappeared. Now, more than twenty years later, this was where it had got me. I had betrayed my staff by never revealing my past and allowed it to undermine my business. I didn't join the police not because I wasn't suited to it – I would have loved a police career more than anything. I didn't apply because I knew my criminal record prevented me. So I did what I thought was the next best thing and threw myself into becoming a private detective.

I told Rory and Simona I was sorry. I sat them down and gave them every unvarnished, sordid, dark little detail.

Colin Torday was a decent, caring human being, nothing like my mum. In fact, as far removed from my mum as it was possible to be. He was nine years older than me. He had a regular job, money and a nice house. I was nineteen when I met him and I fell in love for the first time; I loved him madly, I loved him without limits. Maybe it was because I had been abandoned by the person I had loved as a child, by the woman who had a duty to love me, that I overcompensated with Colin. I moved in with him pretty quickly.

Colin was my entire world; he was my route to a better life and I grasped at him with both hands.

Our relationship was short-lived. I was too volatile and high tempo for him; he found my adoration cloying and overbearing. After a few months together he began to withdraw from me; the arguments began. But instead of understanding and accepting that our relationship was over I clung to its carcase. He asked me to move out. We argued more. He begged me to leave and I eventually slunk off to a friend's sofa, defeat and failure cloaking me. Deep down I wondered if I would always fail at love; I didn't have the capacity to be good enough because after all, no one had ever wanted me. I thought if I could show Colin how much I loved him, that would be enough. If I sent him endless letters, if I called him and woke him from his sleep, he would see that as charming and a sign of my commitment. If I carved our names inside a heart on his front door, he would finally be convinced that we should be together. If I sent him photos I had taken with my camera of him going about his day, he would realise his mistake. When he pleaded with me to stop, when he shouted at me to go away, I thought he was paying attention to me, and I redoubled my efforts to get him to notice me again, to get us to turn back time and get back to what we once had. I did all these things for five months, until the police came calling. Again, and then again.

It took a judge and a court case and hours and hours of hard self-reflection to realise that what I had done to Colin was wrong, that I had ruined his life with my love. I wasn't a blessing, I was a curse. And he would have wished he had never met me.

And in my life that I've lived since then, I have come to realise that I was unlovable and unloved.

I knew it was Helene who had tipped off the press about me. But could I blame her? What the media had published wasn't a lie. I went crazy when my heart was broken, but the work I had done in the intervening decades to make myself a different person wasn't mentioned in the reports. I would forever be the sum of my youthful mistake. Whatever the newspapers and the media did to me that day I had already done to myself. The way I chose to live my life had been a reaction to my loss of control when I was nineteen; never get attached, never get too involved. Always move on. And I had succeeded at that, all too successfully.

Once I'd finished my confession, Rory came over and hugged me for a long time and then Simona joined in and we stood as a little crabby huddle in the offices of the Blue and White. It took all of my self-control not to sob in their arms like a baby.

And then before we could adjust, we were fighting a firestorm with a leaky bucket.

By ten thirty, Mrs Gupta had cancelled her job. So had another two clients. And the hate mail had started on the company's Twitter account. I was trending under the hashtags #menfightback and #banthebitch. I was caught up in the perfect storm of concerns about invasion of privacy, trolls who had an itch in their pants about feminism and men whose wives had stiffed them in a divorce settlement (and that was every man that had ever got divorced). Social media that day showed that I had pricked the boil of feminism, money, and sexual jealousy, and released a river of pus.

When Simona answered the phone to a man saying he wanted to rape her, I sent her and Rory home and closed the office. Against Rory's advice I nipped out to the off-licence, came back to the office and got cuddly with an entire bottle of vodka. Before the booze haze obliterated every sensible reflection, I went through a moment of cold, hard admiration for Helene Moreau. This was her move against me; her way of seeing me off, of sending me a warning –

leave my family alone, walk away from the bad smells and the unanswered questions. Ten to one she knew before she hired me what lay in my past, and she saw an opportunity that might prove useful to her in the schemes she was planning and to gain control of GWM. Privacy is dead, as I've said before. A quick Internet search, a bit of digging in a library, and all my sordid past was there for anyone to find. Could I prove what she had done? No. Could I use it? No. But sometimes a woman just knows.

But before the bottle of vodka was finished, my emotions had changed from self-pity to anger. Helene had overplayed her hand. She had underestimated the danger from a woman who was at risk of losing the only thing she had. I was, at forty-two, unattached and childless. My work was the thing I loved, the thing that gave my life meaning and in less than one day it had been laid to waste. I had within me the passion to be obsessive about finding the truth, the ability to never give up and the need to keep at it until the picture was clear. I was going to find out what had happened to Gabe Moreau, I was going to find out what had happened to Milo, I would understand why Helene had really hired me.

Game on, Helene, I thought. *Now I really have nothing to lose. Unlike you.*

When the bottle of vodka was finished, I thought about Gabe Moreau. About following him down dark streets, watching him unobserved from the security and warmth of a car. Had I been beginning to form an obsession with Gabe, had he turned something dormant back on? Had I been taking the first steps down a dangerous road that would lead back to the behaviour I had shown to Colin? That long night I thought and I examined and I wondered. But it wasn't true. I had been looking for the truth. And it was still to be found.

I pulled out the series of photos that Rory and I had taken of Gabe's mystery woman in Chelsea. I blew every one up to maximum size and studied each one carefully – what could be seen of her tanned face, her blonde hair and her clothes. She was maybe a little older than Gabe, but well preserved, with slim wrists and ankles on teetering high heels that lent her a fragile air that was accentuated when she moved to and fro in front of him. It was almost as if she was dancing for him.

I went back to my phone and sped through the photos, now a jumpy silent cine film. She patted his chest, she leaned in to him, she talked continuously. At no point did Gabe smile or reply, he stood stiffly by as she performed around him and he followed her with leaden steps through the front door of the flat. If anything he seemed scared of her.

I realised then where I had seen that behaviour before. I had done those things to Colin; he had been stiff and silent as I had acted in more increasingly desperate ways to get him to love me, to get him to see me. I had revelled in the power that I seemed to hold over Colin at those moments; I told myself that his silence, his inaction, were signs he was devoted to me. I saw it as love, when really it had been fear.

And fear was what Gabe was showing in these photos. And now he was dead.

CHAPTER 65

Maggie

Six days before

There's a lot of chat these days about online harassment; people complaining about 140 characters floating in the ether, but being doorstepped is analogue torture. You can't close down an app of your home and get back to real life. I like the sunlight – who doesn't? – but there I was in my flat, blinds closed against a huddle of men and women staring up into my window, the doorbell ringing every half an hour as they searched for something quotable, pushing notes through the letterbox, annoying my neighbours in the block, texting, phoning the landline. They didn't give me a moment's peace.

The phone kept vibrating so often on the coffee table that it had become a game to watch it inch towards an edge and fall to the carpet, but as I picked it up a text caught my eye. 'It's Alice. I'm outside your back door.'

I phoned her and she answered straight away. 'Let me in, I need to talk to you.'

'We have nothing to say to each other.'

'Be the judge of that after you let me in.'

I was intrigued and wanted to hear what she had to say. I buzzed her in through the back gate and a little later there was a knock on the door.

I took her through into the lounge and she looked around uncertainly so I sat in the armchair and she perched on the couch.

Considering she had lost her dad, she looked better than expected. Paler and thinner, her whiteness threw her red hair into sharp relief. She was a beauty in her own way.

'You were there with Poppa at the end.' It was a statement, not a question. I nodded. 'Was he in pain?'

I took a while to digest that question. She could have meant in his life in general, but I took it to mean after he fell. 'A little. But not for long.'

She didn't bow her head or cry, she was as tough as they come. 'What happened at Connaught Tower?'

I would have needed a heart of stone to not have sympathy for this abandoned girl, and I certainly had never had one of those. As a grieving daughter she had every right to know, so I told her what I had seen as accurately as I remembered it. I said that Gabe had seemed out of sorts earlier in the evening and that was why I had begun to follow him; he had caught sight of me and understood he was being followed. I told her about going into the gloom of Connaught Tower itself, walking up the cement stairs. I watched her face as I retold events, but something I had heard at the scene was scratching at my memory, a thing that had been on the floors above me that I couldn't catch hold of. But it was gone as soon as I tried to recall it. It was in direct contrast to the images outside the tower moments later, which I was finding impossible to get out of my mind.

Finally I told her I was sorry, and I meant it.

I thought we were done, and I got up so she could leave, but it turned out we had only just got going.

'Do you think he jumped?' she asked. I sank back into my chair. She didn't take her eyes off me. The silence stretched.

'Because I'll tell you that he didn't. He left no note or explanation. He wouldn't do that. He would *never* do that.'

'Ms Moreau, I—'

'I want to know what *really* happened at Connaught Tower.'

'I can't help you—'

'I've come here, because I saw you with Poppa.' I wasn't sure what she was referring to, and felt myself stiffen. 'You loved my father.'

'Steady. Stop making assumptions—'

'I saw you in the Langham with him. I'm not blind, or a child. Most women react to Poppa in the way you did. Most have their heads turned. You owe me answers, at least.'

The wish to have answers, who doesn't want that?

She ploughed on. 'I can't let this rest, I can't get beyond this until I have all the answers. Show me a photo of Poppa's lover.'

'They're at the office, not here.'

'OK, but I want you to find Poppa's lover for me,' she persisted.

I got angry then, and even though she had lost her dad I couldn't contain it. 'Your stepmother did that to me,' I snapped, jabbing my finger at the ogling crowd outside the window. 'Hire another private detective.'

She opened her bag and pulled out a tabloid and threw it on the coffee table. There I was, down amongst the tits and tarts, my shameful past laid out for all to see. She was forcing me to take a look, to know what few options I had left. 'Helene claims she found that woman in her bathtub the night before poppa died.'

'Excuse me?'

'Helene was ranting and raving that she had stolen her keys, had come into the house, had a bath and left when she arrived home.'

'Did Helene say what the woman said?'

Alice shook her head. 'To be honest, I wondered if it had even happened; Helene is often fanciful. And anyway, if it did happen, I mean, it's a sign this woman really loves Poppa, isn't it, that she's prepared to do anything for him.'

I was shocked. Alice was so young, she didn't get relationships, she had no idea how extreme this behaviour was, how provocative. It wasn't a sign of love; an act like that was about power, humiliation and ownership – it was the opposite of love. I remembered what Helene had mentioned in my office a while ago – that this woman might have been following her, maybe even the family. That's why Gabe had been so shaken when I tailed him on his last night, this woman Warriner had blown his secret affair wide open. An end was coming, and he knew it. It was all the motive Helene needed to unleash her deadly passions – or Warriner for that matter.

'It's out of character for Poppa to do what he did,' Alice urged. 'You think there's something wrong about his death. I know you wonder if it's connected to Milo's murder, he and Poppa were too close for it to be chance. You dislike coincidence as much as I do. Well, the first place to start is with this woman – let's see what she knows. You want to find her, and this way you get paid. I'm guessing you're going to need the money.'

Despite everything I'd been through, and against my better judgment, I felt a flicker of interest. Alice was saying out loud what I suspected, but I had another question. 'Helene's taken over Gabe's company. You happy about that?'

She paused and I saw something unpleasant pass across her face. 'I want you to look into Helene. Do a background check on her. You'd better make it very low key. Get your employees to do it, not you. She's taken over GWM, I want to know that everything is above board.'

So she didn't trust her stepmother any more than I did. After that my decision was easy. I'd done a lot of the legwork on Gabe's mystery woman, Ms Warriner, already. Rory at present had less than nothing to do and could hunt for information on Helene. I didn't tell Alice I would have done the work for free. But if she was happy to pay, I wasn't going to refuse.

CHAPTER 66

Alice

Six days before

Maggie let me in the back door of her block of flats and we took the stairs to the third floor. I was shocked at how much she had changed from when I saw her in the Langham Hotel, gurning at Poppa. Then she had been cocky and sexy, her boobs out and the gaudy dress holding her in in all the right places – if you liked that kind of thing. Now she seemed tired and ragged, her nails needed doing and her hair was a mess. She opened the door to her flat, which smelled of food waste, and I saw wine and spirits bottles and beer cans stacking up in the corner of the kitchen. She wouldn't have wanted to carry those out to the communal bins past the waiting reporters.

She walked into the living room where the blinds were drawn against the world and sat back in a chair, made a sarcastic gesture towards the sofa for me. She didn't offer me a drink, which was fine. We weren't friends and it wasn't a social call.

The kitchen might have been a mess of too much drink and too many ready meals but the small living room was tidy. I saw the neat lines of DVDs on a shelf, thrillers and zombie films and other commercial crap: box sets of *Top*

Gear, crowd pleasers from yesteryear such as *The Office*. There were books too, and I reminded myself not to be surprised, people were complex, she was smart. Andrea Dworkin, a book on self-esteem, something on economics.

There were many photos in frames of different sizes, circles of sunburnt faces grinning behind a table full of cocktails, fat shoulders red with sunburn, clichéd Mediterranean sunsets and smiling, toothless babies.

It was a collection of the mess and tangles of a normal life. All her relationships jumbled up on the shelves in here, but she lived alone. It was obvious from the moment you stepped into her flat. I bet explaining her criminal conviction to a hot date was a deal breaker, even now.

I got straight down to the point of my call. 'Why were you following Poppa? What were you doing there when he died?'

She told me the sequence of events. I felt nothing when Maggie apologised for Poppa's death. I didn't want to be here, I didn't want to ever see Maggie again, but I had unanswered questions that needed to be cleared up. Getting emotionally involved with my family had cost her dear and she had been backed into a corner. So we needed each other to get what we wanted in our grief and rage. She made little protest to me hiring her. She needed the money, I needed to find that woman from Chelsea and be reassured about Helene. So we were equal.

CHAPTER 67

Maggie

Six days before

In the afternoon after Alice had come round I went back to the office. I couldn't stand to stay cooped up in that hovel of a flat a moment longer. It was time to face the music.

The first thing that confronted me on my return was the state of the front door of the Blue and White. Someone had drawn a cock and balls in white paint that reached from the floor to the door handle. Pull the handle down to open the door and it looked like you were pleasuring it. #menfightback was scrawled underneath it. Several people were taking photos on phones of the door.

I walked away, turning my head from a honking horn on a car pulling up beside me that I assumed was a reporter.

'Maggie! Get in!'

It was Dwight's voice. He opened the passenger door and I jumped in.

Dwight drove round the corner and began to weave through the West End.

'What do you want?' I asked petulantly.

'I came to see how you were. You've had a rough few days, I'm guessing.'

I rounded on him. 'You don't have any bloody idea!'

He held his hands up in defeat. 'OK, I put that badly. But this will blow over.'

'Have you seen my door?' I snapped.

'Get the council to come and clean it off. They've got a team that deal with that kind of thing. It's a criminal offence.'

'I don't need a council team, Dwight, I just want to get on with my job.'

'What happened in the past, it doesn't bother me, Maggie.'

'Come on, Dwight! That's bullshit and you know it.'

'Stop telling me how I think and feel. Mrs Moreau gave you a proper roasting, that's for sure.'

'Hell, maybe I deserved it.'

He braked in the middle of the street and turned to look at me. 'Don't say that. Don't you ever doubt yourself. What you did was more than twenty years ago. You made a mistake and you paid for it. Don't ever forget that.'

I couldn't look at him and something moved inside me that I couldn't control and which I didn't like. I tried to get out of the car but he pulled on my arm, bringing me back towards him.

'Hey! Nobody can do it all alone, Maggie, not even you.'

I didn't answer and opened the car door. It began to rain, the heat of the past few days giving way to a heavy summer shower. I hated getting wet. It was like the world pissing on you. Simona phoned and the piss turned to shit.

'I thought you would want to know that we're being sued. Remember that guy from a few years back who you caught having sex with a trio of prostitutes in his house when his wife Trudi was at a conference? He's claiming invasion of privacy and damages from the Blue and White, citing unprofessional behaviour and breach of the Data Protection Act because we filmed him at his front door, which is his private property.

'And I phoned a painter and decorator to repaint the front

door. When I told him the address and the company he said that if I was such a feminist I could paint my effing door myself.'

'Get back in the car, Maggie!' Dwight shouted.

The traffic was backing up behind Dwight and horns were being blasted.

I walked away, my phone a shield against my ear.

'Simona,' I said, 'make a list of what needs referring to a lawyer, but first I need you to do something for me. Go and buy some paint for the front door. I'll do it.'

I had nearly finished the first coat when Rory turned up. He stood in the street for a few moments staring at me. 'Stop that right now,' he said.

I ignored him and carried on, using jabby, angry little strokes. 'At least let me paint over the tip of the penis.'

Rory didn't see the joke. He said nothing, just stood still in the street looking at me. I couldn't meet his eye, because I was fighting back tears. In all the years Rory had worked for me I had never shown such weakness to him, never felt so exposed and vulnerable.

'What are you looking at?' I snapped. 'We don't have much other work to do.'

'Any other work,' Rory replied.

I put the brush down and stepped back, still staring at the brush strokes in the wet paint. 'Well, something has come up,' I said. 'Alice has hired us to—'

'Jesus, Maggie, we need to walk away from that family!'

'— to find Gabe's lover, to find out what she knows.' Rory gave me a look that showed his interest was piqued. 'And Alice wants us to dig into Helene's past, see if we can find any dirt.'

Rory began to get excited. 'It would be my pleasure. Helene's up to her neck in something, and I'll never forgive her for what she did to you.' He nodded towards the door. 'We are going to open her up like a tin can. We know what's lurking in your closet. Let's see what skeletons are rattling in hers.'

Then he handed me a tissue and I blew my nose and he used his thumb to wipe away my streaked mascara before I pushed him away and said I could bloody do it myself.

CHAPTER 68

Maggie

Four days before

Alice's cash kept the Blue and White afloat and allowed me to keep Simona and Rory on the payroll. Simona had suspended the Twitter account; we unplugged the phone because no one but reporters and abusers rang it. Rory began digging into Helene's life and so Simona and I tackled the woman from Chelsea. Two days later we had drawn a blank. We looked up Warriner in every directory and site we could think of; we did the trawl round social media, Simona got hold of the guest list for the party at the Café Royal; there was no Warriner on it.

I drove down to the pharmacy on the Old Kent Road where Warriner's pills came from and met the usual shuffling line of the public gathering up their medical panaceas. It was a quiet, ground-down kind of place, the high-rise flats poking skywards from every angle. Warriner's pills were Zoloft, which a quick Internet search told me was used to treat mood disorders and anger issues. It would be important that she took her pills regularly. I showed her photo to the chemist and the cashier, they shook their heads.

I tried a couple of the Middle Eastern supermarkets and a Jamaican patty shop on the same strip as the chemist, showed her photo, got politely and rudely shown the door. They thought I was immigration, they suspected I was from the benefits agency.

I showed the picture to passers-by in the street, women at the bus stops, no one knew who she was. It was like Warriner was a ghost.

I told Simona to get back to Foxtons and find the tenancy agreement for the Chelsea flat. 'Tell them you're probate and you can't find her. That way we should get a previous address or a phone number.'

The only bright spot on otherwise gloomy and exhausting days was when Rory told me that he'd traced Gabe and Helene's wedding witnesses and that Helene was born in Newcastle. He gave me another interesting bit of information: Helene had changed her name. She had been born Helen Davey. She'd lost her accent, made her name more exotic. I wasn't against reinvention, but it made me wonder what else Rory might uncover.

Rory told me he was booking a train ticket to Newcastle.

CHAPTER 69

Maggie

Four days before

While Rory was working on tracking down information about Helene, I went back to Vauxhall to try and talk to Larry, who Dwight had said was a friend and neighbour of Milo's. I sat down on the swings outside Milo's flat. There was no shade and the heat was suffocating, but I was in full view of a lot of windows and corners and dark walkways so I figured someone would see me before long.

After a short while a mother and two kids turned up. I approached the woman, smiling, and asked her if she knew a black guy called Larry and where he lived. She didn't speak English, so no joy there. I caught the attention of a young guy being bossed by his huge dog and asked him the same, and he couldn't help either. I walked round the block and up to the windows of Milo's flat, but the curtains were drawn.

I returned to the playground and sat down again and a few moments later a big black guy approached. 'Why are you looking at Milo's flat?'

I smiled. 'Take a seat.' I gestured to the empty swing next to me. 'He a friend of yours?'

'More than a friend of yours.' He didn't return my smile.

I stood up, pulled the skirt off the back of my legs where it had been stuck by my sweat. I held out my hand. 'I'm Maggie.' He didn't shake it.

'Who are you?'

'I'm a private investigator. I have a client who wants to know if everything possible is being done to find Milo's killer.' He grunted with dissatisfaction and pulled out a cigarette packet. I pulled out my lighter and after a moment's hesitation he accepted. 'Who do you think killed him?' I asked.

He took a deep inhale, blew his smoke sideways. 'Someone who'll get away with it.'

I shook my head. 'That isn't likely to happen. Strange, though, when Gabe Moreau threw himself off that tower.' He looked at me sharply but said nothing.

'I heard Milo was close to Moreau's daughter, Alice.'

He gave me a long look. 'The ginger? Why you so interested in that? The family's hired you, haven't they?' He scowled. 'That Moreau was good at using people, at getting them to do things for him.'

'Was the daughter the same?'

He frowned and then he laughed. 'How would I know? Girls like that, they're trouble if you ask me.'

'In what way trouble?'

'That friend of hers, the fit one with the long, dark hair?' He nodded, a look of wary appreciation on his face. 'That girl, she would bat her eyes, wiggle, give you the come-on and would only lead you to overreach yourself. A payday lender wouldn't be far away.'

I gave him a wry smile. He was a good judge of character. 'But Alice, was she really the same as her friend Lily?'

Larry shrugged and sighed. 'I don't know, man. Milo liked her, I reckon. He talked about her quite a bit. That was different.'

'You were pretty close to Milo.'

'He was a good friend.' He looked at Milo's flat. 'Known him since I was nine years old.'

'I'm sorry for your loss.'

'Not as sorry as I am, man.'

I pulled out my phone. 'Have you ever seen this woman?' I showed him a photo of Gabe's woman from Chelsea.

He peered half-heartedly at my phone screen, trying to shade it from the sun. He shook his head. 'Who's she?'

'Someone I want to tick off a list.'

'Ain't the police doing that?'

'Yes, but this is a personal matter.' I put my phone away. 'Tell me about him. About Milo.'

I was in luck because Larry wanted to talk. He was in pain and talking helped. 'Energy. The guy had so much energy, man. He had many aspects to his life, fingers in many pies, you see what I'm saying? The place just doesn't seem the same without him.'

'Did you have him as a drug dealer?'

He got angry. 'That's bullshit, man. I told the police that. No way was he going to be tarnished by gangs, drugs. That makes me crazy. I mean, Milo had all sorts of plans and schemes.' Larry shook his head, as if he had tolerated one too many of them over the years. 'But they just trampling over his memory with that crap.'

'What's your take on Gabe Moreau falling from up there?'

We both looked up at Connaught Tower. 'I don't care about Gabe Moreau. No way was he trying to sweeten the pill for the likes of us.'

I opened my bag to pull out a card to give to him so that he could ring me if he ever felt he needed to, but he had already stood up and begun to head off and even when I called after him he turned round, walking backwards as he spoke. 'The likes of me, we're fucked. I don't need no private investigator to tell me that.'

I lowered my hand, the card still in it. There was nothing I could say that would make a difference, and he knew it. A moment later he was gone.

CHAPTER 70

Maggie

Two days before

Miss L Warriner was very difficult to find. I went back to that pharmacy three times, spoke to different employees. I tried all the local shops again, accosted a couple of street cleaners pulling crisp packets out from between the railings around a housing block. Every time I showed her photo, everyone shook their heads.

The pharmacy was close to a large estate with a jumble of low-rise units plonked at odd-looking angles with patches of grass sandwiched between them. I walked around for a fruitless hour trying to spot her Porsche.

I was getting pissed off and I was running out of time. I was sick of hanging about here but I had nothing else to do, what with no clients to fill my time and lawsuits to fend off.

If in doubt, follow the money, I thought. Many of the clients I'd followed over the years were men who had paid for sex. It was an exchange the Neanderthals probably understood – here is some bear meat if you let me put it in there – that kind of thing.

I was pretty sure Warriner had been squeezing money out of Gabe, but for what was still unclear. But Gabe made his money not down here off the Old Kent Road but in Vauxhall, so I drove back to the estate. For all I knew there was another flat here she was holed up in.

I pulled off the Vauxhall roundabout and parked near the city farm. I took a long look at the whole area on Google Earth's satellite view, spent time zooming in on the nooks and crannies, the cul-de-sacs and jumbled dead ends. I couldn't do anything about underground car parks, but there wouldn't have been many in this area. The easiest way to look for a Porsche was from the air. I got out of my car and opened the boot, pulled the drone from its black bag.

Simona rang as I was unpacking and getting it set up.

'I got the information from Foxtons about the Chelsea flat,' she said. I was excited but it didn't last long. 'For what it's worth.'

'What do you mean?'

'They had no contract with her. They usually let the flat for the management company, but in this case it was a temporary arrangement and they did it by word of mouth. No paperwork.'

'Why did they do that?'

'Someone from the company phoned up. They simply took a phone number, which is disconnected, and she moved in.'

'Who was paying the rent?'

'She paid in cash, on a weekly basis.'

'Weekly, in Chelsea? That seems unlikely. Who's the management company again?'

'Some outfit called Mount Southern Holdings. I'm looking into them now.'

'OK, let me know how it goes.'

I pulled the drone out of the boot of my car and set it flying over the estate. On my live feed I was searching in all those car parks, side alleys and blocked-off private parking areas for a grey vintage Porsche.

I knew I had little time. In an urban area with lots of people and windows and gardens, someone would complain and complain loudly (if they could even hear the drone over the construction noise) but it was a shortcut, and I needed all of those that I could get.

I watched the images as they came in on the feed, moving the drone as slowly as I dared. I found a Porsche, but it was the wrong colour. I saw upturned faces on pedestrians, dog walkers, mothers with buggies and fingers pointing as the machine passed overhead. I scanned as much of the estate as I dared, and manoeuvred the drone back to me. I got in my car and drove away.

I stopped in a side street in Pimlico and had a closer look at the images I'd taken. London looked so flat and grey from the air, acres of grey roof felt punctured by satellite dishes and air vents and a crazy-paving jumble of triangles of grass and grass-lined paths that cut through the estate. I couldn't find her damn car. I began to watch the film again, but Simona rang before I got halfway through.

'I've been thinking,' she began. 'The instructions on the packet of pills from Warriner's flat say "take morning and evening with food". There were sixty pills in this pack, and it's dated 12th of July. I've checked the medicine online and it's for an ongoing condition. That means she'll be needing a new supply every month.'

There was another maddening pause. 'So?' I asked.

'She'll be turning up to collect a repeat prescription, and since most people are creatures of habit, she'll probably get them from the same doctor and the same pharmacy, probably in the next couple of days.'

I banged the steering wheel of the car with delight. 'You're a fucking genius, Simona,' I almost shouted it down the phone. 'I'm on my way to Peckham now.'

It was the first ray of light in the dark days of the recent past.

CHAPTER 71

Maggie

The day before

Warriner finally turned up at the pharmacy after I'd been waiting for another day. She had changed her hair, it was now dark brown, so the dye in the Chelsea flat was indeed hers, and she wore large dark sunglasses. If it wasn't for her distinctive high heels and good clothes, I could easily have missed her. When she came back out of the shop, her hand was closed over a paper bag. I began to follow her down the street.

Warriner headed off the main road and cut through a succession of large housing blocks and on into a redbrick three-storey block of flats with a set of stairs at either end. She headed up to number 27 and let herself in.

I followed her to the top floor.

The kitchen window faced the walkway and was next to the front door. A net curtain obscured the view.

I knocked on the door.

There was no answer. I knocked again, she didn't open up. I flipped the letterbox and looked into a shabby, narrow hall with nothing in it except a patterned carpet I'd last seen on sale in the 1980s and a scattering of fast food flyers. 'Can I talk to Miss Warriner?' I called. 'I'm a private investigator working for Alice Moreau. I want to ask a few questions about Gabe Moreau.'

There was no movement inside the flat. I tried again. 'My name's Maggie Malone, I'm not working for the police. I'm sure you're aware that Gabe Moreau has recently died, and his daughter is looking for closure. She would like to talk to you.'

There was still no response. I couldn't tell whether she was hiding in the kitchen or the room at the end of the corridor that had a partially closed door. The unkempt flat and its location were at odds with her clothes and car and I was unsure if she was living here. 'It really would be better to open the door.'

I waited a few more moments, but she was stubborn and refused to appear.

Many people in my line of work were reluctant to talk, but rarely the mistresses. Being found out on some level appealed to their vanity. Knowing another woman, in this case his own daughter, had cared enough to hire someone to hunt for them didn't go down so badly. I'd had more than one mistress sit me down, put the kettle on and pull out the biscuits. Justification, explanation, defence, it's hard to not want to tell your story.

But not Warriner. Something was off.

I pulled out a business card and wrote a message entreating her to call me. 'It really would be better to talk to me, otherwise Alice will probably call on you herself,' I said, opening the letterbox and about to drop the card.

I heard a noise from inside. A moment later the door opened.

'You'd better come in, it's boring being shouted at from out there.'

I was finally looking at Warriner up close. She was tall and lithe with an age north of forty, but not by much. She was tanned and well preserved, but her mouth had a downward slant that expressed disappointment.

'Thank you for speaking to me,' I began, 'I have a few questions—'

'Doesn't mean I'm going to answer them.'

She had an accent that was the same as Gabe's. She was from the old country, and that made sense, a rekindling of some trace of his previous life, something Helene could never compete with.

She stood in the hallway, so the furthest I got into the flat was the corridor.

'Alice is looking for answers about what happened to Gabe.'

'She'll wait a lifetime and then some.'

I tried to keep my manner neutral. I could tell she was easily riled and I wanted to keep her talking. 'I understand that you were Gabe's friend, confidante, what would you call it?'

She took a deep breath. 'I was much more than that.'

'How do you feel about his death?'

'What does it matter how I feel?'

'Ms Warriner, Gabe was giving you money, wasn't he?'

'So?'

'Were you sending him threatening notes, writing on his wall? Were you blackmailing him?'

She snorted. 'Why would I answer that?'

'Well, you were pretty aggressive with the bathtub stunt.'

'I don't know what you're talking about.'

I was getting nowhere. 'Is this where you're going to stay, now that the Chelsea flat is no longer an option? It's a pretty fast fall from grace, isn't it?'

I saw a flush on her features, an anger that had bobbed to the surface. 'If it's a fall from grace, then you know all about that.' I said nothing. She had been following the news all right. She must have sensed my defeat because I saw triumph on her face. 'Tell your client I have nothing to tell. No comfort that can be given.'

She began to turn away. I had only one thing left to ask, and I was genuinely interested in the answer. 'Did you love Gabe Moreau?'

She turned sharply towards me and blinked, fast. 'Totally.'

I gave her a thin smile. 'I was there at the tower when Gabe fell. You knew that, but you never asked me what happened, you never wanted to know. That's not a sign of love at all.'

Now it was her turn not to answer. I had put her in her place, but it was a shabby victory. 'Good day, Ms Warriner.' I put my card on the hall table, turned and walked away.

CHAPTER 72

Alice

The morning of

Helene had thrown off Poppa's death too easily. She began to go into work earlier and earlier, taking phone calls late into the evening and acting with a new direction and purpose. I heard laughter in the house again. I didn't like it and I began to indulge in fantasies that Poppa's other woman loved him more, that she was sitting in an armchair with the curtains drawn, sniffling into a handkerchief in her grief.

This morning I found Helene humming in her bedroom before eight a.m.

She turned and saw me in the doorway. 'Oh morning, Alice, I have to go in early today, do you want to come with me or come in later on your own?'

'What are you doing?'

She had laid a black dress with glittering beads on it out on the bed, and was trying to match some scarves against it.

'Tonight I'm having dinner with Peter Fairweather, you know, from Partridger. You met him at the charity auction.' Her face was hidden from me as she was already pulling stockings from a drawer.

I tried to keep my voice neutral. 'Why are you seeing him?'

'He's got a business plan to discuss.'

'About GWM?'

'Yes.'

'What is there to talk about?'

'I expect he wants to talk about buying some or all of the company.'

'But it's not for sale. Poppa never wanted it to leave the family's hands.'

Helene turned and gave a tight little smile. 'I'm aware of that.'

I felt a surge of dislike for Helene. She wasn't there through the early years when Poppa built the company, when I was dragged up by a succession of au pairs and nannies, while both Poppa and I struggled through the grief and absence of Momma in our lives, yet somehow now this interloper was running the show. 'Where is he taking you?' I asked, straining to think well of my stepmother.

She named a fashionable restaurant with high prices. I forced a smile. 'Have a nice time, but tell him the company is not for sale.'

'I know that,' she said. The silence between us stretched. 'Maggie Malone hasn't been in touch, has she?' Helene asked.

I shook my head. 'Why would she?'

'No reason, I guess,' Helene replied. She seemed to visibly relax, then. She packed her accessories into a bag and hung the dress on a clothes hanger and swung it over her shoulder. 'So, are you coming with me?'

I shook my head. 'No, I'll come in later.'

'OK,' she said.

I watched from Poppa's bedroom window as a taxi pulled up and she got in, looking like she had a spring in her step and not a care in the world. I wasn't going into the office today, I decided. I wanted to see if she would even notice. But I knew the answer to that already.

CHAPTER 73

Helene

The morning of

I was desperate to get out and meet Peter Fairweather that evening. An early dinner was the perfect distraction from everything that had happened recently. The more the work at GWM piled up the better I felt. I knew I had made the right decision to fight to take control and run the company. I liked the sound of hundreds of emails pinging in my inbox, I relished the many reports to be read, decisions that needed to be made, meetings that needed to be scheduled. I gathered an excellent team around me, helping me learn the ropes, taking the responsibility for different sections of the business.

I felt a growing confidence as the initial shock of Gabe's death began to lessen. The days had taken on a new shape filled with urgency and purpose, new horizons beckoned; people needed me, a thousand business decisions had to be taken. This was the public face I would show to the world. I would provide Gabe with a suitable and fitting legacy. But there were going to be changes at the development in Vauxhall, a move in a different direction for the company. For GWM to survive it was essential.

Every task needing to be done was a godsend, because it

stopped me thinking about Gabe, about that woman or about Maggie. I had not the slightest regret about the bad publicity that I had unleashed on a woman I used to like and who I had hired. When it comes to love and affection, allegiances can shift like the wind. My tip-off and interviews to the papers about her sordid past would have left her business in ruins and her reputation in tatters. I didn't care. She had overstepped the boundaries of our agreement, she had been unprofessional. She would have realised by now that she had taken on a fight she couldn't win. Life was a struggle – get over it.

I watched the city slide by from inside the taxi. It was better to be inside looking out than outside looking in. I decided it was time to put a restraining order on Maggie. If I was going to take a course of action, it needed to be seen through till the bitter end; there was no point in half measures. I needed to keep her away from the house and, more importantly, the office and our employees, just in case she felt she had nothing more to lose and she might as well stir up trouble by making wild accusations that GWM was responsible for Milo's death. It would keep her away from Alice too. I didn't want Maggie inserting herself into the gap that had opened up between me and my little Alice.

But then I reconsidered the restraining order. Maggie alone knew what Gabe had said in his last moments sprawled in the dust. I needed to find out what that was. I needed to tie up the one dangling loose end.

CHAPTER 74

Maggie

The day of

I woke late, turning over the conversation I'd had with Miss Warriner in my mind. I called Alice. She was at home, and I asked if I could see the texts on Gabe's second phone.

She agreed, and I was about to ask her to come by the office with it but she said she was busy and asked me to come to the house.

She said Helene was at work and would be there all day. We argued it back and forth for a while, as I knew it was better to stay well away from Helene's house, but she didn't relent. I was stuck and since it would only take a few moments I headed over to Islington.

On the way Rory called saying he was on a train coming back from Newcastle. 'You sitting down, because you're going to want to be,' he began.

'I'm too busy to do that. What have you got for me?'

'Do you know how far five hundred quid goes in this town?'

'A long way, I imagine.'

'Wrong,' Rory retorted. 'It's the scariest place I've ever been. I'm lucky to escape with my gonads intact. I'm broke, and I'm coming back before I get lynched. But you're going to want to listen to this. We know our fragrant Helene Moreau started life as ordinary Helen Davey, right?'

'Go on.'

'Well, her mum was a hospital cleaner, dad wasn't around. Our Helen was very pretty. I've paid to see photos of her. And she had a liking for married men. And soon it became a liking for rich, married men. Two divorcees talked a lot about her – I didn't have to pay them, they were happy to relay how Helen Davey had turned the heads of their husbands and ruined their marriages. She had a fancy flat in town paid for by one man, he bought everything for her – clothes, jewellery, he even bought her a car. And then, in the early noughties, when she was in her late twenties, she left. She was run out of town, the way I heard it. That's when she came to London – in that same car, I imagine.'

'Where she ended up meeting Gabe,' I added.

Rory agreed. 'I bet you Gabe knew nothing about her past, or how he was only one in a long line of wealthy wallets she was only too happy to help empty.'

I smiled. Rory could give me a run for my money when it came to cynicism. 'Great work, Rory, I'll see you later tonight.' He rang off and I sat back.

Was I surprised at what Rory had uncovered? No, was the long answer. Women like Helene were found watching every casino table; they were perched on barstools in every five-star hotel bar, smiling at every charity fundraiser. There was nothing wrong with that in itself – grown men were masters of their own actions; nobody was forcing them to cheat on their wives. Helene had had a plan and executed it. But deep down inside was the tiny beat of alarm – how deep did her ambition run, how high did she aspire? Was her love for Gabe an act? Or was the truth that it was easy to fall in love with a rich, charismatic man who had overcome personal tragedy?

I parked around the corner from Alice's house as a precaution and rang on the door. It took her a long time to answer. She was still in her pyjamas with a cup of coffee in her hand and seemed thinner and more serious, her bright innocence dimmed. It was strange being in that house again. Gabe whispered at me from every corner, but the look of the place had changed too; it had become unkempt and messy, with drifts of clothing and paperwork layering surfaces and trailing across floors and stairs. I saw shrivelling apple cores on a footstool in the lounge, a vase of dried-up and wilting flowers. It was as if with Gabe gone, the order under-pinning the Moreaus had begun to collapse.

Alice took me up to the office and found the box with Gabe's things in it. 'It's charged,' she said and handed the phone over before walking into her bedroom. I followed her in and sat down next to her because it was the only place free from the clutter. I called the number, it was unobtainable.

I read the messages; the oldest said 'You can't let me go x'. The next said 'Alice need never know xx' and the third, 'I deserve more x'. The messages were humdrum, if anything.

'Why do you think they're talking about me in the text?'

I shook my head, but I felt a beat of annoyance at her narcissism. But this was how I got paid, and so I said nothing.

'Can I see a photo of her?' Alice asked.

I pulled out my phone and showed her one of the photos of Warriner I had loaded on it.

She stared at it for a long moment and gave a small nod. 'How are you getting on finding her?' she asked.

'Does the name L Warriner mean anything to you?' I asked. She frowned. 'No.'

I told her that I had traced and spoken to Gabe's woman but that she was reluctant to meet his family.

Alice wouldn't accept that. 'I want to see her,' she said.

I held up my hands. 'I can't stop you but I would counsel against it.'

She was silent then and I was unclear whether she was absorbing my advice.

'What have you found out about Helene?' she continued. The hard look on her face told me that things weren't great between the grieving women in Gabe's life. 'Well?' she asked again, her eyes fiery with righteousness and clear moral boundaries.

So I gave her a watered-down and sterilised version of what Rory had found out in the home town of her stepmother.

I was unprepared for what happened next.

Alice screamed. She picked up her coffee cup and threw it at the wall, the saucer straight after it. The coffee splashed like a blood spurt from an artery straight across the paintwork.

'Alice!' I jumped up and grabbed her from behind, trying to pin her flailing arms by her sides. The duvet got tangled in my feet, Alice tried to upend the bedside table.

She was stronger than she looked. I was trained in self-defence but most of the drills were for taking out a male opponent. The role-play hadn't factored in so much red hair that I was temporarily blinded as I tried to grab her arms to stop her destroying her bedroom. For a few terrible moments she was a whirling helicopter of fury on my shoulder, trying to take down anything within five feet.

It took a full five minutes to get her on the bed, calm enough to speak to her.

'I'm going to fucking kill her!' she screamed again.

'You need to calm down!' I screamed back.

She didn't speak, her adrenaline was running so high she was panting, wordless. I realised I was still gripping her arms. Everyone has a tipping point, a moment when they can take so much, and no more, so far, and no further. I thought then that Alice had reached that point, and I feared for what she might do to Helene. If her stepmother did have a role to play in Gabe's death, she needed to be behind bars, not at the end of Alice's fists.

I didn't get off her arms. But a few minutes later her hard breathing had lessened and I felt her go slack under my touch. I climbed off her bed and straightened my clothes. She sat up and I began to reorder the disaster that was her bedroom, setting her bedside table straight and putting the things that had fallen off back on it.

'Grow up,' I said. 'You wanted to know the truth, but you have to be strong enough to cope with it.'

She looked up at me from under her fringe, her face red and stained with tears. 'I'm sorry,' she whispered.

I nodded and she started to cry. She had crossed from angry banshee to dishevelled emotional wreck in a few moments.

'How much do I owe you for your work?' Alice said dully.

'You're all paid up,' I answered. There was nothing more to say. I walked out of her house and back to the car.

CHAPTER 75

Helene

The night of

Peter Fairweather took me to dinner at an upmarket and fashionable restaurant that was taking bookings eighteen months ahead. We were shown to a table past two pop stars and a Hollywood actor but I took the seat facing the wall. I didn't want to be seen enjoying myself so soon after my husband's death. I still wore black, observing my period of mourning for Gabe, but God, it was good to be out! To hear laughter and gossip, to see joy in other people, to watch the swish of waiters moving back and forth in a confident choreographed stream.

Peter had asked for this meeting. I wondered why he didn't just come to the office, but that wasn't Peter's style. He wanted to show me what my life would be like if I sold the company; how easy easy street would be.

He offered me champagne, and I accepted just a glass. We talked about a play at the National, we touched on politics, we kept it all neutral. My real opinions I didn't share.

Peter has very blue eyes and good suits. He offered his profuse commiserations for Gabe, as he had done at the wake. It came across as heartfelt. I used the edge of the napkin to dab at my eyes.

'Will you allow me to speak plainly, Helene?' I nodded. 'What in hell's name were you thinking hiring that detective!'

I rubbed my hand across my forehead. 'Until you've been there, don't judge.' I looked at him defiantly. 'No marriage is easy, Peter, as I'm sure you appreciate.' I gave him a long look of understanding from under my lashes.

Peter leaned in close. 'Was there another woman that Gabe was seeing?'

I had a decision to make. Should I tell Peter the truth? I decided it was better to get out in front of it, stem the rumours that might cause trouble later.

'There was, I'm sorry to say. Whether it contributed to what Gabe then chose to do, we will never know.'

'That is really awful for you, Helene,' Peter said. 'Who was she?'

'I realise now, Peter, that it's irrelevant. She means nothing to me. So much other important stuff has happened. We must remember the good in Gabe and all the love he gave.'

Peter politely probed about why Gabe might have done what he did, if I needed help, the kind of which was left deliciously hanging. I knew what game Peter was playing, but he didn't realise he was up against a master who could play him back.

Peter changed tack. 'I heard about the speech you gave at GWM, about the new direction for the company. It's quite a different vision – a far more aggressive programme – you've got. How does that fit with what Gabe's wishes were?'

'Business directions change often, you know that, Peter. I felt it was important for GWM to be able to respond to new market realities in London property. We need to serve the interests of the people who rely on us.'

A small frown appeared, but he pressed on. 'Still, Gabe was passionate about social housing, about protecting the little guy. There was a certain . . .' he tailed off for a moment, searching for the right word, 'logic, in positioning the company in that way. You're changing that emphasis dramatically.'

'Yes, I am.' I wasn't going to apologise for what I was going to do. Not to anyone. 'As long as Alice is happy with developments, I can do what I like.'

I ran my fingers down the stem of my champagne glass, slid one stockinged leg over the other under the table. I felt the rustle of silk against my thighs, felt the comforting clank of a heavy gold bracelet on my wrist.

Peter was married, of course. They always were. I had met his wife a couple of times. I sensed a door of opportunity opening, should I wish to move through it. Should I wish, in the wake of Gabe's death, to revert to how I used to be, to what I used to know.

Peter was being so warm and comforting. Anything he could do, he insisted, nothing was too small a favour. I sipped my champagne, felt the bubbles bursting on the roof of my mouth, touched the smooth, snow-white laundered tablecloth under my fingers. I knew what Peter wanted, I knew the rhythms of what would come next. What he was offering was attractive, in a way.

The waiter came over and asked if we wanted dessert. Peter looked at me, those blue eyes so clear, his hand close to mine on the table. 'Well?' he asked. His voice was velvet.

I looked up at the waiter and smiled.

CHAPTER 76

Maggie

The night of

The traffic in the West End was horrendous; backed up at every light and mini roundabout, the city a maelstrom of hot tempers and fraying nerves. Simona called as I was trying to get back to Paddington.

'I've traced that company that Warriner was renting the flat from, Mount Southern Holdings.'

'Go on,' I said.

'It's a subsidiary of another company owned by GWM.'

'Very interesting, thanks, Simona.' So Gabe had provided Warriner with a flat – my guess is he had been paying for it too – and when he died she had moved on, or moved back to where she had been before. Perhaps her step up in the world had been short-lived. But it also showed the depth of the connection between Warriner and Gabe – this hadn't been a relationship conducted in hotel rooms or twice a year while away at a conference.

My phone pinged with a text. Alice wanted Warriner's address. I didn't answer; stalling her.

It was late by the time I finally got to the office and Simona had gone home. The room was still baking from the afternoon sun, so I turned on the fan, which instantly blew a fuse. I yanked open the window and while an insipid stream of cooler air began to leak into the room there was nothing subtle about the smell of frying onions that bullied its way in alongside. I'd always hated fried onions.

I sat down in my chair, feeling exhausted. When was I going to win another case to put in my filing cabinet? Would clients ever come back through my door again? The Moreau family had cost me everything I had built and worked for. They hadn't been worth it.

Dwight calling was a welcome distraction. 'You holding up OK?' he asked.

His voice was soft, and I was thankful. 'I can pay the rent on the office this month, but next month I probably won't make it. And I've got no idea how I'm going to keep Rory and Simona on. I'm probably going to be sued, and I'm a public hate figure, so everything's grand.'

'Tough break,' he said, and sounded genuine. 'I thought you might like to know we've had a breakthrough in Milo's case. We've found the murder weapon. It was his cast-iron doorstop.'

'Interesting.'

'It was dumped in the bin of a commercial property that's being squatted.'

'I thought squatting was illegal now?'

'It is, but this guy pays £1,000 a month cash as a back-hander to a security guard who's supposed to keep the squatters away until the place is redeveloped. That's why the bins aren't emptied regularly. He's not supposed to be living there. But best of all, the squatter's got a conscience, because he heard our appeal for information, he got in touch, and he might have seen who dumped it.'

'Who was it?'

'He thinks it was a woman.'

I sat up in my chair. 'What did she look like?'

I heard Dwight scoff down the line. 'I can't tell you that! But we're working at a faster pace, things are falling into place, we've got forensics to concentrate on now.'

'Anything more on Gabe's death?'

I sensed a pause of irritation, but he continued. 'Not that I've heard, but it's not my case.'

'Well, thanks, Dwight.'

'Yeah, keep safe, Maggie,' he said and rang off.

The doorbell rang.

I glanced at the clock, it was gone eight thirty. I pressed the intercom buzzer and waited at the top of the stairs. The door opened and it took me a moment to register that it was Warriner walking up to meet me.

She got straight to the point. 'I need more reassurance that you're going to leave me alone. I need to know that you've told your client that your investigation is at a dead end.'

I sat down on the edge of my desk and held my hand up in conciliation. 'I was hired to do a job, which is now over. I'm not going to trouble you again. But I can't speak for Alice Moreau. She's looking for answers about Gabe's death, and she's going to be pretty persistent. It might be better just to meet her and answer her questions and that would be it.'

She gave a high, nervous laugh. 'I don't think so.'

'Well, if you can't face the consequences, maybe you should have thought a little harder before you started your affair.'

She looked at me with pity bordering on scorn. 'Consequences – you don't get it, but then, why would you? Someone who grew up here, in this place,' she waved her hands, the gesture taking in the vast city and maybe more beyond, 'in this *safety*, can have no understanding of it.' She blinked several times. 'Gabe and I lost so much when we were young, you cannot begin to appreciate, but you think I can't take a risk, can't face a *wife*? War transforms everything.

It crushes who you are, it changes what you do, it ruins every dream.'

So that was it – Gabe had succumbed to the pull of the past, to the feelings aroused by a young beauty he had known before the war, and years later they couldn't resist a reliving of it. 'So you've known Gabe a long time?'

She shook her head, realising she'd become distracted. 'None of this matters. You won't find me after I leave here.'

She swept her hand through her hair, pulling it back from her face as she glanced out of the window. As she turned I caught the profile and side view of her face. I stared at her in confusion.

She saw the change in me. 'What?' She gave a little pout and that banished more of my doubts. I had seen that pout before.

'You look like Alice – you're family . . . but I thought Alice's family were all gone?'

I rose to my feet, coming closer to her. She backed away, and suddenly something that had been so obvious but that I had never seen was staring me right in the face. 'Clara? You're Clara Moreau!'

'What? No—'

'This *client* you're banging on about is your daughter!'

She changed tack then and stopped the denials. 'Not to me, she isn't.'

I took a step across the room. 'You better start talking, before I pick up the phone and bring a whole heap of trouble down on your head. Why did you pretend you were dead?'

She had retreated to the window, as if my words were punches driving her backwards. 'I don't expect you to understand. But it was something I had to do.'

'Did Gabe know your death was a lie?'

'No, not until years later. I took my chance to get away when our car ended up in the water.'

The questions were coming so fast I could hardly get them out. 'But they found your body?'

'No. I was registered as missing, declared dead seven years later.'

I recalled that her memorial plaque in the graveyard bore no dates.

'So Gabe never wondered?'

'He told me that he wondered plenty. But I was very resolute.'

'Not that resolute – you came back in the end. Was that when he'd rebuilt his life and married again? When he was rich? I'll bet you don't like to be forgotten! You made yourself found. Now you're gonna face the consequences. You were tapping him up for money, weren't you? Your new life didn't turn out so good, eh? The grass isn't greener, is it?'

'It wasn't like that, it wasn't about the money—'

'Well, it sure as hell wasn't about your daughter.' My mobile rang but we both ignored it. 'You abandoned Alice – you ran out on her!'

She was unaffected. 'It was something I had to do, for her, for myself.'

The clamour in my brain was reaching such a crescendo it blocked out rational thought. My anger was a sea through which a menacing predator snapped and thrashed. 'A child needs every family member she can find. Take it from me.'

'I don't expect you to understand, but I know you won't report me, this is private family business. It's not about you.'

I closed my eyes. Through my long and lonely childhood I had had a thing about doors. Every time one opened – in a classroom, on the tube, at a friend's house – I would hope for a second that through it would come my mother, arms out to gather me up, that her long search for me was over, that somehow it was all a tragic misunderstanding. I had waited all my life for a moment that had never arrived. 'Not about me, eh? My mum walked out on me when I was seven. I know how it feels to be abandoned as a little girl. I *know* that life!'

I shouldn't have said it, it wasn't my place, but I guess in the end I was a human being with a heart. I had never warmed to Alice, I had thought her spoilt and privileged, she had just been a job to me, a way of getting some revenge on Helene. But now, meeting her mother, hearing her selfish justifications, I felt for her so badly. Some part of what I had done to Colin was because of what my mother had done to me. She hadn't loved me. She hadn't wanted me enough. And I hated her for it. Now here was another mother who had spurned her child and let her husband pick up the pieces.

I took a step across the room, my fists balled. 'I'm never keeping this quiet, even if Alice has to see you from through the glass of a prison visiting room. I'm going to make you face up to your responsibilities if it's the last thing I do.'

She didn't cower, she stood up to me. 'You think Alice is better off knowing about me? I've watched her, you know. I have observed her limitless opportunities, the advantages her youth and beauty bring. She's so lucky and you're not going to take that away from her. You want to make me pay for running out on my flesh and blood? Get real – men do it every day. I'm going to tell you a story that will make you change your mind about what I did.'

She put her hand in her bag and I took an involuntary step backwards, unsure what was going to be coming back out in her fingers.

As I began to tense, something else sprang into my mind like a little firework blasted into the night sky. If Clara wasn't dead, Helene was never legally married. She didn't own GWM. She had no right running Gabe's company, she had no right to his fortune, to anything.

CHAPTER 77

Helene

The night of

The waiter was smiling, Peter was hanging on my every word. Peter's wife came into my mind then. She was a lawyer called Deirdre; they had three children. I could have told Peter that Deirdre and I had talked for a long time at one of the functions that had thrown us together; she had wanted to get the measure of me, not because she saw me as a threat, but because she was actually interested in me. She had known I would have been more fun than those bores our husbands hung out with. Deirdre had had an acid sense of humour. She had made me laugh.

I told the waiter I wanted only coffee.

Peter's smile faded a little. He shifted in his seat. 'I heard that the police think the activist's death is drug related.'

'He's got a name, Peter. He was called Milo Bandacharian. Drugs can trip up even the best of us.'

Peter made a face. 'Still, reputation is everything in this business. Maybe, Helene, you need to take more care about your friends; I heard you two were close.'

That was a low blow, but I smiled as he would expect me to. 'Developments are easier when you have the local community on board. You'll realise that, Peter, when you do your first large-scale London project.' Take that, you Yank fucker, I smiled.

I stood up, put my napkin on the table, looking every inch a woman who was born to this. Quite the opposite, but I'd left my past behind, a long time ago.

Keep the fuck away from my company, Peter, I thought.

Peter stood, defeat like dandruff on his shoulders. He kissed me on both cheeks and I walked out into the night past a doorman.

Yes, I had been a mistress, yes, I had used men for what I could get. But everyone reaches the end of that road. I was fully aware that I had ended up here, in central London, expensively dressed, living a life of comfort, rubbing shoulders with powerful people, because I acted and looked a certain way. But that didn't mean I had a heart of stone, quite the opposite. When I met Gabe everything had changed. And Gabe wasn't even married; I didn't have to act the mistress and we didn't have to lie and cheat and pretend. I could give myself for the first time, body and soul, to someone else.

It hadn't always been easy. But then the best things never are. His first wife still hovered over us like a spectre, with her death she would never be diminished in his eyes. She had died when her daughter was two. There would have been moments when Gabe would have looked over at little Alice perched on her mother's knee and Clara would have soared so high on a pedestal in his mind that nothing would ever knock her off it. I would never be able to compete with that.

And I thought I knew why Gabe couldn't keep his demons at bay any longer, why he took the self-destructive step to end his life. His guilt over what had happened at his hands to Clara eventually ate him out from the inside. Maybe it was Alice reaching eighteen and about to flee the nest that made him think the long struggle of his life could finally be done. He had never shared his insecurities and pain with me, and that was something I would have to live with. But love is complicated, relationships even more so. I forgave Gabe, I would remember and I would mourn, and I would try to learn. I had been blessed to love another human being so completely.

And so what of the woman in the green dress, that threatening presence of the last month, stalking my dreams and invading my most personal spaces? I walked slowly along pavements, past groups of people laughing and talking and enjoying the summer. Hers were the actions of a woman who had lost, a woman whose desires would never be met. She had fallen for Gabe, more fool her. He had unleashed emotions in her she couldn't control. She could almost be pitied. Now that Gabe was gone she simply didn't matter, it was all blood under the bridge, because something so precious had been left behind: Alice. On her I would lavish all the love I had left, she was the last remaining memory of Gabe I had; I could nurture her, help her grow into the beautiful woman she could be. I had her, I had GWM, I had memories of Gabe's love from an earlier, simpler time, it was more than enough; it was more than many had.

A text pinged. It was from Alice. 'I know all about your past, you whore.'

I felt something sliding away from me. I fumbled with the phone and rang her, but there was no answer.

Another text arrived. 'I know about all of it, Maggie found out for me. Don't lie and deny it.'

I phoned her again and left a message, pleading with her to call me.

'Leave me alone,' she wrote back. 'You chucked Poppa out, now I'm throwing you to the dogs.'

I phoned Maggie's cell and her office. There was no reply. I had the sensation of swimming for years to reach dry land but when I was finally there it disintegrated under my feet.

I'd worked so bloody hard to build a relationship with Alice and now Maggie in just a few days had blown it up.

As I re-read Alice's texts I got angrier and angrier. Maggie wouldn't get away with this; not for a moment would I let this stand. If Maggie wasn't at her office I would track her down at her home. Ten minutes later I was on Praed Street looking up at her window.

CHAPTER 78

Alice

The night of

I felt liberated, it wouldn't have been too much of an exaggeration to say reborn. Poppa's death and the fresh revelations about my stepmother made me into a harder, older person. I knew now that my stepmother was a cold, conniving, strategic exploiter of men's weaknesses and desires. Her beauty was a weapon she had used to full and potent effect for her own selfish ends. She had ensnared Poppa, pulled him into her tainted web, but her power over him and over me had been broken.

I would cast her out. The break felt physical. I wanted her to feel it too. I didn't trust anything Helene had ever said. Her love for Poppa was a lie from the start, a calculating plot to profit from a man's weakness and need for companionship and affection.

She was out on the town right then, winking, preening and gurning at Peter Fairweather, at Poppa's business rival, in her widow's weeds, as treacherous a betrayal as any. GWM is my company, not hers.

No wonder Poppa had had an affair. He had been driven to seek the comfort other warming, kind arms and minds could give him.

I left the house and headed to Maggie's office. What I wanted now was to meet Poppa's other woman, this Warriner, and hear what Poppa had meant to her. She must have loved him! Maggie would give me her address and I would find her. I would get her to overcome her shame at being the other woman and talk to me. We could comfort each other – we had a connection! I for one would never condemn her. I felt the sense of an ending, of things shifting into new patterns.

I turned into Praed Street and saw the lights spilling from Maggie's open office window.

CHAPTER 79

Helene

The night of

Maggie's door was ajar and I took the stairs two at a time, hustled into the office and stopped in confusion. Maggie looked shrunken and tired, sitting hunched on the edge of her desk, a far cry from the brash and bold force of nature I had known. Someone was near the window. She turned and I saw with a start that it was the woman in my bathroom. Now she wore a silky striped top, trousers and high heels and her hair was dyed dark.

The room crackled with an oppressive silence that was broken by the sound of footsteps ascending the stairs. A moment later Alice burst into the room. She took one look at me and twisted away as if I was rotting meat. Her eyes caught the woman near the window. It took her only a couple of seconds before she realised who she was.

'Oh God, it's you, talk to me about Gabe, he was my dad you know, yes, he was my dad. Tell me about him! I want to know everything! How you knew him, where you met him.'

The woman took a step back, eyes wide.

Stop it, Alice, I felt forcefully. Stop this right now. It wasn't her place to be asking this, it was mine. This was between Gabe and this woman and me, not his daughter, yet this naïve child only had eyes for this interloper, as if his mistress was more important in her life than me.

Maggie stood up, tense and unhappy.

'What's your name?' asked Alice. 'Don't be afraid, I'm glad you're here to talk to me. When was the last time you saw him?'

'Why was he giving you so much money?' I snapped, hatred blooming in my chest.

The woman looked at me and I thought back to the text messages I had seen on Gabe's phone, the intimacy of them, the way she talked so casually about Alice. My dislike transformed into a cold, hard anger. 'Well, why?' I asked, louder and more insistent.

'He felt he needed to help me,' she said.

'So you had a real connection?' Alice began, her voice hopeful.

'Shut up, Alice!' I screamed at her.

A noise of protest came out of the woman but I carried on. 'Why did he need to help you? What's so special about you?'

'Helene, stop it!' Alice countered with a loud voice of her own. 'What's your name?'

'I don't want to know your name,' I shouted. 'You disgust me. You don't get to claim that you knew him – you knew nothing about him or his life or his struggles.'

'Ladies, please,' Maggie appealed for calm, but I was having none of it.

'You've been harassing my family, you've been screwing money out of Gabe. You've invaded our house – I should call the police and have you arrested.' I felt the moral high ground solid under my feet. 'You're nobody,' I snapped. 'Nobody at all in this family. You'll be forgotten soon enough.'

I grabbed Alice's hand, trying to turn her round towards the door but she snatched her hand away, hissing, 'Get off me right now.'

'Stop it, just stop it, Alice!' I pleaded. The woman stood there mesmerised by our vicious family row, she drank in the depth of our conflict and difficulties and I hated her for seeing it.

'Do you miss your mother, Alice?' The room stilled as she spoke. She had the same accent as Gabe, and I realised that they must come from the same place.

'My mother? Yes, of course I miss her. Did you know her?' Alice's little face was lit from within, it was her greatest fantasy come true, to find someone who had known her, who had been there with her in the past. 'Oh my God, you knew her. I have met so few people from Poppa's past, hardly anyone who knew my momma. Please, tell me more.'

I felt the foundations of my life beginning to crumble. I saw in Alice's face the possibilities of a heritage she could never access opening up through this woman, I felt her turning away from me and towards this other woman whose stories, invented or real – and who would be able to verify? – would change our lives.

The woman smiled. 'I knew your momma, as you call her, very well indeed.'

Alice clapped her hands together. 'This is a miracle, it was destiny to find you! I want to know everything, I have waited all my life for this moment.'

I don't have the strength to tolerate this, I thought. Some bigger part of me knew that understanding her heritage was good for Alice, but what about me, I wanted to scream, what about me?

'Oh tell me about her,' Alice enthused, 'I want to feel as close to her as it's possible to be.'

Maggie took a step forwards. 'Helene, I think it would be better if you waited downstairs—'

'I'm going nowhere,' I snapped. 'How dare you.' I turned back to this woman. 'Just because you once knew Alice's mother doesn't give you any moral right to do what you did! He loved *me*, he married *me*, we raised Alice together, you just met him in sad little flats and skulked in cloakrooms—'

'Helene, I beg you—'

Maggie's pleas spurred me on, '—stealing my keys, stalking my daughter, what were you thinking? What you did is not a sign of love, it's a sign of madness. You were only interested in Gabe's money, that's the real truth here, isn't it? You weren't interested in Alice. You're nothing, you're no one, you will be forgotten soon enough. To the Moreau family you never existed!'

She looked angry then, a vein pulsing above her eye. 'You were wrong at the beginning and you're wrong now. It was always about Gabe and me. I am everything to the Moreaus, I *am* the Moreau family. I'm Alice's mother.'

CHAPTER 80

Maggie

The night of

Helene seemed to fall backwards and it was only hitting the wall that held her up.

Alice stood with her arms hanging limply by her sides, staring at her mother. 'So the car crash into the water, your disappearance, was all a lie?'

'No – that crash was very real. Arguments can make drivers lose their concentration and come off a bend in a road. But I'm a survivor, and I walked away. I was very young, I had to go. Gabe never knew I survived that crash, not until years later.'

'Why did you never tell me, why did you never come back?' Alice asked.

'Because Gabe begged me not to. He said you weren't ready. I used to watch your dad, it comforted me, I saw him at work, saw how much he had achieved, saw this huge tower going up in the richest city in Europe – well, that was something! I watched you too, Alice. I saw you with that handsome young man in Vauxhall—'

'You saw me with Milo?' Alice's face was a moving sea of shock and joy that overwhelmed her. She burst into tears and collapsed into Clara's arms, putting her hand around her neck and laying her head on her breast.

I saw Clara recoil.

'So many years I have loved you and dreamed about you,' Alice sobbed. 'Tell me everything.'

'Of course, child, of course, but it's complicated.'

Alice looked up at her mother, wiping tears from her eyes. 'Love isn't complicated,' she said, 'it's simple!'

I glanced at Helene. We both knew Alice would learn the hard way when she was older how untrue that was.

'What do you think happened to Poppa in the tower?' Alice asked.

A defensive look flitted across Clara's face. It was less than a second long, but I felt the hairs rise on the back of my neck. She pulled away from Alice and stepped backwards, her heels clacking on the wooden floor. Something snagged on my memory, a connection I was trying to make, and then several bits of the puzzle finally fell into place. I stood up sharply. 'You were in Connaught Tower with him at the end!'

'No.'

I pointed at Clara's feet, with every second my conviction becoming stronger, because I understood where I had heard that noise before. 'Your shoes, I heard your high heels on the cement floor above me.' She took a step away from me as I advanced towards her, my fists balled. 'Gabe decided enough was enough, didn't he?' I thought back to the photos I'd taken of him outside Clara's Chelsea flat, his unhappiness, his similarity to Colin Torday. It wasn't love and passion I'd witnessed, it was threats and intimidation. Gabe's fist grinding into Clara's memorial plaque in the cemetery took on a sadder meaning too. 'He said he wasn't going to pay you any more – was that it? You met up in Connaught Tower because he was going to put an end to your blackmail—'

'No!' Her eyes were blazing. 'You'll never understand the bond we had. We had a connection that was lifelong!'

'This is bullshit. Did you two fight? I bet you're capable –

all that history, all that pain and misunderstanding, oh I bet you guys got right to it. Did he fall, unable to hold on with his bad arm?' I held my elbow up, clenched it with my other hand. 'Or did you push him off?'

'How dare you—'

'I know you were there, I know because when Gabe landed at the foot of the tower – he was calling out your name as he died in my arms!'

'So he should have been,' she hissed.

And there it was, her admission, bubbling to the surface on her uncontrollable anger.

CHAPTER 81

Helene

The night of

Never had a secret kept been at such high cost.

I had endured agonies of conjecture over the past weeks that my love and marriage had been betrayed, yet I had been wrong, more wrong than I could ever have known. My heart screamed at Gabe, *Why didn't you tell me?* We could have worked it out, we would have emerged stronger, better. My husband hadn't been having an affair, he was processing the reappearance of his wife from long ago, but that period of his life was over and he had resisted Clara's attempts to resurrect it. He hadn't jumped off Connaught Tower, he hadn't abandoned Alice and me. And if he hadn't jumped, that meant she had pushed him. I started forward across the room.

Alice's voice stopped me in my tracks. 'Maggie wasn't expecting me here tonight, so it was an accident that we met, wasn't it? You never wanted to see me, did you?' Her voice was quiet.

Clara turned back to Alice, and I fancied that she had almost forgotten she was there. 'Come now, child,' she snapped.

I felt a tremor of fear. That was a dangerous thing to say.

Clara didn't know her daughter, this young woman who carried her DNA but nothing else. She had no idea how emotional Alice could get.

'Why don't you love me?' Alice asked, her voice a whisper.

Clara took a deep inhale and paused, and I felt an extraordinary sensation: *Lie*, I wanted to scream, tell her what she wants to hear. This vulnerable girl who has just lost her father is your flesh and blood, trip over your words for her, contort your twisted feelings into something palatable for her – force yourself to do it. Lies make us compromised hypocrites, but sometimes lies make us live.

But she didn't do that. Clara pulled out a cigarette and tapped the end impatiently on the side of the packet.

CHAPTER 82

Maggie

The night of

Clara put the tip of her cigarette between her lips. She twisted, searching for her lighter, instead of giving Alice an answer. Alice stepped forward sharply towards her mother. She shoved Clara once, very hard, in the chest. Clara's face had the briefest chance to register her shock before she teetered backwards, her high heels catching in the cord of the broken fan, her arms cartwheeling too slowly to be any use. By the time Clara's bum had cleared the windowsill I was in full lunge, rugby tackling her round her thighs, figuring my greater weight would pinion her in the room. Too late did I realise she was pulling me out of the window and I was hurtling to the pavement with her.

CHAPTER 83

Helene

The night of

It took me a few seconds to get down the stairs and out into the street. The angle of Clara's neck spoke louder than any hunting for a pulse or putting hands on her chest. She was dead.

My limbs moved like I was stuck in treacle. I looked back up at the window and saw Alice silhouetted against the yellow light one storey up. I replayed her step forward, her hard shove in her mother's chest; intent to cause injury glowing in every cell of her body. It was premeditation in a court of law; a charge of murder sure to follow. I heard brakes in the road and the shouts of passers-by.

Maggie was gasping little breaths of air, blood pumping from a head wound. I knelt down, touched her face and leaned closer because she was talking. 'I saw her fall. It was an accident,' she said.

Her eyes were burning with intensity.

'No,' I said. Shock had robbed me of speech and it came out as no more than a whisper.

Maggie gripped my wrist, folded something into my hand. I took it dumbly. 'I saw it all and so did you. Warriner tripped and fell backwards out of the window and I couldn't save her.'

My hands were rubbery, unable to grip Maggie's clothes. Maggie was making no sense. For a start, this wasn't Warriner, it was Clara Moreau. You couldn't lie to the police, it would never work, Maggie would change her mind as soon as she was able. I had fallen through layer after layer of horror, but here was another. Alice was going to have to face the legal consequence of what she had done. 'No,' I said, stronger this time.

'Yes,' Maggie said, and fainted.

I looked at the object she had forced into my palm and saw a photo.

CHAPTER 84

Alice

The night of

I stayed where I was, looking out of the window at the scene below. That woman had obviously broken her neck. She fell just one floor, but get it wrong, as she did, and that's enough. Maggie was groaning and struggling, she landed right on top of her.

Helene looked up at me, her face entirely rearranged with the shock of what had happened. I turned away.

I came out into the street to find Helene a different woman. She hurried towards me, a look of hunted protection on her face. 'Maggie's told me exactly what she saw – Warriner tripped and fell backwards and Maggie couldn't save her. Is that what you saw?' Helene waited, hanging on my reply, her eyes beseeching.

So this was how she was going to spin it. People were milling around, the sound of sirens was moving closer. I nodded, repeated the lie and hugged Helene. I took a long look over her shoulder at that dead woman.

I noticed that Helene was holding a photograph in her shaking hand. When the first police officer arrived she transferred it to her pocket.

CHAPTER 85

Helene

The night of

We were in the street a long time. So many people had to process us. They took Clara away first, because there was nothing anyone could do for her. Maggie they took longer on, an oxygen mask, a drip and a brace to protect her back. Alice and I gave our statements, as did a man who saw the two of them hit the pavement. The police went up to the office of the Blue and White and we weren't allowed to follow. I could see them intermittently moving back and forth in front of the window, sometimes leaning out and looking down.

The photo burned a hole in my pocket.

Much, much later we were allowed to go home. I had to almost carry Alice into the house; the shock at what she had done was creeping into her limbs, rendering her almost unable to walk but leaving her with the wide eyes of a terrified small animal. I laid her in bed fully clothed and pulled the sheet up under her chin.

'What's going on, Momma?' she said.

I froze. It was the first time she had ever called me that.

I hugged my daughter so tight. *My* daughter. I kissed her on the forehead and stroked her hair and shushed her and a few minutes later she was asleep, adrenaline and lies robbing her of consciousness in a moment.

I quietly closed her door, and then I tore the home office apart. I upended every box, scrabbling for information on every aspect of Gabe, Clara and Alice's life, looking for any and every detail which could explain and disprove that picture in Maggie's bloodstained hand – and then I would destroy it. But the deeper I looked, the less I found. There were barely any photos – a few black and whites of his parents, but no record of the wife he had loved and lost, no photos from his childhood. I found his name change documents, from Buric to Moreau. There was no marriage certificate. I found Alice's birth certificate, but that was it. Her parents were listed as Gabe and Clara Moreau. I found the file about the accident on the bridge, about how his wife was listed as missing, not dead. I found letters from solicitors about the long process of declaring Clara dead.

I picked up the cheap disposable phone that Gabe had used to communicate with Clara. I examined the texts again. 'You can't let me go x', 'Alice need never know xx', 'I deserve more x'.

I pulled out the photo that Maggie had clutched in her hand as she had tried to save Clara's life. No image like it existed in this house. The people in it were all gone, the names on the reverse faded but still clear. I stood up and waited outside Alice's door, listening to the silence.

When I was sure she was asleep I walked into her room and stared down at her. The sheet was thrown back in the summer warmth. I watched her breathing, the small rise and fall of her chest. With every in-breath ugly images of what had happened earlier that night in Maggie's office flashed through my mind.

Alice's red hair was spread across her pillow, the white crook of her arm folded near her ears. She was miraculous, and it utterly broke my heart. I took out my phone and risked using the torch. I double-checked her features, comparing them to the photo in my hand.

A long while later I walked out and closed the door. My doubts had all dried up. I turned towards the stairs, determined to burn the photo in the kitchen sink, but saw instead that the bottom of my dress was stained with Maggie's blood, my knees coated in rust-coloured smears of her pain.

Revulsion swamped me and I ran to the bathroom, threw the cloying dinner dress and my underwear and jewellery to the floor and got into the shower and turned it to boiling. I reached for a flannel and began to scrub.

CHAPTER 86

Alice

The night of

Helene was standing over me in the dark, the light of her phone swinging around the walls of my room, scattering shadows and creating others. She stared for a long time at me and at the photo in her hand before she left.

I got out of bed and crept towards the bathroom door and opened it a crack. I heard the shower running.

Helene had cast her clothes in a heap on the floor, steam was curling in tendrils across the ceiling, her naked body was the faintest outline behind the frosted glass of the screen.

I bent down and pulled the photo from the pocket of her jacket.

CHAPTER 87

Maggie

The day after

I was driven to St Thomas' hospital where there was a free bed rather than carried to St Mary's right next to where I fell. I woke to a view across the river to the Houses of Parliament. Big Ben was practically sitting in bed with me.

I bitched and begged for painkillers. I wanted to stay high as a kite for as long as possible; the police would come to interview me soon enough and I wanted to delay it.

I had been told by a young nurse that I had a broken collarbone, concussion and they were monitoring possible spinal damage, but by late morning I was judged well enough to give my version of events at my office the night before. A police officer came to take my statement. My feelings from yesterday hadn't changed. The lies fell easily and slickly from my lips: it was a dreadful accident, she had been right by the window, the cord from the broken fan was behind her heels; when I saw her trip I instinctively rushed to try and save her and had been pulled out the window myself.

Why did I stick to such a monstrous version of events? Why did I subvert due process and put myself at risk of a perjury charge? Because in that moment when Alice stepped forward, her arms outstretched, a look of wild fury on her face, I saw myself. If it had been my mother, I would have acted the same. I would have thought, don't you dare, don't you fucking dare stand there and pretend you love me. You don't get to come and go, you don't get to lay waste to my life and treat it casually. So Alice Moreau and I, separated by class and background and age and experience, found a way to feel as one. I'd instinctively done my best to stop Alice, but I couldn't condemn her for it.

In the early afternoon Helene came to visit. The cellophane around the extravagant flowers she carried crinkled under her touch, their heavy scent perfumed the room.

She looked as terrible as I felt, with bags under her eyes and skin that looked grey in the summer light. She sat down by the side of the bed, asked me how I was.

'I gave my witness statement this morning,' I said.

She looked at me sharply. 'Did you remember anything else since last night?' she asked.

I shook my head. 'The sequence of events remains quite clear in my mind.' There was a short silence as she looked around the ward, checking who was near.

'I burned that photo,' she said in a whisper.

We looked at each other for a moment before she looked away. Clara's secret was buried so deep it would never resurface now.

'I cannot ever thank you for what you have done for my family, for Alice,' she said. 'I am sorry for the public pain I put you through and the damage I must have inflicted on your business.'

'Forget about it,' I said. 'There is one thing I want to ask you, though. Did you know about my past when you hired me?'

She nodded. 'I did research on you, I'm always thorough. But it wasn't until Gabe died and it was being insinuated that I was responsible that I decided to strike back at you.'

Gabe's name hovered uncomfortably between us. 'I want to make up your financial loss.'

'I don't want your money,' I said.

She opened her bag and pulled out a chequebook. 'I don't care. Rip it up if you want. I won't take no for an answer.' She scribbled with her pen and placed the cheque face down under the vase. There was another silence. We weren't friends, and never would be, but we had reached an understanding of sorts, a mutual respect of what we had suffered. She looked away across the river. 'Do you really think she was with Gabe when he died?' she asked.

'I think it's likely, yes. Whether it was an accident or premeditated I can't say.'

'What did he say after he fell?'

I felt for her then, trying to stay afloat as her life unravelled around her. She didn't deserve it. I wondered whether to sweeten the pill, but I'd told the only lie I was ever going to tell to protect what was left of her family. I shifted in the bed. I took a deep breath and it hurt, in my heart and my head.

'He was mumbling. It was difficult to hear it all. He said "Clara" several times.'

Helene swallowed. 'Did he say anything else at all?'

'I cradled his head so he could speak. He said "Clara my love," or something that sounded like that. He was finding it hard to form the words.'

The colour drained right off her face. It was a harsh thing to hear all right. At his end, Gabe hadn't been thinking about Helene. She stood up on shaking legs and gave me a short nod. Then she turned and walked away.

What a mess. Clara had been absent from Gabe's life for years, he had gone on to make a new life, to love again, yet they held a power over each other unmatched by anyone else and undimmed by the passage of the years. Theirs was a twisted tale of two emotionally damaged people whose relationship had been lifelong.

In the final moments of his life, dying in my arms, Gabe hadn't been calling out for his wife, he had called out for his sister.

CHAPTER 88

Maggie

The day after

The day wore on, the light from the river shifted and moved in ceaseless variation. At one point the sun came out brightly but it couldn't lift my mood. When Clara had come to my office we had argued. I was going to bring the full weight of the law down on her pretty head, and nothing she could have said would have stopped me, until she had shown me a photo. In it were a nuclear family, a smiling mother and father sat behind their son and daughter. Gabe looked about fourteen in the photo, Clara a few years older. She looked so like her brother and Alice it was unmistakable. But she had tapped the photo just in case I still didn't believe her. The girl in the image was wearing a university sweatshirt with Clara emblazoned on the front.

Clara had insisted that theirs was not the dark and twisted tale I assumed; Gabe was two years younger than her, a beloved brother who meant the world and more to her. When she was twenty-one and a mortar shell hit the house and obliterated their family, the emotional pain and chaos made them find momentary comfort in each other. But their moment of madness and grief had consequences. She fell pregnant.

They fled to London together, pretending they were

husband and wife, they changed their name from Buric to Moreau, trying to outrun their mistake and the destruction of everything they held dear. Clara couldn't deal with the consequences of what they had done. As Alice grew, she felt a growing alienation from her daughter, a repulsion at what she saw. She told Gabe she had to leave. There were months of screaming arguments as he demanded she stay for their daughter, that they see it through. And during a vicious row in the car one night, he skidded off the road and into the water and she did indeed go.

But she kept tabs on him over the years, what he was doing, who he was seeing. She saw how, freed from the weight of his broken past, he founded and ran a successful business. When I quizzed her on her daughter she showed little interest, dismissing the importance of her with a lazy wave of her hand. 'She reminds me of a period we wanted to run from,' she said. It remained all about Gabe. When she saw that he had fallen in love with Helene, she felt she had been forgotten.

It was pretty clear from Clara's personality that being forgotten, being rendered invisible, was what she hated most. There were long descriptions of parties before the war, of the beauty of her mother, and by extension herself, of the attention her looks commanded and the ease with which she could win people over to do her bidding. She talked with bitterness about Alice's limitless possibilities and how different her daughter's teenage years had been from her own. I thought back to the pills she took, and knew that for every high came a corresponding low, where her mood would have been very different, where everything would have seemed black and hopeless and she would have railed angrily at the world and her reduced place in it.

And the victims of those actions? Gabe and Alice above all. I remembered Alice's face when Clara revealed who she was. The momentary ecstasy followed by the understanding of the scale of the betrayal. I saw those wiry arms thrust forwards and the tumble out of the window. I had known when I was on my back on the pavement that Clara was dead. I saw Alice, silhouetted in the light from the window above. She was eighteen years old, poised to dive into her life, but about to drown under the weight of events she had no control over from a generation ago.

I had felt the photo still in my hand as I looked up at her and tightened my fist around it. Not all family secrets needed to be revealed. How ironic, for me, the woman who prised apart secrets for profit, to wish to protect my client from this one. My job was to watch and expose but at that moment I turned a blind eye. When Helene saw the photo, read the faded names and the date on the back, she immediately understood. We were middle-aged, our pasts were littered with pain we had inflicted and suffering we had endured. We had wanted to protect Alice from at least some of it.

I fell asleep thinking about forgiveness.

I woke a little later when Rory came in with a plastic bag full of chocolates and bunches of grapes, Simona following with Tupperwares brimming with home-made food. Their hugs and good wishes were balm to my soul.

'What the hell happened last night?' Rory asked.

Lying to Rory was harder than lying to the police. He looked at me sceptically as I related what happened. 'I'm not sure she was worth falling out of a window for,' Rory counselled.

'Good job I landed on her then.' It was a bad joke and no one laughed.

'When are you going to be up and about again?' Simona asked, peeling the lid back on a Tupperware, and a smell of roast tomatoes and basil filled the room.

'A while,' I said.

Rory came and sat on the bed, opening the box of chocolates and popping one in his mouth. 'Why'd Warriner come
and see you?' he asked frowning, pressing for the details he
instinctively knew I was keeping from him.

'She wanted to make sure I was going to leave her alone.
She didn't want to meet Gabe's family.'

'Well, that was a bust,' he said tartly.

'Can I ask you something,' Simona said. 'When you were
plummeting to the ground, what went through your mind?'

'Christ, Simona, what a question!' Rory exclaimed.

'It's important to understand the world,' Simona insisted.
'I'm just really interested. Did your life flash before you?'

'I think it's fair enough to wonder,' I said, as Rory got up
and began walking round the room.

He spied the cheque under the vase and picked it up before
I could stop him. He looked at me sharply. 'So you've decided
she didn't have anything to do with Gabe falling from that
tower?'

'I think I got that wrong,' I said to Rory, then I turned to
Simona. 'Yes, my life flashed before me. I really thought I
was going to die, to tell the truth. It's made me think about
Gabe, he fell a lot further than I did.'

'God, I wonder what went through his mind,' Simona
shuddered.

'I bet you were swearing all the way down to Praed Street,'
Rory said.

I grinned. 'Like a bastard. That shows the difference between
us, I guess. Gabe was talking about Clara before he died.'

'Jesus, a deathbed confession a Catholic would be proud
of,' Rory said. 'Poor man.' He shook his head. 'I'll put this
cheque in the company account, if you don't mind.' He picked
it up off the table and pocketed it. He glanced at me and
did a double take. 'Are you OK?'

A lot of images were crowding my mind all at once, but

one thing was becoming clearer. I threw back the cover on the bed and swung my feet to the floor.

'What are you doing?' Simona asked.

I yanked the drip from the back of my hand and awkwardly pulled on the trousers that were in the cupboard by the bed and slipped shoes on my feet.

'What the hell?' Rory was bewildered.

'I have to go somewhere,' I said.

'Get back in bed!' Rory shouted as I began to walk out of the ward.

CHAPTER 89

Maggie

The day after

Iwas more injured than I had realised. I was feeling sick and sweating with pain by the time I'd hailed a cab on Westminster Bridge and directed it to Vauxhall. I got out and staggered across the lawns by Connaught Tower and asked in the local pub and a couple of shops if they knew where Milo's friend Larry lived. My inquiries drew a blank and exhausted, I took a rest on the swings in a nearby playground. The sun beat down and left me lightheaded.

I spotted Larry an hour later cutting across a patch of grass and I flagged him down with a wave of my hand.

'Jesus, lady, you look like shit,' he said as he approached.

I really didn't feel so good any more and the heat of the day wasn't helping. My head was swimming and something was jabbing painfully inside. 'I just have a few more questions.' I pulled out my phone and showed him a photo of Clara again. 'Is this the woman you saw with Milo?'

He looked exasperated. 'I told you, it's not her.'

'What if she had different hair? She changed her hair colour, maybe quite often. You only saw her from the back.'

He sighed and looked at the picture again. 'I don't know, man! Maybe, maybe not.'

'Did she wear high heels?'

'What? I don't know . . . yes, I guess so.'

'What exactly did Milo say about this woman he was seeing? Was she older?'

'I can't tell you anything! He never spoke in detail about her, told me he couldn't.'

'Why wouldn't he talk to you about her? You shared everything normally, didn't you?'

Larry shrugged, pulled out his fags. 'I guess.'

'Was it because she needed it to stay a secret? That's why you never met her, wasn't it? Because she didn't want it to be public knowledge that she was seeing Milo.'

Larry took a deep drag on his fag. 'He said as much, I guess.'

'What would be a reason for Milo to have to keep who he was having a relationship with a secret?'

'I dunno, if she was married, if she was dodgy somehow, maybe if she was famous . . . A million reasons!'

I smiled in triumph. 'No, not a million reasons. Each affair is different, with many different circumstances and motives, but it needs to remain a secret because it matters in the end to only one person.'

I pulled out my phone and called Dwight.

Dwight answered. 'Maggie, I've been trying to get a hold of you—'

'What was the number that Milo used to call his girlfriend?'

'Why?' Dwight began, but I cut him off.

'The number, Dwight, just give me the bloody number.' A wave of tiredness hit me and I slumped off the swing on to the spongy tarmac of the playground floor.

'I don't have it right here, and I'm not allowed to tell you anyway.'

'Did it end 4472?'

There was a short silence on the line. When he spoke again his voice was almost menacing. 'How do you know that?'

I stared at the sky, which looked tinged with red. It was the same number Clara had used to text Gabe. Clara had wanted to keep her affair with Milo hidden from Gabe.

Rory's comments by my hospital bed about a deathbed confession had made it all come together. In my office Clara talked about how she had watched Gabe in Vauxhall. I guessed she had met Milo there and started a relationship with him.

When I held Gabe in my arms as he was dying, he had tried to tell me something I hadn't understood. It wasn't *Clara, my love,* he was trying to say, it was something very different. It was *Clara and Milo.* He wasn't struggling to explain how he loved his sister in a tragic twist on familial bonds, he was telling me something much darker. His sister had killed his friend. I remembered how Clara had seemed with Alice, her spiteful comments about her looks, her youth, her opportunities. When Clara, with her taut and explosive temper, saw her own daughter's blossoming relationship with Milo, something snapped. And Milo bore the tragic and brutal consequences of her murderous rage.

'It's Warriner's number,' I struggled to say to Dwight.

'Lady, get off the floor!' Larry bent down and tried to pull me upright and something pulled taut inside and I remembered nothing more.

CHAPTER 90

Alice

Five days after

Helene couldn't hide her joy. It was an unbridled, bubbling-over euphoria at what the police revealed to us last night.

That *that woman*, known to the police as L Warriner, was the prime suspect in the murder of Milo Bandacharian. The working theory was that she hit Milo with his doorstop in a jealous rage and dumped his computer and mobile phone to cause confusion for the investigation.

The story that Helene, Maggie and I told after that night in Maggie's office now had justification. Helene looked at me as if thanking me for pushing that woman out the window, but she never mentioned it. She was going to live that lie, and over time it would become real.

It would make Maggie's lie easier for her to swallow.

So, pats on the back all round.

It brought a bittersweet memory back to me, forgotten in my long night with Milo. He had held me close and touched my face, saying 'you look so like someone I know'. It was truer than I had ever supposed.

Helene couldn't stop hugging me. She came over and opened her arms and gathered me up, as if touching me was balm to her soul. Maybe she thought she had healing hands, that she could unpick my twisted and entangled DNA with love alone.

The day had dawned bright and blue and Helene had ditched the black clothes for the first time. The long process of mourning my father had entered a new stage. Helene asked me what I wanted to do, just the two of us.

I told her I wanted to go to Connaught Tower, one more time, for Poppa.

Helene nodded and smiled.

A little later we were walking arm in arm through St James's Park, past tourists and cyclists and Chinese tour groups, ice creams in hand, talking. We were almost happy together.

Helene looked up as something caught her eye. 'Look, the first leaf of autumn.' And sure enough, a brittle brown leaf parted from its host and fluttered soundlessly to the ground. It was a little death in the height of summer.

As we walked Helene talked about her past, explained what Rory had discovered in her home town. She painted a vivid picture of her childhood privation and subsequent happiness, there was no deviation from the usual rags to riches story. She apologised, and begged my forgiveness; I was noncommittal. She told me repeatedly how much she loved Poppa. We passed the Houses of Parliament and Lambeth Bridge, heading towards Vauxhall.

When we arrived at Connaught Tower the builders were busy working on site, but they welcomed us in and handed out yellow hard hats as we entered the foyer.

'I feel a little bit of Gabe will always be in this building,' Helene said, gazing up and around.

It was lighter in here today, as the hoardings at the front of the tower where the doors would eventually be had been removed so that the cement lorry could lay the foundation of the fountain. Helene sat down on the side of the unfinished fountain, staring up at the cavernous, vaulted ceiling. It was possible for the first time to see what a beautiful and inspiring space it would eventually become.

'I love it in here,' I said, sitting down next to her.

'So do I,' Helene smiled, encouraged by my attention to her. 'There's something I need to say, Alice. I've been thinking it over, and I'm sure it's the right thing to do. I'm taking the company in a new direction. It is a fitting legacy for Gabe. You know that he always tried to do the best he could for local communities, and in that spirit I want to turn GWM into a cooperative, invest every penny of our profits back into building homes for Londoners, and everyone who wants to become a Londoner. This tower is allocated to have twenty-five per cent social housing, but I want to make it ninety.

'The block where Milo lived was called Reg Jones House, but do you know who Reg Jones was? He was a local Vauxhall flying ace who died for his country fighting the Nazis, and they named a block of flats after him, where people lived and loved and raised their families. Let's call the tower we're going to build there Bandacharian House, let's call this one Moreau House, not Connaught Tower. Let's celebrate Gabe's and Milo's lives and what they stood for, Alice! I want Gabe's legacy, his lives, to be a celebration of what can be achieved, not of the demons that haunted him.'

'A cooperative?' I asked, stunned.

'Yes!' Helene was warming to her theme now, gazing adoringly around the foyer. 'We can make GWM the most high-profile building company in London. Our family has got enough money, for Gabe it was never about the money, it was about what a person can create. It's a new start, a new way of doing things. We can turn the bad stuff, their deaths, into something good.'

Helene was excited; her eyes were shining, her shoulders tight to her ears with optimism for the future. Oh dear oh dear.

CHAPTER 91

Maggie

Five days after

My ill-advised trip to Vauxhall slammed me right back in hospital and it was several days before I was well enough to see anyone. Dwight was the first one to come and visit. He brought a gaudy bunch of supermarket flowers with the price label still attached and they were perfect.

'We know now that Milo's girlfriend was also the lover of Gabe Moreau,' he explained. 'In her flat in Peckham we found a card that he had written telling her it was over; in it Milo said he didn't like the secrecy and he had found someone else, the daughter of a friend who shared his outlook on things.'

I winced. Poor Milo. I don't think he had any idea of the deadly emotions he would have unleashed by rejecting Clara. On such thin threads do our lives dangle.

'Forensics are working on a match between what the door-stop was wrapped in and fibres from Warriner's flat. It seems likely she insisted on keeping their relationship quiet because Milo had no money and she was seeing the much richer Gabe and didn't want to jeopardise that.'

It made sense from an investigation point of view for Dwight to be looking at the financial angle, but I knew now how Clara and Milo met: Clara would have spotted Milo on the estate while she was watching Gabe. Her head would have been turned, just like Alice's was. And what a way to win a little power back, to feel wanted and admired, than to launch into a relationship with a much younger man who knew Gabe well?

'I'm putting you up for a police reward,' Dwight said. 'It's important. This isn't whether some adult couldn't keep it in his pants. This is murder, the obliteration of a young man's opportunity, his one chance. This is as fundamental as it gets. You got Milo justice, Maggie. You.'

My eyes filled with tears.

I felt more certain then that Clara had taunted Gabe with the violence she had meted out to Milo, knowing he could never reveal it. I could never know when she had told him, but the last evening of his life when I followed him to Connaught Tower something fundamental in him had changed. She had dragged Gabe back into the secrets and pain of their youth, and all the effort he had expended to overcome his past had come to nothing.

I felt Dwight's warm hand on my ankle, comforting and reassuring. 'You seem quiet,' he added. 'What are you going to do once you get out of here?'

'I'm broke and I've got lawsuits pending, but I've been broke before, probably will be again.'

I lay back, looking at Dwight. I felt surprisingly good. Across the river over the Houses of Parliament a cloud floated, grey as a dove. Big Ben chimed five p.m. and we listened to its low boom as it rebounded away over the river. I asked him to come and lie on the bed with me as I shifted gingerly over.

'Nice view,' I said after a while.

'Must be the best in London,' Dwight added.

'The good old NHS, eh?'

'I was born in this hospital, you know,' Dwight said.

I smiled. 'So was I.'

Dwight stayed until he was thrown out by the nurse when visiting hours ended.

CHAPTER 92

Alice

Five days after

I take a long inhale; the smell of the fresh layer of cement, the wetness of it, hangs in the air. 'It's going to be so beautiful in here,' I say.

Helene nods, but she's looking at me. 'You're beautiful, Alice, beautiful and sweet. The trauma and pain are behind you now. I will help you face the future every step of the way.'

I see pity on her face. Every time she looks at me she sees Gabe and Clara and what they did and it repulses her, even as she struggles to shield me from it. It's boring after a few days, let alone a lifetime. What Helene doesn't understand is that I can't stand pity. It's time this charade ended.

My Fitbit glows 13.00. It's quiet in the foyer now, we are mainly hidden from view behind the cement truck. The builders have moved away, probably on their lunchbreak munching chicken and chips.

I punch Helene hard in the jaw with my little fist and she topples over backwards into the base of the fountain. She's so shocked she makes just a small gasp, struggling for purchase in the heavy cement. She gropes forward to get to the edge, trying to wipe the cloying, gloopy mess from her eyes but my hands are instantly round her neck. 'I saw that photo,' I hiss. 'This is *my* life, it's *my* family, you don't get to judge.'

I push her under and I don't let go, I am as strong as a fury. I am as strong as my mother. And as I feel Helene's last struggles, I think, I've always hated weak women.

CHAPTER 93

Alice

Five days after

Helene doesn't take long to die. There's a bit of fighting against the cloying weight of the cement and my hands round her neck but she gives up pretty fast. Like I said, weak. I pull my arms and her yellow hard hat clear of the mess. I sit for a few moments looking at part of her elbow poking skywards. I push it back under the surface. I glance around the foyer, but everything is as quiet as five minutes ago. I walk over to the water tap a short distance away that has a hose attached and wash my hands and Helene's hat and wipe the splashes off my sleeves and front. I look back at the fountain; there's not even a ripple of disturbance on the surface. I give the cement layer under which Helene lies a fine spray with the water hose and wipe its end and hang the hose back neatly where the builder left it.

In a few days when the cement has hardened, the builders will put an even finer layer of plaster on and after that has dried thoroughly they will lay a layer of epoxy, and when that has dried the tiler will arrive and lay the small squares of marble around the sides and all across the fountain's large base, its modern curves an expression of faith and an investment in the future.

I head out of the foyer with the cement mixer between me and where I assume the builders are gathered. At the small hut by the entrance I hang up our two hats and leave Connaught Tower and stroll away in the late afternoon sunlight. 'We leave behind only the things we build and the families we create,' Poppa once said to me. But Poppa wasn't always right.

The victors tell the stories. Now I get to tell my tale my way.

My momma and poppa were happy, they met young and fell in love in a war-torn land and escaped to London and began a new life and built a family and a business and loved their child. Their wonderful relationship was cruelly cut short by a patch of ice on a bridge. Theirs was the perfect love story; they were the perfect couple. I have made them so.

I will change every dark colour of my past into something bright. I like to think it was me, just a tiny collection of cells, multiplying and transforming, who brought them to London, me who has saved the Burics and transformed them into Moreaus.

My parents were shaped by unspeakable events and went on to do an unspeakable thing. On some people that burden weighs heavy. I know why Poppa stood in Connaught Tower with his long-lost sister as they circled each other, insults flying, maybe fists and other hurts. I know why he never told me Clara had come back; because she was a bad person, she was not my mother. You don't get to come back when you feel like it. You don't get to open your arms after sixteen years and expect me to run into them. A mother is someone who cares, who loves. That's the kind of mother I'll be, when the time comes.

I dished out justice for that woman in the end. It was a sensible and moral decision. I'm a very moral person.

I've decided I can do better without Helene.

Poor Helene. I quite liked her. This isn't a story of a loathed stepmother, a cuckoo who set up in my nest and tried to eject me from it. Her only fault was falling in love with Poppa.

People say that parents have a biological imperative to protect their children at any cost, well, I have the opposite, I have a duty to safeguard my parents, to create them in any fantasy I see fit. And thus are the dark bits of the past swept away, like rats or nasty rumours.

I walk east, quite contentedly, through the maze of buildings and warehouses, keeping the river on my left until I come round the side of St Thomas' Hospital and find the riverside walk and look across the Thames at the Houses of Parliament and Big Ben. Ten minutes to five. The calming white disc of the clock's surface and its heavy black hands mark time over the city; order triumphing over chaos.

I turn and look back at the hospital. There is a stream of people coming and going through the doors, ordinary people of every age, colour and nationality. Londoners.

I walk over to where an overflow pipe on the wall of the hospital has created a puddle on the uneven paving slabs. My reflection shows only that woman and Gabe, only the Moreaus, there is no fresh blood in my features, no chaotic collision of DNA that develops in unknown and unpredictable ways. A lesser person, a weaker person, would be repulsed, but I am proud. I have a terrific ability to shut down things I don't want to see, to live life as if certain events never happened. I always wanted the memory of a happy family, a family that overcame. And now there is no one to tell me I never did.

I look down at my hands and begin to pick tiny fragments of cement out from under my fingernails. There is just one tiny flaw. Maggie is recovering in this hospital. She knows the story.

I walk towards the entrance.

CHAPTER 94

Alice

Five days after

I ask for Maggie Malone's ward and wait outside the lifts. I examine my reflection in the chrome of the lift doors. I suppose Helene was a combination of traits, as we all are. A calculated, cold-hearted girl who fell in love when she never expected to and didn't realise how fatally weakened she had become because of it. She was a dreamer, but GWM as a cooperative! Give me a fucking break! In some ways Gabe and Helene were well suited, there was an old-fashioned outlook to their utopian dreams. But her plan will stay a fantasy.

Helene was too trusting generally – she understood every nuance of human nature when it came to what went on beneath the sheets, but not when it came to power plays in boardrooms and pubs and alleyways. But I understand it.

My teacher Mr Dewhurst ended our relationship before it had even begun. He was scared, of us, but particularly of me. He had a right to be. I didn't like being rejected and my invented and fantastical tales of what we did together were my punishment for him rejecting me. Turns out my mother didn't like being rejected either, as poor Milo found to his cost.

The apple doesn't fall far from the tree.

The lift pings and the doors open, but I step away, I've changed my mind.

That woman came back because she was jealous of what Gabe had achieved, of the life he had managed to build after the tragedy of their youth. She was desperate that all her early promise had turned to dust. Yet just one generation later, the opportunities available to me are limitless.

I walk out the doors of the hospital.

Maggie is no longer my concern. She has lied for me, and I didn't even have to force her to!

The sun is out and shining brightly. I walk to the bridge and stare back at the hospital. Buildings today are really only designed to stand for fifty years. The thirteen storeys of the hospital I'm looking up at were built in 1975. It could well be only fifty years when it's blasted to the ground. It will make such lovely apartments. I think Moreau Plaza has a certain classy ring to it.

Tomorrow morning I think I'll go and see Peter Fairweather and then Arkady and Irina Oblomov. Maybe I'll have a joint meeting with all of them! With the upheaval facing GWM and the loss of Helene Moreau, their expertise will be essential to have on board as we expand Poppa's company into a profit-making machine. We have a lot to discuss.

I walk away over Westminster Bridge. The sun dances and sparkles on the moving water. I think about my mother. Before I found you, I say to myself, I was unformed and unfinished, a child created wrong. But now, everything is so different and exciting! Opportunities are everywhere. I am young, I am rich. My family is all gone, a thought that is liberating, not scary. There is nothing to hold me back, no religion or culture or family to temper me. This is London. And my future is bright.

Acknowledgements

Books are written by one person, but they are created by many. With many thanks to my agent Cara Jones, to the great team at Hodder for all their work taming this book – Emily Kitchin, Eve Hall, Helen Parham and Rosie Stephen; to the writerly support offered so generously by Polly Williams, Liz Fremantle and Tammy Perry; and to the Euro gals, because an anecdote of yours ends up in every book I write. Finally, special thanks to Stephen, for always having faith and showing me the way. I couldn't have done it without you.